# THE RISEN SHARD

## THE CHAIN BREAK BOOK 1

### D.K. HOLMBERG

## CHAPTER ONE

Gavin crept along the tall stone wall surrounding the manor house, staring outward against the night. Lights within the house behind him made it easier for him to see, but he still struggled to make out much of anything in the distance. Shadowy forms moved along the pathways leading up to the house, their circuitous route predictable now that he'd been watching for the last few hours.

*How am I supposed to finish the job in this place?* Gavin wondered.

"You need to stop watching and get to doing," a voice said in his ear.

Gavin tapped the small metal chain leading from his ear down to the patch on his chest. The enchantment enabled him and Wrenlow to communicate, though there were times when he wished it wasn't quite as effective as it was.

"You need to be quiet," he whispered.

"You're just mad that you can't talk back to me the way you want to. And here I can go on and on and on and—"

Gavin tapped the metal enchantment again, welcoming the silence, though he knew it wouldn't last long. He needed Wrenlow in his ear. This was *his* plan, after all. The only problem was that Gavin didn't care for listening to the chirping in his ear during the entire mission. While scouting and observing like he had been, it wasn't quite as bad, but as they got closer to completing the job, it would become distracting.

He tapped the enchantment again and heard Wrenlow cut back in. "You still there?"

"I just had to take a break from you," he whispered. Even with whispering, Gavin wasn't entirely sure whether he was making too much noise. The night was silent. A soft breeze sighed through the trees surrounding the house and rustled the thick, waxy leaves he'd seen earlier in the day. He couldn't make out the trees as anything other than darkened shapes, though he knew they were there. Someone could be hiding within those trees and could spring up on him. That was what he planned on doing, anyway.

"Take a break from sitting there. It doesn't make this get any easier."

"It's not you who's risking themselves going down in there," Gavin said.

"I risk plenty every time you go out."

Gavin smiled. It wasn't untrue, though it would take

someone with more resources than most within the city to track the enchantment back to Wrenlow. "What do you propose I do? There are at least five people patrolling the grounds." And the fact that he had seen five suggested that there were probably two more he didn't see.

"Drop down next to the wall. Use the trees. The first one should be only about five paces from your position. From there, you can—"

"I know what I can do. I'm just saying I'm not convinced it's going to work the way you think it is."

"And I'm telling you it will. Just trust me on this."

"Trust you. Trust is a little difficult for me these days. Especially with what happened the last time."

Wrenlow's voice cackled from the other end. It went up an octave, as it often did when he was really amused. "The last time wasn't my fault. You were the one who strayed from the plan. If you would've only followed my suggestion, you wouldn't have had any difficulty."

Gavin shook his head. "You know, Wrenlow, things have a way of going a little different when you're out on the job."

With that, he dropped down behind the wall and surveyed the grounds. The grass was short and damp, and the scent of flowers drifted up to him, almost cloying. Dozens of different fragrances reached his nostrils. He hesitated a moment, listening for any movement near him. The only thing he heard was the sound of the breeze drifting through those leaves.

As Wrenlow had said, the nearest tree was only five

paces away. Gavin darted toward it and pressed against the rough bark, which scratched at the fabric he wore and clung to him. He avoided the leaves themselves, knowing how they could cut if he were to get too close. Though they might look attractive, these bells trees and their leaves could be incredibly deadly.

He hesitated there. Movement could be noticeable in the darkness, and he waited for any sign of being spotted, but he saw nothing. Taking a deep breath, he started forward. The next tree should be only twenty paces away, if Wrenlow's intel was correct. Having scouted here throughout the day, Gavin knew the information was good. The real challenge was whether or not something would go off plan. Something *always* went off plan.

As he neared the tree, a shadowy form headed toward him.

*Balls.*

He unsheathed one of the knives at his waist and darted forward, reaching the figure before they could raise the alarm. A sword started coming free, but Gavin slammed his fist into the guard's chin and slowly lowered them to the ground before they had a chance to unsheathe fully. Still, there was a soft, guttural sound that escaped their lips.

*Please let that sound fade into the night.*

He wasn't sure whether or not his prayers would be answered, but he focused instead on dragging the body closer to the tree. If nothing else, he thought he may be able to prop the body against the tree and hide the guard there. It wouldn't be long before someone would recognize that the patrol was off and sound the alarm. He worried about what would happen at that point. Half of the technique in doing what he did required he get some place quietly and without any alarm raised.

He hesitated near the tree and felt one of the waxy leaves carve through his shirt. He jerked his arm back, clutching it to his chest, and glanced down to make sure there wasn't any blood drawn. The bells tree could inflict pain, but that wasn't the worst of it. At least the sap hadn't trailed through his bloodstream and left him incapacitated. It was unlikely someone in this house knew the trees were capable of that. They probably thought the trees were simply pretty, as most people did. Given the nature of the bell-shaped yellow flowers they bore that gave the trees their name, it wasn't an inaccurate statement.

When he was certain no one else had noticed him, Gavin darted forward. He clutched the knife in hand, hoping he wouldn't have to use it. Now that he was out in the open, he needed to get closer to the house.

As he approached the next tree, movement drew his attention. The patrollers had shifted the course of their patrol.

*Did they hear the guard?*

Gavin didn't think that was likely. Maybe he hadn't watched long enough to observe this part of their pattern —a potentially dangerous oversight. If he didn't pay enough attention, he ran the risk of the guards not only noticing he'd disrupted their patrol but also summoning others.

"How's it going?" Wrenlow asked.

"Can't talk now," he whispered.

"Is the plan working?"

"Not yet."

"You know, all you have to do is take a dozen steps off to the right of the third tree, dart toward the doorway, and you should be in the clear. Once you're inside the house, it's just a simple matter of going up the staircase, down the hall to the right, and it should be the third or fourth doorway."

Gavin nodded. "A simple matter," he repeated.

"Well, maybe not quite as simple as that, but I'm sure you can manage."

Gavin resisted the urge to tap on the enchantment again. He might still need Wrenlow's help as he made his way through the manor house. He looked around and didn't see any further movement. The other patrols had moved off to the side. They were far enough away to not have to worry about them coming to him. He hesitated where he was, staring at the doorway.

He thought about the number of steps involved, keeping the count in mind. Wrenlow was usually dead on when it came to tracking the number of steps required to go from one place to another, but in this case, Gavin wasn't sure if the count was quite right. It seemed as if everything was farther than suggested. Even the next tree seemed more than the dozen paces Wrenlow claimed it would be.

Readying himself, he darted across the lawn. A light moved overhead and shone out into the grass.

*What kind of light was that?*

It wasn't from a lantern. The only thing it could be would be an…

"Enchantment," he whispered.

They weren't cheap. It was a luxury he and Wrenlow shared, and anything much more sophisticated would be incredibly expensive. He prized the communication for their jobs and were it not for a gift he'd been given long ago, he might not be able to have something like this. In Yoran, enchantments were rare. That was part of the benefit of working in this city—there wasn't much magic to contend with.

Gavin sprinted. He was nearly to the next tree when somebody separated from the shadows near him. Not just somebody. Two somebodies.

A sword came swinging toward him. He ducked underneath the blade and slipped his knife forward to block the blow. He expected to meet resistance, but he carved through nothing more than air. The attacker was fluid and far quicker than him.

Gavin rolled off to the side. As he twisted and swung the knife around, the second attacker was waiting. The two fought him in unison. Not only that, but they were far more skilled than most men he'd faced.

He smiled to himself. It had been a while since he had a

fight that would engage him fully. If only he had time to savor it. If he wasted too much time, the target would get away, and the job would go unfulfilled.

Twisting his knife and shifting his stance, he feigned darting forward before backing away, sweeping his leg down, and hooking it beneath the leg of one of the attackers. He drew it forward and stabbed the nearest person in the shoulder. The attacker dropped his sword. For good measure, Gavin jammed his knife into the other shoulder. That left him with just one attacker.

Gavin switched his technique. In the years he'd been training, he'd learned many different fighting techniques. These men were skilled, but he should be far more skilled than them. There was no one within the city of Yoran who posed a real challenge to him.

At least, he hadn't thought so.

The man he faced now was not only skilled but fast. The sword was a blur, and the darkness made it so Gavin could barely keep track of the spinning blade. He traced the man's movements in his mind, having learned to watch not only the blade but the wrist and shoulder too. It was the attacker's leg that betrayed him.

The other man swung his foot, crashing a heel toward him. Gavin reacted by falling back. He pressed his hands against the ground and flipped back to his feet. While in midair, he twisted, swinging his heel around. It connected with the attacker's stomach, driving him back. Gavin didn't hesitate.

"How is it—" Wrenlow said.

"Not now," Gavin growled.

"You don't have to yell at me. I just wanted to know whether or not you needed any help. You know, sometimes you do have a little difficulty with counting. I just wanted to make sure that you—"

Gavin tapped the earpiece, silencing him. If he got through this, then he would apologize, but Wrenlow wasn't going to be able to help him in a fight like this.

He crouched low, gripping both knives. They had long blades, almost like daggers, but they were still short-range weapons. Against the sword like this other man carried, he couldn't get close enough. The man spun his blade, creating a deadly arc around him. He was waiting.

Gavin had to react soon. Otherwise, more guards would appear, and if they were even half as skilled as this man, then he'd be in trouble. He wasn't going to be able to get inside the sword arc. The other man was far more skilled with the blade and had enough reach that Gavin didn't trust himself to get through without being carved up.

*What if I tried something different?*

He rolled to the side and threw one of the knives. It bounced off the sword, landing harmlessly away from the attacker, who hesitated in surprise. Gavin didn't expect the knife to penetrate the swordsman's defenses. All he needed was to find a way to get beyond the blade, which required a little bit of risk.

The opening was what he'd been hoping for.

As the man twisted, Gavin twisted with him, going

low. He curved one wrist around, slicing the blade toward the attacker's thigh. He expected to meet muscle, but there was nothing. Only air.

He swore as he rolled away and leapt forward. He did so just in time. The sword spun, carving through the air over his head, and would have decapitated him had he been standing.

This time, when he switched hands and drove the knife forward, there was enough resistance that he was able to get through it. He felt the knife strike home. The attacker attempted to bear weight on the leg and surprisingly was able to do so far longer than expected. The man leapt to his feet.

"How about that," Gavin whispered. Someone who could tolerate pain. It had been a while since he'd faced anyone like this.

The man moved forward. A hood covered his face, but Gavin detected a lithe figure underneath. The steady grace he attacked with made it so that he didn't even need to bear weight on the injured leg all that often.

Gavin nodded to himself, focusing on the other leg, and then lunged forward. The suddenness of the movement caught the man off guard, and as he backed away, Gavin shoved his shoulder into him. He connected with the man's leg, causing him to crumple to the ground. He jammed a knife into the other leg, the only place he could reach.

As Gavin jumped back to his feet, light filled the entirety of the manor yard. He darted forward, trying to stay on the edge of the enchanted light, but he knew he was going to be too late. Not only that, he'd raised the alarm. He had failed in this job.

The door wasn't all that far from him. It was close enough he thought he might be able to reach it if he sprinted, but it would take everything within him to do so. Even at top speed, he still might not be fast enough.

He tapped the enchantment, and Wrenlow's voice called out in his ear. "Please tell me you're still there."

"I'm here," he whispered as he looked around the yard. Three others were coming toward him from the south side. The only way he could go would be toward the wall, back outside.

"Good. I thought they'd gotten to you. What happened?"

"Patrol. Skilled."

The man he'd cut down started moving again. Gavin was going to have to decide quickly—and act quickly. Doing anything but running would be a risk. There was an obvious answer, but the problem was that sometimes the obvious answer wasn't the *right* one.

He glanced down at the man he'd cut down and retrieved his fallen knife. "How many steps did you say it was to the door?"

"I thought you said you weren't going to be able to reach it."

"I'm not. I just want to know how many paces it is to the door."

"Well, from where you were, it was a dozen paces. I

don't have any idea where you are now, so I don't really know how far it is."

"Considering the attack took me a little bit away from where I was heading, I'm not really sure either." Gavin swept his gaze around the inside of the yard, gripping his knives tightly, and started running. He had to hope that he could be fast enough. At least, he had to be faster than those behind him. He felt movement all around him and worried that this was a terrible mistake.

As he glanced behind him, the activity near the wall caught his attention. Had he gone that way, there would've been others. They had wanted him to think that he could head toward the wall.

Smiling to himself, he nearly reached the door before diving off to the side. Gavin crashed through a window, glass shattering all around him.

"What was that?"

"Window," he whispered.

"We were going to go through a door."

"We were, but given that it was blocked and we didn't have any other choice, we went through the window," he muttered.

He was in a small room. Glowing coals at one end suggested it had been used recently, but as far as he could tell, there was no one else inside. It was dark, and as he hurried through it, he tried to fix the layout of the house in his mind.

*If I go through the door on the other side...*

He pulled the door open. There were enough people

that he wasn't sure he'd be able to cut his way through. His only advantage was that the hallway was narrow, which would limit how well the guards could fight.

Gavin lowered his shoulder, driving forward with his heel, and launched himself at the three people in the hallway. He twisted in the air, spinning the blades out from him. It was a dangerous technique in the best of times, but within the hallway, he thought it was somewhat safer. He could use the walls on either side of him to brace himself so that he could spin even more.

He launched himself up and continued to spiral and pivot. He caught one man in the stomach and another in the side of the neck. He slammed the hilt of his knife into the third man's temple, and the man crumpled. Not wanting to take a moment more to make sure they stayed down, he raced toward the stairs. This was going to be a bloody affair.

"It's a good thing the job didn't say how we had to complete it," he whispered.

"Why?" Wrenlow asked from the other side.

Gavin envisioned Wrenlow sitting in a chair near the hearth in the Roasted Dragon tavern, smirking to himself as he listened to the chaos through the enchantment. The other man was likely sitting with his notebook out, looking down at the notes he'd taken, and contemplating just how many steps Gavin would need to make it to each level.

"Too much noise. Most of the time, they want us to be quiet," he said.

"You? I don't know if you could be quiet if you wanted to."

"I can do quiet."

Wrenlow snickered. "Then prove it."

"Another job."

Gavin found the stairs and glanced behind him. So far there was no one else coming, and he didn't hear anything above him either. That seemed ominous since the target was on the second level. He raced up the stairs, trying to keep his footsteps as quiet as he could, and reached the next landing.

"Which door did you say it was?"

"Fourth or fifth," Wrenlow replied.

"Which one is it?"

"Like I said, the fourth or the fifth one."

He grunted and threw open the fourth door. There was no one inside. When he reached the fifth door and opened it, he realized the two rooms were connected.

"Fourth *and* fifth door," he said.

"What was that?" Wrenlow asked.

"Both doors. They led to the same place."

Gavin stopped inside the room, sweeping his gaze around. The room was incredibly decorated, with richly stained wood along the walls. A massive desk occupied space near the far end, and several sculptures sat atop its surface. One was seemingly made of gold and in the shape of a small rabbit, which gave him pause. He glanced at it for a moment and considered whether he should take the golden statue, but he decided against it. That wasn't the job. A fireplace at one end of the room crackled wildly. Two chairs sat facing each other, with a small stone table set between them. A glass of wine and the bottle it was poured from rested on the table.

As he took in everything around him, he shook his head. He'd been in two places of incredible wealth before, but this was still impressive. Were he a thief, he might find himself preoccupied, but as it was, he had another task set before him.

He picked up the glass and took a sip. The wine was sweet and far more expensive than anything he would've been able to purchase on his own.

"She's got expensive tastes," he muttered.

"What are you going on about?"

Gavin ignored Wrenlow and scanned the room. If she'd heard the noise below, then he could imagine her coming out and hiding. Maybe there was some secret place here. The walls were paneled, and he looked for any cracks that might suggest some hidden room, but given the layout of the house, he didn't see how something like that would've been possible. There was no place for her to hide.

A thumping overhead caught his attention. She *had* gotten out.

Gavin reached the door and pulled it open. He kicked the man that he found on the other side, causing him to double over. Gavin drove his knee up to the man's face with a satisfying crunch as something shattered.

He had to keep moving. If she had gone up another

level, then he'd have to follow. He raced up the stairs at the end of the room and found a door. He hesitated, squeezing the hilt of his knives, and when he was ready, he darted through the door onto the rooftop.

There was no one here. Whatever he'd heard was already gone. Gavin looked around, and he could see movement on the grounds below him, but the woman—the target—had escaped.

*Balls.*

Now he was going to have to go to Hamish and admit that he'd failed. He had no idea how the employer might react, but he wouldn't be surprised if the jobs dried up. Which meant it might be time to move on again.

"Wish me luck," he whispered.

"With what?"

"With getting out of here."

CHAPTER TWO

The street was empty, and Gavin stayed in the shadows, hiding near the buildings. Large sloped roofs covered the street where he stood, shielding him from the gentle rain cascading throughout the city. No moonlight was visible, and were it not for the faint lantern light at either end of the street, he might not have been able to see anything. The rain fit his mood.

He'd silenced the enchantment, though it didn't really matter. Wrenlow wasn't going to be talking to him much at this point. The job was over, though not done. It wouldn't be done until he completed the mission, but given what had just taken place and how much he'd made a mess of things, he wasn't at all sure whether he'd be given the chance to finish it. More likely than not, someone else would be hired. Worse, others would be aware of what he'd done—or failed to do. If it got back to his employer, Gavin knew that he or she—it could be either—would be displeased.

When he reached the end of the street, he hesitated. All he wanted was to sit down, have a mug of ale, and relax. His heart still raced, and sweat made his back moist, almost unpleasantly so. He probably needed a bath and a change of clothes. He was certain he needed to wash blood off, which was part of the reason he stayed in the shadows. There was enough activity from the constables in this section of the city that he worried he'd draw their attention.

His jobs had become increasingly complicated these days. There had been a time when he'd been able to complete a task quickly and efficiently, but that time seemed long ago. Now, most of the jobs involved targets that were difficult to nearly impossible for him to reach. Then again, his employment situation had changed. Ever since he'd been hired by his mysterious employer, he'd found the assignments to be increasingly complex.

A couple staggered down the street nearby. The thin woman leaned on the man for support, and they both seemed intoxicated. It was a little early for such intoxication, though there were places within this city, much like in all cities, where people drank all day. He studied the thin woman, noting her cloak. The weather wasn't quite warm enough for the heavy gray wool. Even the man was overdressed in a thick jacket and pants.

He remained in the shadows and headed past the pair.

Their quiet conversation shifted, cutting off as he passed them, and he could hear them start to murmur.

*Did they notice my bloodstained clothing?*

He had managed to escape the manor house without killing too many, though that really wasn't his greatest concern. All he'd wanted was to get out of there safely, and since he'd accomplished that, he figured the rest of it was a success.

As he rounding a corner, he glanced back. Was it just his imagination, or was the woman leaning on the man a little differently? He thought she'd had her arm wrapped around his waist with her head resting on his shoulder, but now it seemed as if she were upright, looking at him. Something was off. The years he spent training—and fighting—had taught him to trust his instincts and not to ignore when an alarm was raised within him.

Ducking around the corner, Gavin reached a nearby alley and slipped into it. As soon as he did, the couple appeared.

"Where do you think he went?" the man whispered.

"He couldn't have gone very far."

That didn't sound intoxicated to him at all. Worse, it meant that they were following him.

*How could they have been following me when I'd encountered them by chance? Unless it wasn't a chance meeting...*

He tapped the enchantment and leaned his mouth close to the chain. "Wrenlow, if you're there, I'm going to need your help," he whispered.

He tried to keep his voice little more than the barest of whispers, not wanting to draw any more attention to himself than he already had. If these two began searching the street, realizing he couldn't have disappeared very far, they might still find him. He would have to turn this into his advantage.

Gavin backed into the alley, looking for some way up. The pitch to the roofs was such that it would be difficult for him to maintain his footing, but he might be able to find enough grip. He wouldn't be able to move from building to building up there, but perhaps he could spy on them and get a better sense of who they were and who they were working for.

There wasn't anything for him to grab onto. Just the buildings. Thankfully, they were close enough together that he could wedge his feet out from him. It was an awkward position, but as he pressed each foot against the sides of the narrow alley, he shimmied his way up until he could reach the rooftop. From there, he gripped it and pulled himself up. When he swung his legs over, there was movement at the mouth of the alley where he'd just been. He pressed himself flat against the rooftop and stayed in place.

"I could've sworn I heard something here," one of them said.

"If he was here, there isn't any place he could've gone."

"Maybe he knows somebody in this part of the city."

"That's not the intelligence we have."

"Maybe it's wrong."

*Intelligence? Who are these people?*

They could be constables, but Gavin had been careful to avoid drawing their attention. The moment he did, he wouldn't be effective in Yoran any longer. The kinds of jobs he'd taken didn't get reported to the constables, though, so he hadn't needed to worry about that yet.

He stayed on the rooftop, leaning close enough that he could hear and hoping the angle of the roof made it so they couldn't see him.

"We should keep moving."

As they headed toward the alley, they stopped. Shouts rang out in the distance, and Gavin froze.

"What do you think that's about?"

"Probably him," the woman said. "We need to find him, and from there…"

Gavin couldn't hear what they said next, but the message was clear. Somebody had sent them after him, and all of it was troubling. Now he had to hide from the recent target, as well as whoever was pursuing him. There was also the matter of how skilled the guard at the manor had been.

He waited on the rooftop. "Did you hear any of that?" Gavin whispered.

"Some of it," Wrenlow said. "You have someone following you?"

"That's the way it seems."

"Why?"

"No idea."

Gavin dragged himself along the roof until he reached the main part of the street. He was able to look out from here, and the location afforded him enough privacy that he didn't think anyone could see him.

*I'm hidden here, but for how long?*

He didn't want to stay up here all night. It got in the way of his dream of drinking some ale, relaxing by the fire, and filling his belly. "Do your digging and see what you come up with," he said.

"There are plenty of different outfits working within Yoran. That's why we came here," Wrenlow replied.

"I know that's why we came. It's just…"

They hadn't been here all that long before the first job offer had come in. Then the next. Each one was a little bit more complicated, and each one seemed to drag him deeper into some unknown challenge. Now he had no idea whether or not this was all some sort of test, but he didn't want any part of getting caught up in the politics of the city.

"When are you coming back in?" Wrenlow asked.

"When it's safe."

"What if it's not?"

Gavin grunted. "It will be."

He listened to the sounds of the city as he lay on the rooftop. Wrenlow fell silent, though Gavin didn't expect anything more from him. Not until he found anything. Likely he was reaching out to other contacts, searching for information about what had happened and who was after them. Hopefully, he would find something, but even if he didn't, Gavin wasn't entirely sure that it mattered. Maybe it *was* time for them to move on.

Yoran was just one more city, though maybe it was more than that. There were other cities and other places they'd gone, and there were plenty of ways for him to supply his trade. He'd found an easy benefactor here, but that wasn't what had brought him to the city. He'd come to see his old friend Cyran Black but hadn't worked up the nerve to go to him yet. There was too much history between them.

"I haven't found anything," Wrenlow said. "I'm going to keep looking, but I think you really need to come back in."

"And I told you that I will."

"Maybe this has something to do with our benefactor."

"Maybe," Gavin said.

"I've been digging, you know."

"I suspect you were."

There was a pause. "You're not angry?" Wrenlow asked.

"Why would I be angry?"

The rooftop was uncomfortable. Gavin shifted and nearly rolled off. Were it not for him positioning his feet off to either side to catch himself, he might have.

"I don't know. You get… touchy… about things sometimes. Especially if you think I should be doing something else."

"You've helped plenty, and I've been trying to uncover information about our benefactor as well," Gavin said.

"You have?" Wrenlow asked. His voice was soft and clear through the enchantment.

"As much as I can."

"I imagine that involves wine and women."

"Not always in that order," Gavin said, smiling.

The street had been empty for a while, and he rolled over, dropping down from the rooftop. He looked around, but there was nothing suspicious. He hurried along the street until he reached an intersection. From there, he hesitated another moment before heading onward. He started taking a circuitous route, instinct guiding him. He wanted nothing more than to head back to the tavern, to sit by the fire, but given what he had encountered tonight, that wasn't safe. Instead, he wandered through the city, winding his way back.

The sense that he was being followed began to build. That must've been why his instinct had been to take this roundabout route. At one point, he paused and spun around, but there was no one there. That didn't change the feeling that there was some activity behind him. Gavin started back the way he'd been, turning at random corners and sweeping through the streets.

Yoran was a massive city built before the Reclamation War. It had barely been affected by the warfare, not the way that so many other cities had been. Much of the ancient structures remained with stonework that was incredibly ornate. The pale white stone gleamed in the sunlight, but in the gray overcast of night, it looked run-down, almost dirty.

Gavin rounded the corner, then paused at the next intersection. He looked around for any sign of movement, but there wasn't anything. Again he changed direction, heading back the way he'd come. By the time he reached the wealthier section of the city, he was certain he was being followed. It was nothing more than a feeling, but he'd learned to trust his intuition.

A massive tree grew in the middle of the street. It had an enormous trunk, and the thick, velvety leaves were nothing like those on the bells tree he had nearly cut himself open on while approaching the manor house. This was a sacred place in the city to some; a place where they came to worship the tree that had supposedly been planted long before the city had been built. If so, that made the tree over a thousand years old, which Gavin found almost impossible to believe. He reached the tree and traced his fingers along the trunk, feeling the smoothness of the bark that was in sharp contrast to the trunk of the bells tree.

"I understand that you weren't successful," said a voice behind him.

Gavin spun, knives already out, but hesitated. "You really should be careful, Hamish."

Hamish was an older man with graying hair, and a gold chain hung over the robe he always wore. It marked him as a priest of sorts, though he was like no priest Gavin had ever met. Each time Gavin encountered Hamish, the man was dressed in a different garishly colored robe. The darkness made it difficult to tell what color it was tonight. Deep eyes stared at him, the look within them almost knowing, as if Hamish recognized some secret Gavin had yet to find.

"Why must I be careful? Isn't it your job to ensure that you are cautious with your blades?"

"I suppose it is," he said.

"Not so cautious tonight, though."

Gavin's gaze flickered toward the end of the street. The manor house that he'd been asked to attack was not so far away.

*Had it been chance that had brought me here?*

He liked to think that it had been, but maybe he'd been guided. If so, he didn't care much for that.

"I was as cautious as I could be. The job wasn't to be silent with my actions."

Hamish surprised him by laughing. "I suppose we should be much more particular with the assignment then."

"We?"

"You know you aren't working for me, Gavin Lorren."

There were many things about Hamish that Gavin didn't like, and knowing his full name was just one of them, especially as he had certainly never shared it. Names made it far too easy to uncover things that needed to remain hidden. "When do you intend to tell me who I'm working for?"

"In time. Now, should we talk about the price for failure?"

"Price? I haven't completed the job, but it's not a failure."

"I'm afraid your failure must be punished, but the type

of punishment depends on your attitude. So says our mutual employer," Hamish said.

"And I'm telling you that I'll finish the job."

"I'm afraid that isn't going to be possible. You see, now that you have failed this time, the defenses around your target will be shifted, and anything else will be far more difficult for you to reach."

Gavin frowned.

*How much more difficult could it get?*

Getting to that woman had already been incredibly challenging, and he couldn't imagine it being harder. "I could bring others in, and all it takes is for us to—"

"No. We aren't looking for warfare. Besides, that isn't the point. Now that you have attacked—and failed, I must add—our target will move." Hamish glanced up at the sky. He glowered at the rain drizzling down around them. "I don't suppose you understand just how difficult a position you place me in."

Gavin smiled. "And how difficult a position is that?"

"Trying to argue for the merits of keeping you employed."

"I've completed every assignment you've asked of me."

"Not every one," Hamish said.

Gavin shook his head. "Fine. Not every assignment but almost every assignment. And I will complete this one." Failure wasn't something he was accustomed to, though there were times when he hadn't completed tasks before. Usually that was because he chose not to; not at all like this one.

"That is why I'm here. I needed to see for myself."

"To see what for yourself?"

"Whether or not you could be trusted."

Gavin found himself smiling again. "Trusted with what?"

"With the opportunity to finish your task. Seeing as how you have failed us, our employer thought it best you be removed from the equation, but I have argued against that. You see, I recognize the value you offer, even if they are sometimes skeptical of you."

"Do you really think our employer would find me easy to remove?"

"How many of your own kind do you think you could outrun?" Hamish asked.

The way that the man had said "own kind" left a chill through Gavin. There were plenty of mercenaries like himself within Yoran, and he knew it would be difficult to outrun many, but the statement could also be interpreted as something else—something that left him even more troubled.

*What exactly did Hamish know about me? Could that be why they had sought me out as soon as I had arrived in the city?*

Gavin hadn't revealed his presence to that many people, and he hadn't come openly either.

"Now, I know you are quite talented," Hamish continued, "but if we hired five. Seven. A dozen. How many of them do you think you would be able to overpower?"

Gavin resisted the urge to let out a sigh of relief. Maybe they didn't know after all and really did just mean other mercenaries. "As many as they hired to come after me."

"Is that right? Well, perhaps in time we will find out whether or not that is true. For now, know that I have spoken on your behalf. Our employer has decided you will complete this assignment."

"I've already told you I will."

"You're going to complete the assignment, or you will be removed from Yoran."

Gavin met Hamish's eyes, holding them for a long moment. "Are you threatening me?" He squeezed the knives. He didn't want to cut Hamish down, but he would.

"I don't think it's necessary for me to make a threat. Merely a promise. Now, when you complete the assignment, you will be paid as agreed. In this case, seeing as how difficult this task has proven to be, our employer has even agreed to increase the wages offered."

Something didn't fit quite right for Gavin. "Why would they offer me more when I haven't completed the job?"

"Consider it hazard pay. They recognize the job will become more difficult."

"Just how much more difficult?"

If there were others as skilled with the sword as the one man he faced, then perhaps Hamish was right that it'd become more difficult. It might even be worthwhile to take on the hazard pay, though he didn't know how much more hazardous the job could be.

"Unfortunately, I cannot predict that for you. Neither can I predict where you will need to go to find your target. That will be on you. If you fail, the consequences involve you, Mr. Grayson, and all of the others that you have frequented the Roasted Dragon with."

This time, Gavin took a step back. Hamish was far better connected than he had expected. Not only did he know about Wrenlow, but he knew about the others he'd started to spend time with at the tavern.

"You'd better be careful, Hamish," he said.

"And why is that, Mr. Lorren?"

"If you push too hard, you might find I don't take it well."

"If I push too hard, you'll break. Like so many have broken before you." Hamish stepped back and glanced toward the tree, then turned and looked behind him in the direction of the manor house. "Finish the task." With that, he circled around the tree.

Gavin hesitated before following him. By the time he caught up to where Hamish should be, the man had already disappeared.

*Balls.*

"How much of that did you catch?" he said into the enchantment.

"I didn't hear anything. There was too much interference. It's breaking up."

Wrenlow's voice was crackly and difficult for Gavin to hear clearly. It seemed to come from a great distance.

"Interference?" Gavin moved away from the tree. If nothing else, maybe this special tree was disrupting his communication through the enchantment. It was either that or something Hamish had carried, though that sort of enchantment would be incredibly specific. "Is that any better?"

"It's getting a little bit clearer, but something was interfering with me hearing you. I don't know what happened."

Gavin backed away from the tree until he was on the far side of the street. The clouds had started to part, the rain fading. A hint of moonlight drifted through the clouds and caught the leaves of the tree. With the rain they'd had, the moonlight glistened off of the leaves, making it seem as if starlight danced within the tree. He could almost imagine it being something mystical; the way the people envisioned it to be.

"It seems that my employer has decided to take a very different approach to their assignments," he said.

"What approach is that?"

"If I fail, they're going to have me, you, and everyone at the Dragon killed."

Wrenlow started to laugh, but it died off when he caught on that Gavin wasn't laughing with him. "You can't be serious."

"I'm afraid I am. I don't really know how they know about all of you, but they seem to. Given how easy it was for Hamish to find me, I suspect they have the resources to do so."

"How do you propose to keep us alive?"

"I'm supposed to do my job."

"Weren't you going to do that anyway?"

Gavin nodded. "I was. I will. But now I think I might need to do something else."

"What's that?"

"I need to figure out who the hell I'm working for. Then I need to decide if they deserve to live."

CHAPTER THREE

The inside of the Roasted Dragon was rustic and simple. Rough wooden walls surrounded Gavin, and heavily grooved boards ran the length of the floor. Other than the fire crackling in the hearth, light was provided by a few lanterns hanging along stone columns throughout the inside of the tavern, creating a cozy feel. He had loved it from the moment they had stepped foot inside when they'd first come to Yoran. It was a place that they'd happened upon by chance, but now he couldn't imagine being in any other tavern within the city.

He found Wrenlow sitting alone near the back of the tavern. The man had his book resting on his lap, much like Gavin had envisioned that he would. Untouched food rested on the tray in front of him. Wrenlow even had two mugs of ale sitting there, neither of them empty.

Gavin nodded at the people within the tavern and glanced toward the kitchen. Jessica strode toward them, chestnut-colored hair pulled back in a braid and her apron cinched up beneath her bosom, carrying two trays to patrons on the far side of the tavern. When he took a seat in front of Wrenlow, the other man barely looked up at him.

"I would've asked you if you were followed, but given what Hamish told you, I guess it doesn't matter."

"It doesn't matter," Gavin agreed.

"I don't like it. You know I support everything we're doing—at least most of the time." Wrenlow looked up. He had a lean face, and though he hadn't shaved in nearly a week, barely more than a faint scrub of a beard covered his face. He rubbed the knuckle of his left hand into his eyes and blinked. "If he's going to threaten us—"

"I'm not proposing we do nothing."

"Good. I was a bit worried you were going to let him get away with it."

Gavin shook his head. "There isn't much we can do about it right now. I need to finish the job, which means we have to figure out where this woman went."

"You don't think that she went back to her manor house and simply increased security?"

Gavin sighed. After he'd lost track of Hamish, he'd wandered back toward the manor house, staying as hidden as he could. When he'd reached it, he'd crawled up a hidden section of the wall and looked in the yard. There had been no movement or light in the windows. No evidence of anyone there.

"It's empty."

"Then he wasn't lying about that."

"Nope."

"Which is why you're concerned the other things he's told you are also not lies."

"Somewhat," Gavin said, stretching forward briefly to scan Wrenlow's book. He couldn't tell what was written there, though it looked to be a diagram, probably of the house he'd been in earlier in the night. Notes along the side of the diagram had been crossed out.

"That doesn't mean he's going to be able to get to us," Wrenlow said.

Gavin leaned back in his chair, gazing around the rest of the tavern. The smell of the fire drifted toward him, a pleasing and comfortable sense. It reminded him of his childhood, back before he had started his intense training. Not only was the fire comforting, but the smell of the food was as well. There was simply something about a well-cooked meal, and the Roasted Dragon had many of those. They were all tasty, and given how long they'd been staying here, he'd had an opportunity to eat almost all of them.

"I don't know," he said. "We haven't encountered anyone quite like him before."

"You can't say that. We don't really know anything about him."

"Exactly. Which is why I can say we haven't encountered anything quite like him before. I just want us to be careful. I get the sense that if he wanted to, he could have us eliminated."

The idea that they were the targets would've been amusing were it not for the fact that Wrenlow wouldn't be able to do much against someone like Hamish, though not for Gavin's lack of trying. When they'd first met, he'd tried to train Wrenlow, but the man just didn't have the knack for it. What he did have was a mind unlike anyone Gavin had ever met. That mind had proven increasingly valuable the longer they worked together and was the reason they'd survived as long as they had over the years.

"He's giving you a chance to finish the job, though," Wrenlow said.

"He is, and I have a feeling Hamish thinks he's being generous in doing so."

"He's not?"

"If he were being generous, he would've realized the job was more difficult than he had let on initially."

"I thought he'd made that clear," Wrenlow said.

"He didn't warn us quite as much as he should've about what we were going to face."

Wrenlow looked at Gavin, a question in his eyes. They had been through so much together in the time since they'd met, and they struggled with some of the same things. It had made them fast friends, at least so much as Gavin could have friends. It was rare enough for him to do that. Most of the time, he found it easier to work on his own, and were it not for Wrenlow's persistence, he might still be alone.

"That's why you have me," Wrenlow said. "With a little more time, I can—"

"You seem to be back a little early," Jessica said, swinging by their table.

Gavin looked up at her and flashed the widest smile he could. "I figured I would see what you might have special for me tonight," he said.

"What makes you think I have anything for you?"

He chuckled and shrugged. "I don't mean it quite like that."

"How *do* you mean it?" She leaned forward, a playful smile curving her full lips. A strand of her brown hair hung in front of her eyes, and she shook her head slightly to flip it out of the way.

"How do you want me to mean it?"

Wrenlow slammed his book closed and looked at the two of them. "Do you need me to step away? I mean, I know I'm only sitting right here, but I can step away while the two of you flirt."

"You don't have to go anywhere," Gavin said, pulling one of the mugs of ale over to him and taking a drink.

Jessica smiled and winked at Wrenlow. "If he doesn't mind if you watch, I guess I don't either."

"Would you stop?" Gavin said.

"What? You want him to watch, right?" Jessica said.

"You know he doesn't like it."

"He doesn't like watching, or he doesn't like women?"

Gavin looked over at Wrenlow, and he started to smirk. "You know, I don't really know."

"Well, he does spend quite a bit of time with you."

"Can you blame him? I mean, I'm worthy of spending time with." He chuckled as he said it.

"Listen to you, thinking you're so special."

"That's not what you were saying to me the other night," he said.

"You don't know what I was saying the other night. You fell asleep before you had the opportunity to hear. Or find out."

Wrenlow cleared his throat again. "Fine. If that's the way you're going to be, I *am* going to go. There are things I need to uncover to complete our task, after all." He headed away from them, and Gavin waited until he was gone before shaking his head.

"He really gets quite jumpy about things," Jessica said, taking a seat across from him.

"He struggles around women," Gavin said.

She leaned forward. She had a bright smile, a round face, and chestnut hair that hung in waves past her shoulders, which she kept tied back with a colorful ribbon. "Considering all the time he's spent here, I think I've seen him more than you. Maybe I should spend time with him. At least he's around."

Gavin laughed and took another drink. "Any news?"

"I'm not sure I want to share."

"You'd rather leave me guessing?"

She glared at him, crossing her arms under her chest. It drew attention where she wanted it to, and she grinned as he dragged his gaze back up to her eyes. "There hasn't been any activity, if that's what you're concerned about.

I'd let you know if there was. I'm not going let anything happen to you or Wrenlow while you're staying at the Dragon."

"I didn't think you would."

"No? Then why all of the questions?"

Gavin debated how much to share with her. She'd been an ally ever since he'd come to Yoran, and not only had she welcomed him to the Dragon, but she often had insight into activity within the city he wasn't able to get anywhere else. Her contacts often allowed her to learn information he didn't otherwise have access to.

"A job went sideways earlier tonight."

She turned back to him, smirking. "So that's why you're back so early. I wasn't sure if you simply missed me."

"Jessica—"

"I'll keep my ears open for any news. Maybe you should do better with completing your jobs."

She said it with a hint of a smile.

*How much does she know about what I did?*

Gavin had been intentionally vague with her over the time he'd been in Yoran, not wanting her to know what it was that he did. Stealing. Capturing those who needed to be moved. Killing, when it came to it. He didn't think she would judge him in any way, but it was more to protect her. It was easier for her to deny that she knew anything about him when she didn't know his line of work.

"Are you in trouble?" she asked. Her smile faded as a

look of real concern appeared on her face and within her deep blue eyes.

"No more than usual."

"Seeing as how I don't know you all that well, I don't know what 'usual' involves."

"These days, it involves me working for someone whose face I've never seen, doing jobs that are increasingly dangerous, and trying to keep from having my friend brought into the middle of everything."

Jessica watched him for a moment before shaking her head. "Are you telling me you've never met your employer?"

"Not yet."

"How do you get the jobs then?"

"They always use an intermediary."

"And you're okay with that?"

"It's not so much that I'm okay with it as that I don't have much of a choice. The jobs pay well."

"That's all you care about?"

He frowned. "Is there anything else I should be concerned about? I mean, I need to find well-paying jobs to ensure I can pay for my lodging."

She grinned at him. "I'm sure we can speak to the proprietor. I suspect she wouldn't have any problem with you finding alternative methods of payment."

Gavin found himself laughing. Despite what he'd gone through tonight, sitting and talking with Jessica always put him at ease.

"There is more than financial benefit you can take from your work," she said.

"Really? What other benefits do you take from your work?" he asked.

"You mean, other than having the benefit of spending time with men like you?"

"How many other men like me are you spending time with?"

"You'd be surprised, Gavin." She got up and tapped the table. "Let me bring you some food and fresh ale, then you can relax." She looked over to where Wrenlow had moved. He was sitting alone on the far side of the tavern, his book open on his lap once more, the pen moving rapidly as he made notes. "Maybe I should send one of my girls over and have a few words with him. Do you think that would make him feel better?"

"No, it would probably make him more nervous than anything. I need him focused."

She grinned, tapped the tabletop, and sauntered off, weaving her way to pause in front of Wrenlow's table. Gavin shook his head as she leaned over, revealing a flash of her ample cleavage. Even from here, he could see what she was doing.

"That one can be a bit difficult," Gaspar said, taking a seat across from Gavin.

The old thief was grizzled, with one eye constantly narrowed, and there was a perpetual sense that he was seeing more than what he let on. The heavy hide cloak he wore always had a stain, though never in the same place.

Gavin had always found that amusing, something of a mystery about the man, almost as if he were getting it cleaned and then dirtying it again.

"You're back early," Gavin said.

"Now you sound like her," Gaspar said, nodding to Jessica.

Gavin smiled to himself. "I suppose I do. I figured you'd be gone for most of the night."

"Not tonight. Too many preparations for the next job."

Gaspar rarely spoke about his jobs, preferring to keep the details to the crew he hired. Seeing as how Gavin was never part of those crews, he found out about what type of things they did only when the jobs were over.

"I figured you'd be gone longer too," Gaspar said.

The way he said it suggested he had knowledge of what Gavin was involved in. Knowing the thief and the connections he had, it was possible he did know. He was well-connected within Yoran and often able to use those connections to find information others wanted to keep hidden. Gavin wouldn't be able to conceal much from Gaspar if the man deemed it desirable to know.

"The job went sideways," Gavin admitted.

"Still don't know who you're working for?"

He shook his head. "Not yet."

"Yet?" Gaspar arched one bushy eyebrow, leaning toward him. "Something changed. You never really cared before."

"I cared. It was just…"

Gaspar leaned back, laughing. "Turnabout."

"What was that?"

The man chuckled. "Turnabout. An assassin gets turned on. Never would've expected it to be your employer, but I guess your employer never expected you to fail him."

"Or her."

"Do you think?"

Gavin looked around the inside of the tavern. "I don't really know. Outside of Yoran, I would've said no"—the neighboring cities were nothing if not harsh on women—"but inside the city? With the people I've met here, I really don't know."

"Maybe it's her," Gaspar said, nodding to Jessica.

It was Gavin's turn to chuckle, though there was a part of him troubled by the idea. He didn't think it was Jessica, but it could be somebody else he knew. Hamish knew things about him and had information he really shouldn't; not without having insider information as to the kinds of things Gavin was involved in. Somehow, the other man always had an upper hand.

"I didn't say that to get you upset, boy. I was just—"

"You didn't upset me. I was just thinking I keep assuming that my employer is somebody with money and who's well-connected, but maybe it's someone I haven't paid any attention to."

"You don't think your employer has money? I thought you were taking jobs to get paid. What kind of assassin are you if you aren't willing to work for money?"

Gavin flipped the knife out of its sheath, slamming it

onto the table quickly. It was a flurry of movement, faster than most people could track. He expected Gaspar to jerk his head back, but the old thief simply sat there, watching him.

"Not an assassin," he said more harshly than necessary.

"Those *are* the jobs you've been taking."

Gavin glowered at him. They had been, though they weren't the kinds of jobs he preferred. He didn't like killing unless he knew the person deserved it. That was where Wrenlow came in. Even tonight's target wouldn't have been handed over to Hamish until Gavin knew more about her.

"I get paid. I'm starting to wonder if perhaps the person paying me is hiding in plain sight." It was going to force him to look at everybody with a different level of suspicion. Perhaps that was Hamish's plan—if there was a plan at all.

"Care to talk about it?" Gaspar asked.

A minstrel took up a position in the far corner. They started slowly strumming a long-necked lute, and the music drifted into the tavern. When they started singing, their warbly voice sounded something like an injured animal. Gavin shook his head, looking across the tavern to Jessica, who grinned as she locked eyes with him.

"Damn that woman," he muttered.

"You don't like the music?"

"She knows I don't like music. I think she's been hiring the worst minstrels in all of Yoran just to torment me."

"Why would she torment you with minstrels?"

Gavin got to his feet and grabbed the knife, placing it back into a sheath and shaking his head again. "Because she wants me out of the tavern."

As he started past Gaspar, the thief reached for his wrist. Gavin grabbed the man's hand, pulling it off and twisting. A slender, dark-haired woman sitting in the corner jumped to her feet. Gavin noticed the narrow blade strapped to her waist and stiffened. Imogen often worked with Gaspar, so Gavin should have known she'd be here, but he hadn't seen her. She could be sneaky. Wrenlow watched Imogen, but he hadn't moved. Not much help for him there.

Gavin released Gaspar's hand quickly, letting out a slow sigh. "I'm sorry, Gaspar. Force of habit."

"Never apologize. I shouldn't have laid a hand on you. You're quicker than you look."

"That's sort of my trade," Gavin said.

"Right, but I guess I wasn't expecting you to be nearly as quick as that. Anyway, don't go angering that one," he said, nodding to Jessica.

"I have no intention of angering her."

"Don't go hurting her either."

Though he and Wrenlow were in Yoran for now, if this job didn't work out, he was perfectly willing to move on. He had to be careful not to get attached. With Jessica, that had proven increasingly difficult.

"I'll do my best," he said.

Gaspar chuckled again. He tipped his chair back, teetering on the back legs and balancing. "Your best.

Sounds like the way things went for you tonight, your best isn't always good enough."

Gavin scowled at him. "What do you know about it?"

"I don't know anything. Just that you seem awfully distressed and that there was a high-level house targeted tonight." He cocked a brow at him. "That wouldn't be you, would it?"

"No."

He crossed the tavern, putting distance between him and Gaspar. He liked the old thief, but sometimes Gaspar tried to stick his nose into places he didn't need to. It was the kind of thing that would end up getting the old man hurt.

The warbling singer continued to torment Gavin's eardrum as he crossed the tavern. The only part that sounded decent was the strumming of the lute, and even that was terrible.

"I'm going to go back outside," he said as he leaned close to Wrenlow.

"Why? Did you learn something?"

"No. I just need to stretch my legs. Besides, it's far too early for me to be in here drinking."

"I thought you wanted a night free."

Gavin looked across the tavern to where Gaspar was visiting with Jessica, then to the singer, and finally back to Wrenlow. "I thought so, too, but I don't think tonight is going to be my night for a quiet time."

He stepped outside into the darkness, where there was still a gentle breeze blowing through the city. He paused in the shadows outside of the Roasted Dragon, taking in the smells of the city itself. This area had a bit more decay than in other sections of the city, and an undercurrent of filth was carried with the breeze. Many of the shop owners attempted to mitigate the smells with flowers planted outside of their shops, producing a mixture of competing fragrances. Somewhere nearby, he detected the scents of bread baking and the savory aromas of meat and vegetables. Music drifted out of the Roasted Dragon; a jaunty tune sung by the tone-deaf minstrel inside.

Shadows moved with him.

"Not already," he muttered as he unsheathed his knives, preparing for the attack.

CHAPTER FOUR

Gavin rolled the hilts of the knives in his hands. He ran his fingers along the leather to get comfortable with it again as he slipped back along the street, moving in the shadows. It would be better for him to avoid a fight, though given his mood, maybe it wouldn't be the worst thing for him.

It would be better for him to move away from the Dragon so he didn't create chaos right outside. He didn't want to cause trouble for Jessica and the others inside by drawing the constables' attention to the tavern.

Gavin continued to move up the street, backing as quickly as he could until he reached an intersection. Then he shifted, spinning and moving deliberately. There were others out in the street, but when they saw his cloaked form with a pair of blades in his hands, they scattered.

He wasn't accustomed to being the one running. Most of the time, he was the one doing the chasing. In Yoran, everything had gone sideways. He kept talking about how this job in particular was the one that was trouble, but truth be told, many of the jobs had been off ever since they'd come here. Most of that was because his employer was hiring him to take on increasingly difficult jobs. Some of them involved getting into places that were incredibly fortified, while other jobs involved high-level targets.

Gavin had avoided most of them but refusing ran the risk of losing future jobs. Besides, in Yoran everyone was guilty of something. Situated on the outskirts of the kingdom of Henethell, the city had more thieves and criminals than he'd seen anywhere else. Most of them were like Gaspar, the kind of criminal he was accustomed to working with, but others operated from places of wealth.

Gavin reached an alleyway and darted along it, backing into the shadows. From there, the street opened in front of him. He might be trapped here, but with the way the buildings were situated, he thought he might be able to scale them and escape if it came down to it. Any fight here would force his attacker into face-to-face contact, which gave Gavin the advantage.

He moved toward the back of the alley, the darkness swallowing him. As he did, he watched for any signs of movement. No one passed on the street ahead. Gradually, the shadows started to darken and grow, and he frowned. Someone must have extinguished the lantern along the street.

That would put him at a disadvantage. He had decent

eyesight, but not as good as some. There were times when he wished he'd paid for enchantments that would augment his sight, but they were dangerous.

A figure appeared at the mouth of the alley. Gavin stayed motionless, waiting. When the attacker came, he'd either drive his knives into their stomach and move on, or he would wait for them to leave and pursue them. If somebody was willing to come to the Dragon for him, he was determined to see why they would and who they were working for.

Maybe it was for his employer.

That didn't feel quite right though. He expected his employer to give him more time to complete the job. Hamish would've bought him enough time to at least have another try at the target, even if only another night.

The shadowy form continued moving along the alley toward him. They were thin. And not alone.

There was a second one, and Gavin smiled to himself. He had chosen the alley intentionally, wanting to make sure the fight was one-on-one, and having two come down the alley would only help him. The close quarters would put two attackers at a disadvantage, running the risk of them getting tangled up in one another.

When they were near enough, he lunged forward at one. He swept in a quick arc with his left hand, bringing his right underneath. They caught both arms with a blocking movement, preventing Gavin's strike from hitting its mark. The attacker moved quickly—almost as quickly as he did.

That surprised him. Twice in one night?

Gavin gritted his teeth and switched his fighting style. He thought about a different technique, moving into a close combat type of style where he could attack more easily. He flashed forward, flipping the knife up and bringing his left hand in at a lower angle. Both attacks were blocked by the other person in the alley. Almost too late, Gavin realized that the second attacker was no longer there.

Movement behind him caught his attention, and he spun, realizing they'd somehow scrambled up the walls and gotten behind him.

*Balls.*

The alley might've been a mistake. He was pinned. He stabbed with one hand but found the other attacker driving their elbow down onto his arm. Pain screamed through his arm as he nearly dropped the knife. Ignoring that pain, he kicked behind him. A grunt was his reward, and he flipped the knife, driving it back and hitting only air. He darted forward and switched hands, using his good arm to slash at the first attacker. That one seemed quicker.

Something cut through his cloak. Gavin swore under his breath and dropped low, crouching for a moment and then driving up. The angle was such that he launched himself, using the crown of his head as a weapon. He hammered the underside of his attacker's jaw, freeing himself from being trapped.

Gavin rolled over his attacker, putting himself on the

other side of the alley, closer to the street. Now the attackers were behind him. At least he had only two.

Light from the street made it difficult for him to see them. He studied their dark cloaks and their lithe figures, and with the way they moved in their attacks, he almost groaned.

El'aras.

That had to be who they were. It had been years since he'd faced any of them, though there was a distinct style to their fighting—fluidity and speed. This was not what he expected. This was not the kind of job he would've taken.

The El'aras were athletic and almost universally thin. The men making their way toward him had angular faces, and their cloaks shimmered as they moved, giving them an appearance of something almost supernatural. In a way, they were supernatural. The El'aras were a magical people who lived beyond the reaches of humans, and it was rare for him to encounter them. There was a time when humans and El'aras mingled more frequently, but war had a way of separating people.

War and sorcerers.

Now the El'aras rarely risked the cities of humans for fear of sorcerers. When they were found, they were like this: small clusters, all dangerous.

*What purpose did they have here?*

Gavin wasn't going to be able to win against them. Normally, he had the upper hand in fights. It came from his own heritage and his own quickness, but in this case, he had nothing.

The nearest attacker darted forward, sweeping his long dagger toward him. Gavin dodged to the side, pinned the man's arm up against the wall, and kicked. At the same time, he jabbed with his good arm, driving his knife blade into the man's arm.

It sunk in, and the El'aras attacker dropped the blade. Gavin kicked it, sending it skittering down the alley. He drove his heel into the attacker's knee, which would slow him, but not enough. Not nearly enough.

He gathered himself and pulled on all of the strength within him. It was one thing he rarely had to do, especially since coming to Yoran. He'd been taught this technique by his mentor all those years ago. He could gather his strength as a way of focusing his mind, focusing his body, and getting ready for the job at hand.

Mastering his core reserves involved concentration. It was his way of calling on power deep inside of him, holding it together, and preparing it for the possibility that he might need to use it as an explosion of energy. Time and training had allowed him to hone that power, to turn it into a weapon. It was because of his control over his core reserves that he'd gained the nickname while training with Tristan.

Chain Breaker.

Gavin rarely had used his power in that way, but he needed to use every advantage he had when facing two El'aras—and the possibility there were others within the city. Summoning that power, he flipped backward.

He drove one heel into the forehead of the nearest

El'aras. As he kicked, he spun and drove the toe of his other foot forward, which collided with the man's neck. Gavin completed the flip, landing on his feet, his back to the alley.

Something crashed into him from behind.

Another El'aras he hadn't seen.

Gavin cursed to himself and tried to get up, but his body ached. There was pain within it, and everything hurt. He had no idea how badly he was injured, only that he'd been struck in the middle of his back, which could be shattered. If that were the case, he wasn't going to be able to get up easily.

Once again, he summoned the power within him. He felt it gathering deep within his stomach. He focused on the power instead of the pain, steeled himself, and then launched.

He flipped up and over the third attacker and scrambled down the alley. He staggered, trying to stay on his feet, but the pain within him continued to build. When he reached the end of the alley, he barely paused, looking down to see the three El'aras coming toward him.

One of them moved quickly. That would be the one Gavin hadn't harmed, but the other two were coming at him far more rapidly than they should've been. They were already recovering.

That was one of the challenges when facing El'aras. Their magic allowed them to heal quickly. It was something he often wished he had, despite knowing that wishing for magic was a recipe for disaster. Any time he'd dealt with magic had always ended in chaos.

He grabbed for the El'aras' dagger, then staggered along the street and moved as quickly as he could. He continued to hold onto the strength focused within him, even though there was a danger in doing it. He'd trained his body long and hard using this technique in order to help fortify himself. There was a risk that he could draw on too much strength and summon too much power.

*Still, what choice do I have?* Gavin thought.

If he didn't call upon all the strength within him, then he wasn't going to be able to get away.

Gavin streaked up the street, the technique allowing him to ignore the pain within him. His mind distantly processed the various injuries. His back had been struck, and as far as he knew, something might've been broken when the El'aras had jammed into it. His arm certainly had been injured, and then there was the cut along the other arm. It was a wonder he was still walking. He thought he still had his knives, and at least he had the dagger. An El'aras dagger was incredibly valuable to the right person. Gaspar might be able to find a buyer for it, though that was assuming Gavin survived.

He turned at another intersection and raced forward. Everything was starting to go black along the edges of his vision. He had a destination in mind but reaching it was going to be difficult. He needed more healing than what he could get at the tavern. With his vision starting to fade, he wasn't sure he was going to able to see anything well enough to figure out how to reach Cyran's place.

Cyran was another student who had trained with Tristan, and one who had been the closest thing that Gavin had to a friend while working with his mentor. In the time that he'd trained with Tristan, it was difficult to have friends at all. Cyran had been that person, though it had been a complicated friendship.

Another street.

Gavin paused, looking at the buildings to register where he was. There was movement behind him, and in his mind, he saw the El'aras streaking toward him. He doubted they'd be willing to fight out in the open. That had been his mistake. He'd gone into the alley where it had opened him up to their attack far more easily. Had he stayed on the street, they wouldn't have been willing to attack. They preferred the darkness and the shadows because it was easier for them to use their powers without someone else seeing. During the day, they could blend in effortlessly, as they looked little different than anyone else in the city.

Gavin hesitated, sweeping his gaze around and seeing nothing familiar. He looked at the buildings, searching for anything that would help him know where he was within Yoran. He couldn't see anything but there were certain smells. He followed the scent of death and the poisons his friend had long dealt in.

It was an awful thing to be aware of, but it guided him nonetheless. He turned a corner, and in the distance, the faint lantern light revealed where he needed to go. He could practically see Cyran's shop in his mind. He hoped Cyran was there, but more than that, he hoped his friend was willing to help.

Staggering down the street, Gavin's strength faded, and he stumbled. He lost track of how long he was lying there before he sat up. When he finally did, he took in a deep breath and looked around. There was no sign of the El'aras. There were others in the street, but they avoided him.

*Did they think I was intoxicated?*

More likely they saw the blood on his arm and his other injured arm. They might've even seen something wrong with his back. He had no idea what the El'aras had done to him.

He squeezed the knives, holding onto the El'aras dagger. If nothing else, that was his prize for everything he'd gone through tonight. As he scrambled to his knees, he took in a few more deep breaths and focused again. That distant sense of power was still there, bubbling within his stomach, faint but enough to find the strength to keep going.

He stood up slowly and took a step. Then another. Then a few feet. With each step, it felt as if he were walking through mud. Everything around him felt off. His body felt off. His mind didn't seem to work the way it should. Everything seemed wrong.

Gavin stumbled again, and he didn't know if he could

get back up. It took a force of will to keep moving. Then he saw it.

Cyran's home was at the end of the street. It was near the outer edge of the forest, and he could see the darkened trees ahead of him. A single light glowed in the window. Gavin staggered toward the door. When he reached it, he rested his hand on it, trying to knock. He didn't know if he had enough force with which to knock, but he tried. Then again.

"I'm coming," a muted voice cried from inside. "You don't need to beat down my door."

When the door opened, Gavin fell forward, no longer able to hold himself up.

"Gavin?" Cyran crouched down, rolling him over. It took all of Gavin's remaining strength to look up and see his old friend. "What happened?"

"Just wanted to visit."

Then the rest of his strength faded, and the room went dark.

CHAPTER FIVE

Gavin awakened slowly. He'd been having dreams where he'd seen Tristan, his old mentor. Tristan had been instructing him on how to focus his energy, using his mind to call forth everything within his body in order to concentrate that power and hold it in place. It was a trick, nothing more than a way of gathering his strength. It allowed him to find some place deep inside where he could ignore everything but the innermost parts of himself. The lesson had been one of the hardest but also one of the most important.

Something roused him. When he opened his eyes, there was darkness around him. He started to sit up, but pain made it difficult. He reached for his head, wanting to tamp down the throbbing within it. His arm ached, though with what he remembered, the pain was less than it should have been.

He remembered racing toward Cyran's home and

vaguely remembered reaching it, but he didn't remember getting inside. Gavin took a deep breath, then let it out slowly. He followed the same techniques he'd used all those years ago, the way Tristan had instructed him on preparing himself. It was interesting that he'd also done so in his dream, almost as if Tristan were still there with him. Of course, there were many times when he felt his mentor's presence. Not the least was when he was taking jobs that involved the El'aras.

As he focused himself, finding that inner strength, he called it through him. It allowed him to move and helped him ignore the pain. This was just one more lesson Tristan had wanted him to learn. Not only had he needed to learn how to channel his strength to his source of power, but he also needed to know how to ignore any pain or agony he might experience.

"Pain is just a concept," Tristan had said.

Gavin remembered sitting on the wooden cot, one arm bandaged. It was the first time he'd ever been seriously injured working with Tristan. They'd been sparring in the hidden garden, the smell of the pine trees growing around him. He had been learning the fighting technique of the Zar, which was one of darting and exposing oneself, a high risk but high reward type of style. When Gavin had first practiced it, he'd found that the risk often involved injury—a lesson Tristan had seemed more than willing to teach him.

"I don't like the style," Gavin had said, fighting through tears.

"You have to ignore it. When facing a more skilled opponent, you will likely be injured, but it's how you handle that injury that will allow you to move forward."

Gavin had whimpered, which had been met by one of the many harsh looks Tristan gave him. The old man had never looked upon him with much fondness, certainly not when he was whimpering in pain. The only times he had gotten anything other than a harsh look was when he successfully did something that surprised his mentor.

"Now get to your feet. We will do it again."

"But my arm—"

Tristan reached over and squeezed the injured arm. Gavin had cried out, and even now he could still remember vividly how much it had hurt. He'd cried, waiting for Tristan to release his arm, but the man didn't. Gavin realized that he had to find some way to move past the pain, to fight through the agony, to ignore what suffering he faced. Tristan wasn't going to let go.

Gradually, the pain started to drift into the background of his mind. It happened slowly, but as it did, he began to have some control over it. Eventually, he was able to tamp that pain down. His eyes stopped watering, and he stopped whimpering. He slammed his fist into Tristan's shoulder, and the man finally released his arm.

Tristan nodded. "Are you ready?"

Gavin looked down at his wrapped arm. There was been a slight deformity, and he distantly wondered how long it would take for it to heal. "I'm ready."

Shaking back the memories, Gavin looked down at his

arm now, in the dark of the room. It was wrapped in a similar way as it had been all those years ago. Even now, though it throbbed, the lesson of ignoring the pain came to the forefront of his mind. He was able to control the pain, pushing it down and burying it. He wouldn't allow pain to fill him.

Getting to his feet, he stumbled for a moment before reaching the door. He pulled it open and found Cyran sitting at a table, a stack of books in front of him. Cyran was about his age, with dark hair, glasses, and a thick beard Gavin suspected he kept to give him an air of wisdom. He looked up when the door opened.

"You should be resting," Cyran said.

"I don't think I can rest any longer."

"You were attacked. You probably should be dead, especially given what happened to your back. I don't know how you survived that."

Gavin paused in front of a mirror on the wall. He twisted, but he couldn't see anything. Cyran had removed his cloak but left him in his shirt. His back looked fine. He started to lift his shirt, but the movement caused another brief flare of pain that stopped him.

"What happened to my back?"

Cyran turned around and adjusted his glasses so that he could regard Gavin for a long moment. "I thought I would ask you that. When you came in here, you looked as if you had been crushed by a boulder. That's about the only thing I could think would hurt the Chain Breaker."

Gavin grunted. Cyran might be the only one who

knew that name, other than Tristan. It was something they'd called him after Gavin had learned to escape the various bindings Tristan had placed him in, each one progressively more difficult.

"Not a boulder." He blinked for a moment, thinking about the El'aras dagger. "Where are my knives?"

Cyran crossed his arms, glaring at him. The bushy beard made the gesture look ridiculous. "You come in here as injured as you were, and your first question is about your weapons?"

"That wasn't the first question," he said absently, thinking back immediately to the way he'd once antagonized his friend. "I would think given the state I was in, having access to my weapons would make sense. Even you should be able to understand that, Cyran."

"Even me? What's that supposed to mean?"

"It's not supposed to mean anything." Gavin's strength started to fade, and he sagged.

Cyran was there in an instant and caught him, then he guided Gavin over to the table and sat him in the chair. "I told you that you still needed to rest. I'm surprised you can handle the pain in your arm."

"I heal quickly," Gavin muttered.

"I know that. You forget I've seen you like this many times before."

"It's been a while though."

"It has been a while. I didn't think you coming to Yoran would lead to you being injured like this."

"What did you think would happen when I came to Yoran?"

Cyran sighed, shaking his head. "There was a part of me that thought maybe you would be able to give up the lifestyle."

"It's the only thing I know. It's the only thing Tristan taught me to do."

"It's not the only thing he taught you to do."

Gavin stared at him. There were lessons buried within, just like the pain he'd learned to suppress. He had never become the ruthless killer Tristan wanted, but there was still time. "Just because you gave it up doesn't mean I can. My talents don't translate quite as well as yours."

Cyran swept his gaze around the inside of the room. It was tidy, much like him. Well, other than the beard. A shelf contained all of the medicines, all of the various leaves and berries and other medicinals he'd collected that helped him work as a healer. They were the same sorts of things he'd once been taught to collect when he served as a poisoner.

"I'm sure I can find something for you here that doesn't involve you using those talents the same way," Cyran said.

"I'm sure you could, but I don't know if the pay would be quite what I want."

"That's what you care about?"

Gavin licked his lips, looking around the room briefly before settling his gaze on Cyran again. "I need money to keep going."

Something in Cyran's eyes softened. "You aren't still looking for them, are you?"

"The only thing I'm looking for is who was responsible for killing my parents. That hasn't changed."

"Even though you came to Yoran?"

"You sent word that I might find answers here," he said. They hadn't stayed in close contact, but enough that when Cyran had sent word to him, Gavin had listened and responded.

"Not necessarily that you might find answers, only that the city is unique." He gestured around the room they were in. "I've been here for the better part of the year. It's a reasonable city and being situated on the edge of the Jaren Forest has certain advantages." Cyran turned toward him and shrugged, then studied him for a moment. "Have you found what you're looking for?"

Gavin took a deep breath and let it out slowly. "I don't even know if there's anything to find," he said. He squeezed his eyes shut for a moment. He had searched for what'd happened with his parents, wanting to know the truth of their slaughter and why he'd survived. There had been no answers, much like Tristan had always told him, though he believed there had to be some truth out there, if only he had a way of finding it.

"I think your quest is going to end up with you dead."

"Maybe." Gavin leaned back and rested his eyes for a moment. He felt himself drifting, succumbing to exhaustion.

Focused himself as much as he had and trying to call

upon the core reserves of his strength had drained him. There were limits to how often and how much power he could summon when he did that. He needed to relax and replenish his stores of energy.

"I noticed something with your weapons," Cyran said.

"You did."

It wouldn't surprise him to know that Cyran recognized the El'aras blade. His friend had been trained in much the same way, and though they hadn't faced quite the same challenges, Tristan had been harsh to both of them.

"I did."

He ambled over toward a shelf and grabbed the knives and the El'aras dagger. He placed the knives on the table and slid them over. Gavin reached for them, and he was just a half a breath too slow. One of the knives almost collided with his stomach when it slid faster than he'd been expecting. He looked across the table to Cyran, who examined the El'aras dagger in his hand.

"I haven't seen anything this well made in quite some time," Cyran said as he turned it from side to side.

"You know what it is," Gavin said.

Cyran looked up from the dagger and rotated it, handing it to Gavin hilt first. "I know what it is, but what I want to know is why you have it here."

"Because I was attacked by the El'aras."

"There are no El'aras within Yoran. In none of the free cities. Not since the war."

"Right. And there aren't any sorcerers in Yoran either, now are there?"

Cyran's brow furrowed a moment. "The city outlawed them. They figured it was safer that way."

"That doesn't necessarily keep them away." Gavin shrugged as he studied the dagger. All El'aras blades were made of their metal. It wasn't found anywhere else, and it was harder than steel, the blade able to stay sharp far longer than any other metal. It was what made them so valuable and so rare. The only way to acquire an El'aras blade was to take it off one of the El'aras, and very few people survived the attempt.

"I wasn't expecting to see any El'aras here either. And it's more than us being too far from their lands."

Gavin flipped the dagger over. It was incredibly well balanced, though he wouldn't have expected anything different. The El'aras smiths were the most skilled artisans in the world. They certainly should be, considering how many years they had to perfect their art, much more than human smiths had.

There were a few letters engraved along this blade. Gavin didn't recognize the writing, though he'd never learned to read El'aras. There had been no point in it because the nature of his work had never brought him to the El'aras lands. For all Tristan's skill, he'd never taught Gavin how to read the El'aras language.

"What do you think it says?" he mused.

"I don't know. I only recognize a few of the letters."

"You recognize it?" Gavin looked up, unable to hide the

surprise. He wouldn't have expected Cyran to have learned it.

The other man shrugged. "He wanted me to know how to read some of their language. I think if I would've stayed with him, he would've wanted me fluent. He said it was valuable; a benefit to me as I collected various books and other items."

Gavin rested the dagger back on the table, turning it toward Cyran. "If you can read it, tell me what it says."

"That's just it. I can't read anything about it, but I recognize the words for sun, springs, and stream. Nothing more than that."

Gavin turned it from side to side. "Sun. Springs. Stream. Not the dangerous language I would expect from one of the El'aras."

"You do realize there are different groups of the El'aras."

"Actually, I didn't."

"Were you not paying attention when he was teaching us?"

"You know, my lessons were quite a bit different than yours. Most of mine involved trying to stay alive."

"So were mine," Cyran said, his voice going distant.

Gavin's lessons had involved learning fighting styles to become a warrior, skills that he'd turned into his current line of work. Cyran had learned something entirely different, studying poisons, plants, and other things that were dangerous and deadly. He'd always had what Gavin thought to be a much gentler training.

"What do you mean?"

"How do you think he taught me about poisons? Do you think he did anything different to me than he did to you?"

Gavin hadn't given it much thought. They'd been friends when they were training with Tristan, which was easy since they rarely had to fight one another. There were other students that he sparred with who ended up becoming challengers, and it was difficult to be friends with men he was expected to fight, often to the point of injury. That wasn't the case with Cyran. In that time, friendships were rare for both of them. That was probably why they both valued it as much as they did.

"I didn't think about it," Gavin said.

"No one really thought about it. Everybody thought he was too easy on me. I suppose, in your eyes, the type of suffering you experienced was a much more acute, more obvious sort of suffering, but it doesn't mean the kind I encountered wasn't nearly as bad." He looked down at his hands. "He would have me take poisons to learn the agony I would need to know, to master those effects so I could use them when it came down to choosing which poison I needed."

"I'm sorry," Gavin said.

Cyran grunted and glanced at something near him on the table before looking back up. "You don't need to apologize. None of this is your fault. I blame him." Cyran watched him for a moment. "You took the attention away from us, but we never really appreciated it. Not the way we should've."

Gavin shook his head. "I wasn't trying to take the attention away from anyone." It was strange thinking about Tristan this much again. It had been years since he'd spent any time thinking about him. At least, until he'd received word from Cyran that he was in Yoran. At that point, Gavin had felt as if he had no choice but to see his friend, especially as his and Wrenlow's jobs had dried up. Yoran was a different city for them, and as soon as they had arrived, they'd connected with Hamish and the mysterious employer. The jobs had all been perfect for Gavin. "All I wanted was to survive."

Cyran chuckled. "You wanted to do more than just survive. We all did. We wanted to get out."

"And I wanted him to tell me that I did a good job," Gavin said softly.

Cyran watched him another moment while he took a deep breath. "When he died, I decided I'd had enough. I didn't want to kill. I think I never really did, but he didn't give me much choice in the matter when he was still alive. When he was gone…"

Gavin nodded. After Tristan had died, they'd all gone their own ways. Gavin had embraced his training and used it, though perhaps not in the same way Tristan would have envisioned. His mentor had wanted to use him for power. Gavin had wanted to make money, but he also wanted to find out what had happened to his family.

This was something Tristan had always said he'd share, but the bastard had died before he'd been able to do so.

"I'm glad you're in Yoran." Cyran smiled slightly, though it didn't really reach his eyes. The darkness of the room seemed to linger there. "It really has been too long since we've had a chance to spend time together."

"I've been meaning to stop by…" Gavin had, but he'd been reluctant as well. Going to Cyran meant that he would potentially open wounds that had started to heal. It brought back memories of Tristan that he'd suppressed.

"I know you have." Cyran smiled again, this time the corners of his eyes softening. "I was thinking maybe we'd be able to work together and talk without needing to kill someone."

Gavin grinned. "Where's the fun in that?"

"I don't see fun in killing."

Gavin twisted in place. The pain in his arm was already starting to fade, and the pain in his back had also retreated. In time, he'd recover. He didn't need Cyran and his healing to know that he'd fully recover. He'd always healed quickly, which was one of the reasons Tristan had prized him. Favored him, in some ways. Because of that, Gavin had advanced quickly and developed his place with the old assassin. He had learned but had always been tested. Always challenged. "Thank you," he said.

"That's it?"

Gavin started to stand. "I need to get back. There was a job that went sideways."

"I gathered. I guess I didn't realize you'd get involved with the El'aras, but..."

"But what?"

"But if they're here, then you really should stay out of it. Whatever they're doing is dangerous. Not only for you but for the city. They shouldn't be here. If they're willing to risk... whatever it is that they're willing to risk... you don't want any part of it."

Gavin flashed a smile. "What makes you think I'm not the one they should fear?"

Cyran grunted, scratching at his chin. One hand was stained with ink or soot. "I saw how injured you were. I know just how badly you were hurt. You might be able to shake it off, and with everything he taught you, you might be able to withstand more than most people. Even you'll eventually reach a point where you can't overpower things. Even you have your limits."

"Let's hope those limits aren't anytime soon," Gavin said with a laugh as he walked to the door.

He knew he should listen to Cyran. Not only was he a skilled healer and a friend, but he had a quick mind. That was an aspect Tristan had also valued. He'd used that mind, that knowledge, and had twisted it, perverting it for his own purposes.

"I'll stay safe. If you hear anything about what they're after, send word to me at the Roasted Dragon."

"I know where you are," Cyran said.

Gavin stiffened.

*Cyran knew how to find me?*

It wasn't that he thought he'd managed to hide himself all that well. His employer now knew where his base of operations was, so he shouldn't be surprised that someone who'd trained with Tristan did too. "If you know where I am, then why haven't you come to visit?"

"What makes you think I haven't?"

Gavin paused at the door, looking at his old friend. There was so much history between them, so much that they'd experienced together, that he wanted to stay and visit. At the same time, it was difficult for him to linger when there was so much more he needed to do.

"If you need anything, just send word," he said.

"You know the same goes for you," Cyran replied.

Gavin stepped out in the street, pulling the door closed. The sun was setting, which meant he'd slept through the rest of the night and most of the day. That might be why he'd recovered as much as he had, but it had been too long, especially since he needed to figure out what had gone wrong on the job.

Pain occasionally flared, though he held onto his focus. As he walked, he thought about the training Tristan had given him, his mind going back to some of those earliest lessons. Seeing Cyran did that to him, but there were times like these that did too. Times when he needed to regain some of his strength, when he found himself thinking back to all those years ago where he could use that knowledge to focus his energy and strength.

When he reached the end of the street, he glanced back. Several lights were on in Cyran's home. For a moment, he thought they were shadow figures moving near the home, and he hesitated, tensing.

*If I've brought the El'aras to Cyran...*

Not that his friend couldn't take care of himself. Even though he'd abandoned Tristan's training, it wasn't as if he was helpless. Cyran was trusting, which had always put him into a precarious situation with their training. It was why Gavin had felt he needed to protect Cyran from Tristan and why he'd tried to keep him from suffering the way that so many others suffered under Tristan's attention.

He watched for a moment longer but didn't see any other movement along the street, certainly nothing to suggest the El'aras had reached the home. After a while, he headed back, winding through the streets and taking a circuitous route toward the Roasted Dragon. Though he didn't know how late it was, it was certainly late enough that he thought it was time to return. Wrenlow would be concerned about him. Jessica as well.

Thinking of her put a smile on his face, and he moved quickly. There was nothing like a glass of wine and a woman like her to take his mind off of a job that had gone wrong.

CHAPTER SIX

Gavin rolled over and pulled his arm out from underneath Jessica. She mumbled something in her sleep before dozing again. He pulled the sheet up to keep her covered and sat on the edge of the bed. She'd been sleeping when he'd gotten back after wandering past the manor house again without finding answers.

The lantern glowed softly in the corner. He always preferred to have a little bit of light, just enough to push back the shadows so he wouldn't be surprised. It was a habit that had saved him before.

Getting to his feet, he stood and stretched. The bit of rest had helped. He didn't need much sleep—training had forced him to learn how to function on very little. Now that he was awake, his mind started racing, thinking through what had happened with the job.

He needed answers. First, he needed to figure out where his target had gone, but now he needed to know more about her. Since he'd failed with his first attempt, it was time to do more detailed scout work. Though his employer might not have given him many details, that didn't mean there weren't details he could find. Or Wrenlow, who was much more likely to succeed.

Gavin slipped on his clothes and slid the El'aras dagger into his belt while making sure his knives were there. He padded down the hallway to Wrenlow's room and knocked softly.

When Wrenlow opened the door, he did so with sleepy eyes. "Gavin? What time is it?"

"Time to get working."

Gavin pushed into the room and paused. Wrenlow's room was a disaster. He had stacks of notebooks spread all across the table. His clothes were strewn about, and a blanket was piled in one corner.

"Gods, you really should take better care of your room."

Wrenlow rubbed his eyes and blinked. "You come to me now after you were gone all day? What makes you think I'm not taking care of it? I know where things are. You don't have to worry about my organization."

"I'm sorry I got jumped and not you. Besides, I just want to make sure you can find everything here."

"What makes you think I can't?"

"Look at this place."

"I *have* looked at it. I *am* looking at. There's nothing here to be concerned about." Wrenlow groaned. "You don't have to train me to be you."

Gavin stiffened for a moment. "I'm not trying to train you to be me. I don't think you could be me."

"Thanks."

Gavin shook his head. "I don't mean it like that. I just mean that you don't need to be me. You're enough the way you are."

Wrenlow looked at him and blinked, then rubbed his eyes again. Finally, he turned away. "I know where everything is that we need. You don't have to worry about that with me."

Gavin opened his mouth to say something but bit it back.

*What was there to say? Nothing. Not really.*

They had traveled together long enough and knew each other well enough that Wrenlow understood he was the only person Gavin trusted.

He smiled at the thought. He took a seat on the bed, shifting the blanket to clear some space for him to rest. Now that he was awake, he felt much better. There was still a twinge of pain in his back, but nothing like it had been. The other injuries had almost completely faded.

"I need you to do a little bit of digging."

"I *have* been doing some digging. I want to see what we can find out about Hamish and track him back to your employer, and then—"

"It's not just Hamish." Gavin pulled the dagger out, and he handed it over to Wrenlow. The other man had already been in bed by the time Gavin had returned to the Dragon, and when Jessica had found him and dragged him upstairs, all thoughts of mentioning the El'aras to Wrenlow had gone from his mind.

"What is this?"

"An El'aras dagger."

Wrenlow's breath caught. "How did you find this?"

"They found me." Gavin told him about the attack in the alley the night before and how he'd barely survived. Wrenlow listened, gradually looking more alert the longer he shared. By the time he was done, Wrenlow was staring at him.

"That's what you were off doing. You should be dead."

Gavin nodded. "I should've been dead a long time ago."

"No. I mean, if you were cut, you would've been poisoned." He grabbed Gavin's arm and pulled his sleeve up, seeing the bandage. "Everything I've read tells me the El'aras use a special poison on their blades. Sorcerers are the only ones who can stop the El'aras."

Gavin had heard the stories the same as any. The El'aras had been pushed beyond the borders of the Relanar Forest through the effort of the Sorcerer's Society. Were it not for them, all these lands and cities would have been overrun by the El'aras.

"I'm sure they're poisoned," he said, realizing he should've considered it before. "Part of my training has been to help me deal with poisoning." That was likely the reason that he'd struggled so much getting to Cyran's home. At the time, he hadn't given it much thought, but it made sense. That meant his friend would've known to treat him for the type of poisoning.

Of course he would. Cyran had seen the El'aras blade.

"The poison should've been fast acting. I don't know how you would've been able to survive. Honestly, Gavin, how is it that you're even still standing?"

"Let's just say that the poison isn't as terrible as you believe."

Wrenlow shivered. "I can't imagine *any* poison not being as terrible as what I believe." He looked down at the dagger, running his finger along the hilt but making a point of not touching the blade. "There was a time long ago I saw a book that had some of the El'aras writing in it. I wish I would've taken it. Then again, I never would've expected that I'd be talking to someone who actually fought the El'aras. At least, faced them and survived."

"I almost didn't survive. Don't be too impressed. It's luck, nothing else."

"How many did you face?"

"Why does that matter?"

"It matters because if it was one or two, then sure, I'd believe it was luck. If it was more than that…"

"That's all it was," Gavin said, sighing. There were times when he wished he could tell Wrenlow the entire truth about him, but there were certain things the other man didn't know and didn't need to know. The truth would end up causing only trouble for both of them.

Wrenlow continued tracing his fingers along the hilt, staring at it. "It's an impressive blade."

"I need you to look into who might've hired the El'aras within the city. Do so carefully. From what I understand, there's some sort of treaty that should prevent them from being here. The fact they're here suggests that either they're willing to violate the treaty or they have the express permission of someone powerful within the city to be here."

Wrenlow looked up. He handed the dagger back. "I don't like this."

"You and me both."

"No, I don't like the idea that you've suddenly gone from taking jobs to taking jobs that involve sorcerers."

"This isn't sorcery."

Wrenlow glowered at him. "We don't work around magic, Gavin."

"We use the damn enchantment with each job."

"That's different. That's minor magic at best. And you know what I mean."

"I know," he whispered.

It wasn't his intent, and he certainly didn't want to bring Wrenlow into something he wasn't comfortable with. The man had been a friend, an ally, and in the years they'd been working together, Gavin wouldn't have completed some of the jobs he'd taken had Wrenlow not been a part of them. Together they had accomplished more than what he would've been able to do on his own.

When he'd first started traveling with Wrenlow, however reluctantly, he wouldn't have said the same thing. Over time, Wrenlow had proven himself and shown that he could be incredibly useful. In the first job they'd pulled together, Wrenlow had trailed behind him. Gavin had been stabbed in the side—not the first time and definitely not the last time—and Wrenlow had dragged him away, giving him time to recover. It had made him think twice about having somebody looking out for him. If he had, he wouldn't have been as likely to be jumped.

"We're not going to get involved in sorcery," Gavin said.

"Are you sure?" Wrenlow's gaze drifted to the El'aras blade. "If the El'aras are involved, then magic is already a part of it."

"I think…"

He didn't really know what to think. All he knew was that Wrenlow was right. The El'aras were involved, which meant an element of magic was involved. The timing of the attack combined with what he'd faced when he'd gone after the target made him suspicious.

*Could my employer have known?*

The idea that his employer knew about his capability, along with his history, bothered him. But then, Hamish had made it perfectly clear that he knew more about Gavin than what he would've wanted anyone to know. That was the most troubling thing. Maybe this was a job he needed to keep Wrenlow out of. Which meant going after information on his own.

"Stay on the periphery of what you can find," he said.

"The periphery? What does that even mean?" Wrenlow asked.

"It means don't go and do something foolish."

"I'm not going to do anything that'll get you hurt."

"It's not me I'm concerned about. I know your feelings about magic," Gavin said.

Wrenlow grunted. "I'm not sure you do. You weren't there when my family was slaughtered. You weren't there to see how helpless I was." Darkness clouded his face.

"I've seen others who have gone through something similar."

"I know you think that was what happened to your family—"

"It was," Gavin said.

He had so few memories of that time. He'd been little more than a toddler, and the memories he had were faint. He remembered an explosion and the sense of power, and nothing else. After that, Tristan had claimed him. He'd begun training and working with the man who'd become his mentor. The lessons had been easy at first, but they had become increasingly difficult.

"Promise me that if magic is involved, we'll move on," Wrenlow said.

Move on. It meant leaving the city. Leaving consistent pay. Leaving the Dragon. Maybe they *did* need to do that. He was getting attached, something that he'd learned was a danger.

"I promise," said Gavin, hoping it was a promise he'd be able to keep. "Just see what you can find out."

"What about you?"

"I still have a job to do. I think I need to keep at it. If I don't complete this job quickly, Hamish has made it clear that we'll suffer."

"We don't even know what he's going to do to you. You're too valuable to him."

"I would've thought the same thing, but now, especially with the El'aras in Yoran, I don't know if that's true." He tucked the dagger back into his belt. "I'm sorry I woke you. I couldn't sleep, and I just wanted to get started on this."

"I suppose if you faced the El'aras, I can understand why you couldn't sleep. I'll get working on this in the morning." He flashed a smile. "There's not a lot I'm going to be able to find out at this hour. I have a few contacts within the city I can go to, and we'll see what I can come up with."

Gavin smiled. He appreciated that about Wrenlow. It wasn't just how quickly he'd been able to develop a network of contacts all throughout the city. The man had an easy-going nature about him, and it made it so that others trusted him. In a way, it was almost like magic, though Gavin knew it was a skill Wrenlow had honed over the years, no differently than how he'd honed his fighting ability. It was that trust that he needed now.

Heading back down the hall, he wandered into the tavern and took a seat at a table. The tavern was empty, and the scents from the night before lingered in the air: from the fire that no longer burned, old food, and ale that had gone stale, turning a little bit sour.

He stood and began to move through the fighting patterns Tristan had taught him. At first, his body was stiff, tense. As his body warmed up, he began to work more rapidly. He could feel patterns flowing through him as he let the training come back.

It was easy to embrace the various fighting styles, and he stayed within the confines of each before cycling to the next. When he was engaged in combat, Gavin often mixed fighting styles, rarely keeping to one in particular. They had all merged in his mind so that he could pull upon the most useful aspects of any of them. There were times when it was better for him to get back to the basics, to focus on the initial lessons he'd learned. Working through those patterns also calmed his mind.

The tavern was empty enough, and he'd pushed the tables off to the side so that he had space to work. Even without that space, he could still slip through the openness of the tavern and find the patterns to dance from one to the next.

It bothered him that Hamish knew as much about him as he did. Yoran was small enough that Gavin wasn't surprised Hamish had found him, but it was the fact that the man had dispensed that knowledge with a hint of a threat that troubled him most. The threat meant that his allies were in some danger. Some of them worked within the city's underground and were accustomed to danger. Then there were those like Jessica. She didn't deserve that threat.

He shifted to the Jasap style. It put some pressure on his back, and he twisted, using everything he could to move through that style so he could limber up. He needed the flexibility. The longer he worked through those patterns, the quicker he fought. If there were El'aras in the city, Gavin was going to need all the speed he possessed. Hopefully, he wasn't going to have to face any of them again, but he had to be prepared. That involved his body—along with his mind.

When he was done with the Jasap style, he moved straight into the Bo style. This one was more aggressive, whereas the Jasap was more of a flow from movement to movement.

Gavin jerked his hand forward and pulled it back, then swung his feet around.

He lost himself in the patterns as he switched from style to style, going through everything he'd learned and embracing the calm the training brought him. This was one of the many things he still did that Tristan had taught him. In doing so, he could find the speed and focus he needed.

Memories of those training sessions, times spent sparring with Tristan, flashed in his mind. He thought of his older and much more experienced mentor, the way that he had brutalized Gavin in the earliest years, forcing him to develop or suffer. He'd had little choice but to improve. Over time, the beatings hadn't been nearly as severe, though he had never bested Tristan.

When he was done, he'd worked himself into a nice sweat. The sound of clapping came from behind him and caught his attention. He spun and found Jessica watching him.

"I didn't know you liked to dance," she said.

Gavin shook his head. "It's not dancing. It's practicing. Preparing to fight."

She stood up and started to stretch her hands out from her. As she did, she moved them in a rhythmic fashion. He couldn't deny there was something similar to the different patterns he'd gone through, much like he couldn't deny that there was something appealing about watching her as she worked through those patterns. She had wonderful curves, and as they flowed from position to position, he could practically envision how those curves felt beneath him.

"It seems just like dancing to me," she said, smiling at him.

She reached out, taking his hands. He squeezed as he fell into the same rhythm. There was a hint of a Malian rhythm to it, though part of it was Porth as well. By mingling his fighting styles, he was able to mimic at least enough of her dancing technique. He continued through the movements, embracing the way she danced.

"Didn't I tire you out?" she asked, leaning close to him.

"You did, but my mind was working too much."

"I'd rather have your hands working." She shifted one of his hands, sliding it on her hip. She leaned in, breathing in at his neck, and smiled again. "Of course, I value your mind as well."

She kissed him, and he kissed her back.

Ever since coming to Yoran, Jessica had been the one constant. He appreciated that she was there for him, never asking for more than what he could give. Considering he didn't know how long he was going to stay in the city, he didn't know how much he could really give her. He had a sense of what she wanted, but he also had a sense she knew he might not be able to offer it to her.

"I'm going to be busy for a little while," he said.

"It's an even better reason for us to spend more time together for what's left of the night. Especially since you left me last night."

"I didn't have much choice."

"No?" She traced her finger along his chest.

"What I'm doing might be dangerous."

"I gathered that. I suspect everything you do has the potential to be dangerous."

"Not always… but often."

She looked up at him, and her gaze lingered on his, her eyes seeming to pierce some deep part of him. "I'm not looking for love, Gavin."

He smiled, but he could see the lie behind her words. "You don't need to—"

Gavin never got the chance to finish as the door exploded open.

There was a burst of fire, followed by an immediate enchanted darkness that was overwhelming. He pushed Jessica behind him, positioning himself in such a way that he could block her from the attacker. He reached for the knives and came across the El'aras dagger instead. As he pulled it free, it started to glow softly.

"Shit," he whispered.

"What is it?"

"Bad news."

"I take it that whoever's coming isn't friendly?"

Gavin shook his head. If the El'aras dagger was glowing, it meant there were others coming with it; that their magic was being used.

He flicked his gaze upstairs and thought of Wrenlow. Thankfully, he was in bed. There were others upstairs who were also sleeping, others who might be able to help him. It was late enough that the tavern was completely empty. He should be thankful for that. If it weren't empty, then everyone who was here would be dead.

Instead, it would be only him.

## CHAPTER SEVEN

Gavin leaned toward Jessica. The inside of the tavern was quiet. His breathing and the hammering of his heart were the only sounds, other than a faint creaking of boards. Everything within him was on edge as he scanned the inside of the tavern by the light of the glowing dagger, looking for movement. He didn't see anything. He'd have to handle this on his own, but first he had to ensure Jessica would not be injured.

"I need you to go upstairs," he said, pushing her toward the stairs. "Hide."

The El'aras dagger started to pulse even more powerfully. He could feel the energy within the dagger, and he didn't need access to magic to know that what was coming was more than what she could withstand.

He focused on his core strength. It was strange that he needed to do this so often these days. He'd gone nearly a year since using that technique, and here he had done so several times in one night. Thankfully, he'd had enough sleep that he'd replenished his energy.

"I'm not going to leave you here. If you need help, I'm able to—"

He pushed her toward the stairs again. "I know you're willing to, but I'm saying you aren't *able* to. Go. This isn't a request."

She glared at him, then stormed off. Her footsteps up the stairs were much louder than they should've been. She was bound to wake the entire tavern, though knowing her, that was probably what she wanted.

Gavin focused on what he could feel through the dagger. He'd never had an El'aras dagger, so he didn't know what the glowing meant, but he suspected it wouldn't be good.

The darkness remained, filling the inside of the room. El'aras magic.

Creeping forward, he held the dagger out from him, trying to use it to pierce the blackness. As he swept the dagger through it, it started to clear. Other glowing blades were visible. He counted five.

Five El'aras.

The only advantage he had was that they might not know about his training, but the fact that they'd sent this many at him suggested they realized he posed some sort of threat. He'd have to act as quickly as possible and then hope for enough time to overpower this wave of attack.

Then he and Wrenlow would have to move on. At least, *he* would have to move on. If he'd drawn the attention of the El'aras to the Dragon, then he couldn't stay here any longer.

Gavin lunged. The suddenness of it should've drawn the El'aras off guard. He twisted in the air, swinging his legs up and around, his muscles still loose and warmed from his practice.

He connected with something, but the speed of his attack threw off his ability to determine what was taking place. He drove his heel all the way through, whipping his leg around, and kicking. As he slashed with the El'aras dagger, he was greeted with a flash along the blade. He had no idea whether that meant he'd connected, as the blade was so sharp and deadly it might only mean he'd cut through a table. He kicked off again.

In the darkness, the only thing he could see was the various daggers all around him. There were still five, though one of them now rested on the ground. Gavin lunged for it, rolling and sweeping it away from whoever was there, and he now held it in his other hand.

Both of the daggers glowed. There were four El'aras still out there, though the fifth might be alive. He picked out another target.

Focusing his energy and thankful he still had enough reserves remaining, he brought the daggers back together, swinging them around in an arc as he darted forward. He swept them on either side, slicing at the El'aras as he dodged out of the way.

One of the blades connected. He could feel it this time, though he wasn't sure what he cut. Twisting the blade, he attempted to carve through the El'aras. Something surged through the blade. He rolled toward the far side of the tavern and landed near the entrance. He needed to get out, but as he reached for the door, he found it blocked. He dove off to the side, bringing the dagger up.

It was just in time. Another blade swept toward him. There was a clang of metal on metal, a sound that rang out like a bell. He swept his leg around to kick at one of the attackers, who grunted. Gavin focused his power within himself, then flipped back to his feet and stabbed with the dagger.

The blade caught nothing but air. His momentum carried him forward, and he twisted to the side. If nothing else, he needed to end up back on his feet. He landed near the door again.

One of the El'aras nearby carved their blade toward him. Gavin ducked and brought up his own dagger, slashing above his head. It sunk into the wooden frame of the building. He jerked his hand back and punched with the dagger clenched in his fist, twisting it at the end as he brought the blade toward the El'aras. Again he caught nothing but air.

The strength he'd recovered was already starting to fade. He didn't know how much longer he could withstand this kind of a fight, especially here in a confined space. He needed to get back outside where there was an advantage in fighting on the street. The El'aras wouldn't be able to use the darkness against him as easily out in the open. And those he cared about would be less likely to be harmed.

He jumped, flipping into the air and spinning his legs. One foot connected with an El'aras, and he landed on his shoulder. Pain flared, but he ignored it. His mind processed the pain and knew it was dislocated, though he'd done that before.

He got up and popped his shoulder back into place, then darted toward the fallen El'aras. He wasn't fast enough. The attacker was already moving.

Gavin backed toward the wall. Three came toward him.

*But where is the fourth?*

There should've been another here, and though he'd kicked or punched one—he no longer knew which—he didn't know where they'd gone.

A voice shouted in his ear. "Gavin? Jessica said—"

He hurriedly tapped the enchantment, cursing to himself.

*What was she thinking, waking Wrenlow up? He wasn't going to be of much help here.*

Movement dragged across the floor near him. There was no sign of a glowing El'aras dagger near it, which meant that whoever was coming close to him was one of the disarmed attackers.

Gavin jumped and crashed into something that knocked him back to the ground. His head throbbed, and he shook off the sudden dizziness that rolled through him in waves of agony.

Light bloomed from the far end of the tavern. It allowed him to see the El'aras turn. He reacted by jumping forward, and he jammed his daggers into the back of one of the El'aras and kicked. He spun, swinging toward another, but this time found an emptiness where the El'aras had been.

There were two or three remaining. Still too many.

At the bottom of the stairs, lantern light revealed Jessica's face as she looked out at him. "Gavin? I can't see anything here. I roused the others—"

Jessica fell silent. Gavin's heart stopped. He didn't need to see the El'aras dagger to know the blade had punctured her belly.

He cried out. It wasn't pain. It was rage. He embraced that anger.

Tristan had always warned him against fighting angry. He would get sloppy if he did. In this case, he no longer cared. It was his fault Jessica had been stabbed. The El'aras were here because of him. He should've known better than to come back to the tavern.

One of the other El'aras got in his way. Gavin jumped, twisting up over him, kicking off the ceiling, and driving the dagger down into the attacker's mouth. He plunged it all the way to the hilt, withdrawing it as he landed. The El'aras crumpled to the ground.

He darted forward, reaching the other El'aras who turned toward him. With the lantern light illuminating everything, he made out the El'aras's features. He was thin, like all of his kind, and his face was shadowed. He seemed deeply tanned, though that might've been the lantern light reflecting off of him that made it seem that way.

Gavin jammed his blade forward. The El'aras blocked, but Gavin countered, twisting his other blade and sweeping around. He wasn't fast enough. The El'aras was quick and turned toward him, swinging the blade in a furious pattern. It was a fighting style Gavin didn't know, but it didn't matter. All that mattered was that this El'aras had harmed Jessica.

He needed to act quickly. It was possible something might still be able to be done for her, but he needed to get her to Cyran before she bled out. Even that may not be fast enough since Cyran was on the far edge of town. There were other healers closer to the Dragon.

*But how many of them can I trust with her life?*

None. That was how many.

The El'aras continued toward him, driving him backward. Almost too late, Gavin realized what his attacker was trying to do. There was another El'aras behind him.

Gavin turned, kicking outward. His foot connected and he jumped, avoiding something sweeping at him. He couldn't see it, but he could feel the energy as it whistled beneath his feet.

An El'aras sword. It started to glow softly.

El'aras daggers were rare. An El'aras sword was rarer still. They were mostly ceremonial. As far as he knew, there were no known El'aras swords outside of their lands.

Power burst within blade. Gavin kicked once again, trying to get beyond the reach of the sword, but he couldn't. The swordsmen caught him on the leg, causing him to stumble. If the blade was poisoned, he wouldn't be able to fight for much longer. Now he needed more help than just for Jessica.

He hobbled on one foot. The other attacker came toward him, moving with confidence now. Gavin did all he could to keep his blade up. "You bastard," he said.

"You made a mistake, halfling."

Gavin sneered at him. "I made no mistake. I didn't do anything to you or your kind."

"You made a mistake," the El'aras said again. He lunged, and the movement reminded Gavin of the guard he'd faced the night before when he'd gone to the manor house grounds. He hadn't been an El'aras. Gavin would've known if that were the case.

*Wouldn't I? What was going on here?*

Given the slowly burning pain in his leg he struggled to ignore, he didn't think he was even going to have the opportunity to figure that out.

The El'aras came closer, holding his dagger in hand. Suddenly, he fell.

Gavin blinked. Gaspar was behind the El'aras, a club in hand. Unable to stand any longer, Gavin dropped to his knees. He jammed both daggers into his attacker's shoulders, pinning him to the ground. He rolled over to the side, stretching toward the other El'aras. He was just out of reach, but his sword…

Gavin lunged, but he missed the El'aras. The blade flickered, and again he dove for it. This time, it was farther from him, far enough away he couldn't reach it. He scrambled toward the blade, but with the injured leg, he couldn't get there fast enough.

*Could the El'aras be leaving?*

That wasn't like them. They remained until the fight was over. In this case, perhaps the fight *was* over.

He tried to get up, but pain surged in his leg. He forced it down, all of his training going into ignoring that agony. He struggled to move forward to get closer to the El'aras before they had a chance to escape. Given what they'd done to Jessica, his only thought was of revenge.

The El'aras continued away. Gavin went forward but Gaspar grabbed him and turned him around.

"You can't do anything now, boy."

Gavin jerked his arm free and reached the door, leaning out. Rage boiled within him. But the El'aras was gone.

Someone had lit the lanterns behind him. The inside of the tavern danced with the bright light, and the bodies of the El'aras that he'd carved littered the floor. It was difficult for him to find any sympathy within him.

He scrambled toward Jessica, limping on his injured leg. He lifted her head and propped his arm up underneath her, cradling her head. Blood pooled around her, and she moaned softly.

"Why did you have to come back down?" he whispered. He stroked her wavy chestnut hair, brushing it back from her face.

He had to summon his reserves. Reach Cyran. Get help for her. That was how he would help. Turning to Gaspar, he said, "Stay with her. I'm going to get help."

Gaspar joined him and rested a hand on his shoulder, shaking his head. "You and I both know nothing can be done for her. Stay with her."

Gavin glared at him. "I'm not leaving her to die like this. There has to be something that can be done for her. I know someone who can help."

"Unless they know sorcery, there won't be anything they can do."

He said nothing as he got to his feet, staggering toward the door. With each step, the pain started to fade. He held onto his focus, tying his power together and using everything within him to draw that energy together so he could move through the tavern. He grabbed one of the El'aras daggers and walked back out onto the street.

The dagger was clutched in one hand, even though he knew he probably shouldn't move so openly with it in hand. It would draw only the wrong kind of attention. Of course, it was late enough it might not even matter. There wasn't anyone else on the street. He didn't expect to encounter additional trouble, but then, he hadn't expected to find any trouble in the first place.

As he headed through the streets, he made a straight line toward Cyran's. With each step, his pain continued to fade. His anger did not. When he neared the home on the far edge of town, Gavin knew he'd already taken too long. He beat on the door, not mindful of anyone else who might be around or the noise that he was making. He cared only about waking his friend.

"Answer the damn door," he shouted.

A light started to glow inside the window, and finally Cyran opened the door. He rubbed sleep from his eyes, though he hid a knife underneath his robes.

"What are you doing, Gavin?"

"A friend of mine needs you. El'aras attack. Dagger to the belly. Grab whatever you need."

Cyran rubbed his beard. "If there was a knife to the belly, there won't be much that I can do."

"Dammit, Cyran! See if there's anything you can try."

Cyran regarded him for a moment before rushing inside, gathering a few things, and then closing the door behind him. Back out on the street, he passed a small vial over to Gavin. "Drink."

"I don't need to drink."

"Drink, if you want me to go with you. I can see you're struggling. I don't know what exactly happened, but you need to regain your strength. This will help, and it'll help with anything else you might've been exposed to."

Gavin took the vial from Cyran, tipped it back, and swallowed. The taste of it was awful; like drinking ash. He hurried through the street, guiding Cyran, and with every step, his energy returned much faster than he would've expected.

"Do you care to tell me what happened?"

"After."

"If the El'aras attacked—"

"I told you, after."

Cyran fell silent. They rushed through the streets and reached the Roasted Dragon, lights glowing inside. He found Gaspar at the door, guarding it with a slender sword he'd never seen the man carrying before. He nodded to Cyran when he came inside, and Gavin guided him toward the center of the floor where Jessica lay motionless.

Cyran crouched next to her, running his hands along her before pulling back the folds of fabric around her stomach, revealing the wound. Not only was it still bleeding, but the flesh around it had blackened. The blade had been poisoned. Gavin was surprised that he hadn't suffered from the same poisoning, but maybe Tristan's training had helped him more than he'd realized.

"Gavin, there isn't anything I can do," Cyran whispered.

"There has to be something you can try."

Cyran shook his head. "Even if I could, I don't know if I should."

"What do you mean you don't know if you should? Look at her!"

Cyran stared at the wound. "I *am* looking at her. I'm afraid you aren't. She's gone, Gavin."

Gavin sat down next to Jessica. So much of his time and life was spent dealing with death that he knew it would come for him eventually. It was when death found those he cared about that he struggled most.

This wasn't supposed to happen. Jessica wasn't supposed to be targeted. The tavern wasn't supposed to be targeted. He'd only taken jobs that involved marks that wouldn't retaliate. He'd only taken jobs for those that needed to be removed.

Now it had cost him.

He lifted Jessica's head onto his lap and smoothed back her hair. He stared at her face, touching her cheek, feeling how cold she already had become.

"I'm sorry," he whispered.

## CHAPTER EIGHT

Cyran mixed several different powders from his pouch, all different colors and some with strange aromas to them. He motioned for Gavin to help, who crouched down next to his old friend and looked down at Jessica. So far, she hadn't moved, though he believed that she could still come around. All it would take was time. Healing. Whatever Cyran might be able to offer.

"I need a drink to mix this with. I don't know whether or not this is even going to work. I can't guarantee it'll be effective."

Gavin looked up at him, holding his gaze. "Whatever you can do."

Cyran studied him. "You care about her."

"She didn't deserve this." He scrambled to his feet and grabbed a mug of ale from the kitchen, then handed it over to Cyran. "You're going to have to use this."

He grunted. "I've used worse." He dumped the powder

in and began to swirl it around. When it was done, he nodded to Gavin, who slipped his arm underneath Jessica's neck and propped it up.

Cyran brought the ale to her lips, shaking his head. "I don't know if this is even going to work," he muttered.

"If you're responsible, it's going to work," Gavin said.

"You're giving me too much credit," Cyran said softly.

He poured some of the ale into her mouth, stroking her neck to force her to swallow. Jessica coughed and then began to drink. He poured more of the ale in, making her drink most of it. When he was done, Gavin leaned her back down.

"Let her rest," Cyran said. "If it's going to work, it's going to take time. She's going to be weak." He looked around the tavern. "If the El'aras were involved, it's possible they had poisoned blades. Recovering from something like that will take quite a bit of time. I stitched it as well as I can, but it might not hold."

"I know."

"Most people aren't like you, Gavin. Most people don't bounce back as quickly as you do."

"I know."

Gavin scooped Jessica up and hurried up the stairs to the room that he'd taken to sharing with her. He set her on the bed, and she moaned softly. He debated whether he should change her clothes but figured that, for now, it was best that she have a chance to rest.

Looking around the room, his gaze settled on the small table near the window where she kept the rose he'd brought her. It was a flower that he'd taken after his last job, stealing it from a garden that he should never have been in were it not for Hamish hiring him.

He closed the door behind him, making his way back to the tavern. He nodded to Gaspar and took a seat at a table, pulling a mug of ale to him and resting his head in his hands.

The mug of ale sat untouched in front of him. Tables had been put back in place, an attempt to give the Roasted Dragon a semblance of order once again, though there wasn't anything orderly about what had happened here tonight. The smell of death lingered within the tavern, mixed with sweat and fear.

Anger remained within Gavin.

"Who was she?" Cyran asked as he sat next to him. He looked exhausted, having worked on the others in the tavern who'd been injured. Other than Gavin, Gaspar and Imogen had participated in the fight. He didn't know Imogen that well, but she was a skilled fighter according to Gaspar. Both had sustained bruises, and Imogen had come away with a small scrape. Cyran had rubbed an ointment on it to ensure it wasn't poisoned. Wrenlow sat near Imogen, watching her.

"She's a friend," Gavin whispered. He took a long drink of the ale, setting it back in front of him and staring at the mug.

"She must be a good friend."

Gavin looked up and nodded. "She wanted something

I wasn't able to give her. That doesn't change the fact that she didn't deserve this."

"What about the people you target, Gavin?"

"That's not what I do." He tipped the mug back again, drinking it down in one massive gulp. When he slammed it back down, he started to get up, but the effect of the ale started to work through him. He hesitated a moment, letting it settle.

"That's not what I hear."

"And what do you hear?" Gavin snapped.

Cyran flicked his gaze to the back of the tavern. "Just that your jobs are the kind of thing that Tristan would've wanted you doing."

"That's not how it is."

Silence fell between them for a moment. "After you left earlier, I uncovered something," Cyran said. "It has to do with the El'aras. I looked into the treaty they forged with the free cities. I figured if they were here, there'd have to be some reason they were willing to violate the treaty. What I found was that the treaty was with the Shoren El'aras, not the Yassir El'aras."

Gavin shook his head. "I don't even know what the difference is."

"They aren't one people. The Shoren El'aras are closer to Yoran's border. Typically, they're the ones we encounter."

"No one encounters the El'aras."

"You have."

"I'm different," Gavin said, once again attempting to stand.

When he did, he looked around the tavern. Gaspar and Imogen were talking quietly. Neither of them looked nearly as tired as Cyran, but both of them needed to get back to sleep. He doubted anyone would be sleeping much tonight. Wrenlow should've been oblivious to what was taking place, but with the enchantment, he would've heard everything.

"The Yassir El'aras don't have the same treaty," Cyran said.

"What does that mean?"

Cyran stared at him for a long moment before shaking his head. "I don't really know. I just thought you should know it's not as straightforward as you might think." He nodded toward the corner where the El'aras bodies were.

Gavin had made certain to ensure they weren't getting up. One of them had a dagger through his skull, so there was no questioning he was going to stay dead, but the others had been knifed in less vital organs. Or they had been until Gavin stabbed them each in the heart. Now they weren't going anywhere.

"If the Yassir El'aras have decided to come into Yoran, this isn't the kind of fight that you want any part of," Cyran said.

"They brought the fight."

"Are you sure about that? Didn't you tell me you don't even know who you're working for?"

"What's that supposed to mean?"

"It just means how do you know you aren't working for one of the El'aras?"

The question made Gavin's heart skip. It was no mean feat considering everything they'd been through already today. He hadn't given any thought to that possibility. Hamish certainly wasn't one of the El'aras, but that didn't mean the person who employed Hamish wasn't. More than ever, he needed to know his employer.

Gavin got up and started pacing. It was the only thing he could think of doing. Finally, he looked over to Cyran. "I'm going to need your help."

"I knew you would."

"I don't need you to return to the life you abandoned."

"You say that as if leaving our training is something I should be ashamed of."

Gavin frowned, shaking his head. "I would never say you should be ashamed of it. I'm just saying I want you to recognize that…"

He wasn't entirely sure what he wanted his oldest friend to recognize. There wasn't anything Cyran really owed him. In fact, if anything, Gavin owed Cyran, who'd been the one to leave. He'd been the first one to prove that they could get away from Tristan and the life he'd tried to teach them. Because of Cyran, he had known there was something else he could do. A different life for him.

"I just want you to keep looking into what you can," he finished.

"If it deals with the El'aras, there's a limit to how much I'm willing to dig."

"It's not just the El'aras."

"I know it's not just them. It's the factions of the El'aras, and however they might be tied together. And I know you don't necessarily believe me when I tell you these factions are all interrelated, but they are."

Gavin shook his head. "I believe you. When have you been wrong before?"

Cyran grunted. "You don't know what things have been like since we trained together, Gavin. You've changed." He took a deep breath, letting it out slowly. "I've changed. And I've been wrong plenty of times." He turned his attention to the table.

Gavin headed to the door and paused. Faint sunlight started to stream in the distance. It was going to be a bright, beautiful day. The kind of day Jessica would love and the kind of day that left him feeling even emptier at her condition. He stood there for a long time and looked out, thinking about what had been and unable to shake the thoughts of what might have been.

"If you're going to do this, you're going to need help."

He turned to see Gaspar looking at him. The old, grizzled thief had an intensity to his eyes. He didn't know Gaspar all that well. In the time he'd been in Yoran and staying at the Dragon, Gaspar had never provided him with much reason to feel as if he could be trusted.

"What kind of help are you suggesting?" Gavin asked.

"I care about her too," Gaspar said.

"The same way?"

Gaspar grunted. "Maybe if I were ten years younger."

He looked toward the back of the tavern for a moment, uncertainty flickering in his gaze. "No, not the same way as you, boy. That doesn't mean I don't care. More than a few of us here at the Dragon care about her—and what would happen to the Dragon if she were lost."

"Are you sure you want to help?" Gavin motioned to the pile of bodies in one corner. "This isn't the same kind of job you normally take."

"What do you know about the jobs I normally take?"

Gavin shrugged. "I suppose I don't know anything."

"You're damn right you don't know anything. Now, are we going to begin or not?"

"Now?"

"If you want my help, then we're going to start now."

Gavin turned. Imogen sat at a table, and Wrenlow waited at the bottom of the stairs, watching her. She leaned against the wall, her fingers tracing the hilt of her slender sword. Cyran sat alone, staring at his hands.

*This was going to be my crew?*

It was more than just completing the job for his mysterious employer. That would be his and Wrenlow's task. Gaspar and Imogen cared more about what had happened to Jessica, finding the El'aras and what they were involved in. Unfortunately, it seemed as if the two were intertwined. Finish the job. Find the El'aras. Figure out who hired him.

All without getting someone killed.

Maybe this was all that he *should* bring with him.

Gavin walked over to them. "Let's begin."

Cyran cleared his throat, getting to his feet. "Not me." He looked around the inside of the tavern. "I don't know what you're going to do, though I have an idea. That's not why I'm in Yoran."

"Cyran, I could use an old friend on a job like this."

Cyran held his gaze and seemed to debate a moment before shaking his head. "Not this friend. I didn't come to tangle with El'aras. I helped as much as I could," he said, gathering his powders and replacing them in his pouch, "but you don't need me." He glanced toward the stairs. "I would like to know if she comes around. Will you send word?"

Gavin inhaled deeply then nodded. Cyran slipped out into the street, closing the door behind him. Gavin looked at the others. Wrenlow would help, but he didn't know Gaspar or Imogen too well. For Jessica, it would have to be enough.

## CHAPTER NINE

Gavin slipped along the edge of the street, his eyes darting all around him. Hamish had a way of avoiding Gavin's tracking ability. That alone was surprising, but even more surprising was how he often appeared shortly after a job was completed. Gaspar had managed to uncover some rumors about where to find Hamish, which was more than Gavin had ever obtained. It left him skeptical, but it also left him somewhat suspicious. Hamish knew things about him that he shouldn't.

*Could Gaspar be involved?*

"How does it look?" Wrenlow's voice crackled loudly in his ear.

Gavin almost jumped. There were times when he forgot about just how annoying the enchantment could be. Most of the time, it was beneficial, and he was thankful he had Wrenlow giving him advice and the opportunity to ask questions. But there were other times when he wished for silence.

"It looks the same as it did the last time you asked," Gavin said.

"I was just asking. You know, it's hard for me to be stuck here in the Dragon while you're out on the street, looking for excitement."

"I'm not necessarily *looking* for excitement. Excitement tends to find me."

"What I wouldn't give for a little excitement."

"How about we trade positions?"

There was a moment of silence, and Gavin almost smiled.

"If Gaspar's information is correct, you need to head down to the South Street Market."

The cloudy day meant they didn't have to squint against the sun to search. Wrenlow had taken most of the morning to search and had come up with a possible location, though they didn't know if it would work.

The way that Wrenlow said it suggested not only that he didn't believe that Gaspar's information was correct but that he'd be annoyed if it was. Not that it surprised Gavin. Wrenlow prided himself on his ability to obtain information, and if this was something that Gaspar had been able to acquire much more readily, it would make Wrenlow feel as if he'd disappointed Gavin, even if he hadn't. Gavin understood that everyone had different access to information. In Gaspar's case, he was a native of Yoran and connected in ways Wrenlow just wasn't.

He slipped forward, tapping the enchantment. "I have a hard time thinking Hamish will simply be found at the market," he said.

"I know, which is why I don't know how much you can trust what Gaspar told you."

"I also have a hard time thinking he's wrong," Gavin said.

There was silence on the other end. "If you trust him so much, then head to the market and see what you can uncover."

Gavin started to smile. "I'm sure you'll find something useful as well."

"You don't need to patronize me."

"I'm not patronizing. I was just—"

"You're patronizing me. I'm not from Yoran. You should be impressed with how quickly I established my own network and less impressed with how well-established his network is."

"Have I made it seem otherwise?"

"A little appreciation every now and again would be nice."

"Wrenlow, you are very much appreciated," Gavin said, laughing again.

As he turned the corner, he found a crowd forming in the distance. The market.

The South Street Market was a place where caravans from outside of the city would gather, along with local farmers and other merchants. It was chaotic and boisterous, teeming with life and activity. Gavin had often chosen to use it to hide his activities. It was the kind of place that would be all too easy for someone to slip through unnoticed.

*How would Gaspar have known that Hamish would be here?*

"Do you remember when we first met?" Gavin asked.

"I remember. Why?" Wrenlow answered.

"I was just thinking about the crowd we have here."

"We didn't meet in a crowd."

"We met outside of a crowd," Gavin said.

"Only because you were trying to catch me."

"Trying?"

"Fine. You caught me. Is that what you want me to say? You want me to admit that were it not for you and your willingness to let me live, that I'm—"

"I wasn't trying to do anything like that. I was just thinking back to that time."

"I think back to it all the time." Wrenlow's voice went soft. "Had you not been willing to take me in, I don't know what would've happened to me."

"I know what would've happened to you."

"You do?"

"You probably would've ended up behind bars. The constables of whatever city you were in at the time would've taken you and imprisoned you. You know what happens to little pups like you in prison."

"I don't."

"They end up eaten by the bigger dogs," Gavin barked into the earpiece, and Wrenlow swore at him from the other end.

Gavin chuckled to himself, heading forward until he reached the outskirts of the market. He plunged deeper into the crowd, and the noise and the chaos surrounded him.

"Do you see him yet?" Wrenlow asked.

"I'll let you know when I see him," Gavin whispered.

Now that he was in the crowd, he had to be a little more careful speaking. It wouldn't do for somebody to question why he was suddenly talking to himself. People would have a different set of questions about the enchantment. Especially in Yoran. Magic wasn't so much feared as it was forbidden in order to keep the people of the city safe.

He reached the outer edge of the stalls. Acrobats danced along the side of the street. They were dressed in colorful clothes, bright pants of silky orange with jackets of a vibrant green that rippled in the wind and flowed with their movements. The women wore the same type of clothing as the men, which made sense considering the way they flipped and spun in the air.

He hesitated, watching one of them somersault in the air. It was exquisite. Gavin had trained a considerable amount of time to be able to use the techniques that he did, so he knew what went into the acrobats' training and just how much skill that involved. The crowd around them wasn't nearly as sizable as what they deserved. He flipped a copper penny toward their jar and nodded to the smallest of the acrobats, a man who was balancing on his hands while another was balancing on his outstretched feet.

Gavin continued on. Every dozen or so paces, he came across some new performer. Some, like the acrobats, were performance-based—singers or storytellers or minstrels. Others were artists offering to paint something for those passing by. Still others were beggars. He was surprised by how much coin even the beggars managed to acquire. If it were up to him, he would've given the beggars nothing.

*What value did they have if they weren't willing to demonstrate some skill for their coin?*

He reached the square and passed through the booths, looking around him as he studied the people. It wasn't the merchants he paid attention to—it was the people wandering through the crowd. That was where he was going to find Hamish. The man had a distinct look, but finding him among a sea of people was going to be a challenge, even for Gavin. He moved carefully but wandered almost aimlessly, letting his gaze drift along the crowd to search the people here.

"I'm not seeing anything," he whispered.

"What can I say? You're going by Gaspar's information. What if he was wrong?"

"I don't think he would've intentionally led us awry."

"What if he was involved in what happened?"

"I don't think he was."

He didn't know Gaspar that well, but he recognized the hurt of a man who didn't care for what had happened to Jessica. It was the same hurt he felt, the same pain he knew, a pain that came from watching her almost die in front of them.

The market was enormous, and the square was filled with all manner of people in various styles of clothing. Some were like the acrobats he'd come across, dressed in silky and brightly colored clothes. Others had more drab dress. Some women had low-cut dresses, revealing far more than what was typically considered proper, whereas others had their collars buttoned high on their neck. It was a place where people from all over the city, and beyond, congregated. Places like this felt almost claustrophobic to Gavin. There were simply too many people, all of them crammed in and forcing their way through, practically shoulder to shoulder. The noise was chaotic. Thousands of voices mingled as the hawkers attempted to shout over the din of the crowd, and an undercurrent of music came from dozens of minstrels.

"How can all of these people be from Yoran?" Gavin asked.

"Most of the people of the South Street Market aren't from Yoran."

"No?"

"Well, I figured Gaspar would've told you, but seeing as how he neglected crucial pieces of information, I suppose you're going to need to hear it from me."

Gavin started to smile. He could imagine Wrenlow sitting more upright at the Dragon, preparing his notes. "Please. Go on."

"The South Street Market generally serves people

coming in from outside of the city. You get some locals here, but mostly they want to sell their wares rather than buy them. They view it as overpriced."

"Is it?"

"I don't know. I'm not there. You have a good eye for this sort of thing, so why don't you tell me?"

Gavin paused at a textile merchant. The booth was set up in such a way to display the fabrics. There were silks, colorful and blowing softly in the breeze. There were some of cotton, and even from here, he could see how delicate the weave had been made. There were others of linen; a rougher fabric he didn't particularly care for.

As he leaned forward, listening to the merchant, he tried to get a sense for what they were charging for the fabrics, but he found that it was difficult for him to overhear. The woman bartering with the merchant bobbed her head rapidly. She was far too eager.

Gavin stood off to the side, listening as the merchant continued to haggle. He didn't move much on his price, whereas this woman continued to come up. Gavin shook his head. He waited for a little bit longer to get a sense for how much the woman would end up paying, but the merchant was far more skilled at haggling than she was.

When he moved on, he found a silversmith. That was something he had a better eye for, and he quickly realized the silversmith overcharged. Not that it made much difference. The people around were more than happy to pay exorbitant prices. The quality was decent, though he'd seen better in many of the Northern cities.

He grunted, stepping away. "If we wanted to, we could make a killing here."

"Isn't that what you do anyway?"

"Somewhat," he said, laughing. "Listen. Even you should be able to hear what's taking place here."

"I've been listening. I have a feeling they don't know how to get the best bargain," Wrenlow said.

"You could show them," Gavin said, laughing softly again.

He continued to meander through the market, pausing at stand after stand. Each time, he found the same. Overpriced goods. The quality adequate, sometimes more than that, but the price always far more than what he would've been willing to pay. Of course, if the market was meant for people from outside of the city, it was possible they simply didn't know they could obtain similar—or better—quality by staying in the city and haggling. Looking around this place gave him a better sense for the kind of man who would spend time here.

That involved a different type of work. There were some who simply didn't want to take that time, who didn't have time to be away. He could imagine some of these people needed to get as much of their market shopping done as quickly as possible, even if it involved taking a little bit of a loss.

Even the food vendors were overpriced. His stomach rumbled, though he'd eaten before heading out. He wished he'd brought something to snack on, knowing assignments like this could sometimes take a considerable part of the day. A lot of it involved scouting, patience, and being ready for when the opportunity presented itself. In this case, he didn't know if he was going to be able to find anything more than what he already had.

"Is Gaspar anywhere around you?" Gavin whispered.

"He left early this morning," Wrenlow said.

Gavin grunted. "I don't suppose he said anything more about *where* I was supposed to find Hamish?"

"If he did, he didn't tell me. See? What did I tell you? You aren't able to trust him."

"Why would he lie about this? The market isn't—"

Just then, Gavin caught a flash of a familiar fabric.

"Isn't what?" Wrenlow asked.

"Quiet," he hissed.

Hamish's clothes had a certain cut to them, but it was more than that. He always dressed flamboyantly and preferred colorful clothing; almost always robes rather than more practical pants and jackets. Today was no different.

Even from a distance, Hamish's purple velvet robe clashed with his surroundings. His balding head bobbed through the sea of people. Gavin started to weave toward it. He moved carefully, not wanting to get close too quickly. He would take his time, get near Hamish, and then confront him.

Or not.

He could also just follow Hamish until he left the market, then continue trailing him to learn more about him—and his employer. Gavin fought his way through the stalls and finally reached the outer edge. Once again, he encountered singers and acrobats and storytellers. They weren't nearly as numerous here as they were closer to the main part of the city. Hamish continued to weave through the crowd, getting further ahead.

*Where was the old bastard going?*

"What's happening?" Wrenlow asked.

"He's leaving the city. At least, it *seems* like he's leaving the city. I don't know where he's going, only that he's wandering outside of the market."

"Where would he go from here?"

"Your guess is as good as mine," Gavin said.

He hurried forward and realized that he was making a mistake. The suddenness of his movement was too much. Hamish paused and turned slowly, his deep purple robe flowing around him. Gavin tried to sink into the crowd, to fade back so he wouldn't be identified, but he wasn't sure that he acted quickly enough.

"Balls," he whispered.

"He saw you, didn't he?"

"I don't really know. All I know is that he stopped."

"Maybe he's meeting with your employer."

"I don't know that we're going to get quite that lucky," Gavin said.

He tracked through the crowd, staying off to the side, moving as carefully and quietly as he could. Even as he did, Gavin thought that he wasn't moving as effectively as he intended.

The crowd was thinner here. Behind him, the

merchants were loud, their voices a cacophony of shouts. The nearest street performer was a trio of acrobats, and they were nearly silent. It would've been easier for him to approach Hamish near a singer, but there were none to be found.

That wasn't quite right. As he circled back around, he heard a warbly voice. Gavin recognized it as the same singer who'd performed at the Roasted Dragon. He was certain of it.

He frowned.

*Was Hamish talking to the singer? Could* that *be the source of his information?*

"I need you to talk to the performers at the Dragon," Gavin said.

"Which ones?"

"All of them, I think."

"Why?"

"We've been trying to figure out how Hamish acquired his information. I think I might've just discovered it."

"You think he's talking to the musicians?"

"It's possible."

Gavin remained motionless, though standing as he did would draw its own attention. He had to move on. He drifted, trying to carefully follow the flow of the crowd in a way that wouldn't draw too much notice, but he still had a feeling that Hamish was aware of his presence. He turned to pretend like he was examining a stall's wares, and by the time he turned back, Hamish was gone.

"Balls," he said again.

This time, he said it more loudly. The man nearest him looked over and started to smile, which faded when Gavin glared at him.

He reached under his cloak and felt for the El'aras dagger. It might've been a mistake to bring the dagger with him, but there was something comforting in having it with him, especially seeing as how the dagger was responsible for so much pain he'd suffered. He knew it wasn't this dagger in particular, but…

The dagger was glowing. It hadn't been doing that previously, he was certain of it. That it was glowing again now suggested there was magic being used near him—El'aras magic.

Could it be *Hamish*? He hadn't thought him El'aras. In the interactions they'd had, nothing suggested that, and he didn't think it could be the case.

Gavin moved toward the outer edge of the market, pausing as he looked for any sign of the man. He continued until he reached the perimeter of the market, but he still couldn't find a trace. There was nothing. Hamish had seen him and slipped away, likely into the city where he'd disappear.

"He's gone," he whispered. "But there's something else."

"What is it?"

"The blade is glowing."

"What do you mean it's glowing?"

"Isn't that clear enough?"

"It's clear, but why would it be glowing?" Wrenlow asked.

"Didn't I tell you how these things work?"

"You did, and I'm not dense. It's just that for it to be glowing, it means there's someone near you who can make it do so."

"You can say it. Magic," he whispered.

"I don't want to," Wrenlow said.

Gavin smiled to himself. He turned back toward the crowd, sweeping his gaze around. If the El'aras were here, it meant they'd followed him. Given that they'd been so willing to attack him openly, he shouldn't be surprised they'd come after him here.

"Better you than me."

It would be a simple thing to stick a knife in him, drop him when there was a crowd around him, and move on. It was the kind of hit he'd made before, and there was something practical about how easy it was to slip off into the crowd. No one saw it as anything more than a random act of violence that had taken place, and he was long gone before it attracted the constables' attention.

Gavin wasn't about to be the victim. He paused at each of the few performing acts, using that as an opportunity to scan the crowd again. He held one hand on the El'aras dagger as he did, but he still found nothing. If he'd lost Hamish, then it would be better for him to return to the Dragon.

The blade continued to glow. If the El'aras were there, they were trailing him. More likely than not, they did a much better job than he had trying to follow Hamish. It shouldn't be *that* hard to find him. The bastard was dressed in purple, after all.

"Maybe I should've had you come with me. The two of us would've been able to spot him sneaking away."

"I don't know what he looks like," Wrenlow said.

"With Hamish, you don't really need to know anything more than what color he's wearing for that day."

"What color was he wearing today?"

"Purple."

"I like purple," Wrenlow said.

"You'd like Hamish then."

Gavin moved toward the next performer. This was a storyteller who shared the legend of the exploits of Vonald, a sorcerer who'd supposedly lived hundreds of years ago and who'd also supposedly conquered the El'aras. The storyteller called them something different, and he also didn't call Vonald a sorcerer, though Gavin had heard the story often enough that he knew that was essentially what he was. It did surprise him that somebody would be willing to share a story like that in a place like Yoran, so unaccepting of magic. But then, the people here might not know what the storyteller was actually referencing.

Despite his need to focus on finding Hamish, he found himself listening before he tore his attention away.

"You can go back," Wrenlow said. "I was quite enjoying that, though I'd dispute a few of his details about Vonald."

"You're now an expert on such things?"

"You know I've spent time researching sorcerers. I figured I needed to."

"We don't deal with sorcerers."

Gavin moved off. Arguing with Wrenlow when people were around him only ran the risk of revealing that they were using something magical, or at least something magically endowed. He glanced down at the dagger, testing to see if it was still glowing and found that it was. As he started back into the main part of the market, he caught another flash of purple fabric.

"There you are," he muttered.

"You found him?"

"I found something."

He hurried forward, staying low and concealing his height as he weaved through the crowd. Every so often, he would stand up taller, poking his head up to search for the flash of purple fabric that told him he was on the right path. When he saw Hamish, he continued in that direction, moving ever closer.

Finally, he reached his target, who stopped at a booth. Gavin couldn't tell what Hamish shopped for, as he was trying to stay low and remain concealed. He wanted to listen in and see what Hamish was after, but the man lingered only a moment before moving on.

When he was gone, Gavin popped his head up, looking for the person Hamish had been speaking to. They now seemed preoccupied with the next customer in line to buy fabrics.

He lingered for a moment. "I wish we had a layout of this place."

"Give me a little time, but I might be able to come up with a traditional layout for the market," Wrenlow said.

"It won't matter by then."

He snuck forward through the crowd, following the flowing purple robes. He paused when Hamish paused, then waited for a moment before heading onward. After a while, he started to wonder whether Hamish lingered intentionally. It seemed as if he weaved through the stands casually and not with the same intentional stride that he had before.

Gavin remained cautious. "I think he knows I'm here," he whispered.

"If he knew you were there, would he linger like this?"

"I don't know. It's Hamish. I don't really know what he might do. He—"

Gavin cut off as a man bumped into him and pressed something against him. He reacted instinctively by grabbing for the man's wrist.

The man looked up at him, his eyes narrowed. "I was told to give this to you."

Gavin took the scrap of paper and released his wrist. The man backed away before he turned and ran, disappearing into the crowd.

"What was that?" Wrenlow asked.

Gavin looked back up, but the purple flowing robes were gone. "Dammit," he whispered.

"What is it?"

He unfolded the scrap of paper, recognizing the flowing script. It was neat. Tidy. Almost too decorative. Much like the hand that had written it.

"I guess that answers the question of whether or not Hamish knew I was here," he said.

"Why?" Wrenlow asked.

"Because he just sent me a note."

## CHAPTER TEN

Gavin lingered at the edge of the forest. The note had been quite descriptive as to where he needed to go and how he needed to leave the city in order to reach this spot without someone following him. He didn't know what he might find here, which was why he hadn't come alone.

He looked over at Gaspar. The old thief had an annoyed look on his face as he leaned back against one of the trees. A bow was slung over his shoulder, which seemed somehow fitting for him. When they were making their way from the Dragon, the bow had been almost comical and out of place in Yoran, but as soon as they reached the edge of the city, the bow seemed far more appropriate.

"Do you think he even knows how to use that?" he asked Imogen.

She was dressed in a traveling cloak, its heavy leather

folds covering her petite, slender body. She had a pouch visible beneath it, along with the narrow-bladed sword she kept on her. "He can use it."

She rarely spoke, though he wished she would now. Coming out here with Gaspar was problem enough. Bringing Imogen, as silent as she was, felt like adding an unnecessary challenge.

The trees created a ring around them, forming the small clearing. In the center of it, the trunk of an old tree rested along the ground. Small shrubs rose to about his waist, and several of them had tiny purple flowers growing on them. Thorns caught at his pants in ways that they didn't in other parts of the forest.

Gavin nodded, then headed across the small clearing and reached Gaspar. "This is where we're supposed to meet Hamish."

"Are you sure?" Gaspar looked around the woods, his gaze flickering quickly. He had something in his eyes that suggested he'd done this before. Since Gaspar was a thief, Gavin suspected the man was accustomed to being on edge, always surveying everything around him.

"You read the note the same as I did," he said.

"I read the note, but that doesn't answer the question."

"What do you think the note meant?"

Gaspar pulled the bow off his shoulder and pressing his lips together in a frown. Wrinkles around the corners of his eyes deepened. "The note told you to come here. It didn't say you're going to meet Hamish. It didn't say you're going to meet this target of yours either."

"If it wasn't to meet here, then what point was there in giving me the note?"

"He's your employer," Gaspar said.

"According to him, he's not the employer."

"If he sent you, then he's the employer."

Gavin grunted. He started to look around the clearing and noted Imogen picking her way around it.

A troubling thought nagged at him; a reminder of what Hamish had said to him when he'd failed to reach the target at first. Hamish might've wanted to get them out of the city to eliminate him. He didn't think so, though.

"Do you see anything?" he whispered.

Wrenlow had hidden high up in one of the trees nearby, overlooking the clearing. Gavin hoped that he remained hidden well enough that no one else would be able to see him, though he didn't know if it would work.

"So far, nothing."

"I didn't think so, but keep looking."

"You know I am. It's just that—"

Gavin tapped the enchantment when a flurry of movement caught his eye. He spun, reaching for the dagger, only to find a squirrel scampering up a tree.

He wasn't the only one spooked though. As he turned, he realized Gaspar and Imogen were both on edge, though he couldn't tell it from her. Gaspar had an arrow nocked and ready to draw, whereas Imogen only stood a little more stiffly than usual.

"I guess I'm not the only one startled," he said, laughing softly.

"A squirrel?" Gaspar said. He started toward the tree, holding the arrow slightly drawn. He didn't put any tension on the string, which told Gavin all he needed to know about the man: He understood how to use his bow. "With what I saw, I expected something more than just a squirrel."

Gavin moved out of the center of the clearing, closer to the trees, and tapped on the enchantment again. "Do you see anything?" he whispered to Wrenlow.

There was silence.

"Wrenlow?"

Nothing.

Gavin glanced at the others. "Stay here," he said.

"What are you doing?" Gaspar asked.

"Wrenlow has gone quiet."

He hurried from the clearing, unsheathing the El'aras dagger. The tree Wrenlow had climbed wasn't far from them, and as he neared it, he paused and looked up. There was no sign of anything there, certainly no sign of movement, but Wrenlow was missing. Something had happened to him. Gavin lingered at the base of the tree and then slipped the dagger back into his belt. Climbing up the tree, he reached the upper branches and began to pull himself up more rapidly.

"If you're up there and simply not answering, I'm going to throw you out of the tree," he whispered.

There was still nothing. Gavin hurriedly worked his way up.

*What would've happened to Wrenlow here?*

He was high enough that nothing should've been able to reach him, but *something* must have. There had to be some reason he'd gone silent.

He neared the branches where he thought Wrenlow would be and found a few that were bent, confirming his suspicion. There was no other sign of his friend. He lingered for a moment and looked down. From here, the forest spread out beneath them. The branch was quite high with a good vantage point, and he understood why Wrenlow had chosen it. Sitting here afforded him the ability to survey a wide area of the ground beneath them.

He looked at the branch, but there was nothing here. No sign of where Wrenlow might've gone and no sign of what had happened to him. Were it not for the bent branches, it'd be almost as if Wrenlow hadn't been here.

Gavin started climbing down when another flicker of movement caught his attention. He tensed, hesitating.

At least up in the tree, he was able to see around him more easily. From here, he could make out the edge of the clearing. Gaspar was there, along with Imogen, but there was someone else too.

*Could it be Hamish?*

"If you're listening, I need some sort of indication," he said into the enchantment.

Maybe Wrenlow had seen something and moved forward, and he'd fallen silent because he couldn't speak.

"Give me a cough. Anything."

The sound of wind picked up in his ears. He considered that a response.

Gavin slipped along the trunk and dropped back to the ground, and then he darted forward. He unsheathed the dagger before deciding to switch back to his knives. He glanced down at the dagger to look for any glowing that signified magic was being used nearby, but he didn't find anything. At least that much was reassuring.

He flicked his gaze from side to side, searching for anything else that might be in the forest with him, some other sign of danger. Again he saw nothing. As far as he could tell, Gaspar and Imogen were where they'd been before.

But like he thought, they weren't alone. With them was a figure who was solidly built, slightly shorter than Gavin, and appeared to be wearing long flowing robes. It didn't appear to be Hamish.

*The note* had *come from Hamish, hadn't it?*

He leaned forward, listening.

"You can come out of the trees, Mr. Lorren."

Gavin hesitated. The newcomer's back was to him, and it seemed that it'd be a simple matter to hurl one of his knives and sink it into this person's back. But he knew if he did that, he wouldn't be able to understand why they'd been summoned outside of the city.

As he looked around the clearing, he didn't see anyone else here and could sense no other danger. He slipped the knives back into their sheaths and rested his hand on the hilt of the dagger instead. He didn't withdraw it, but he was prepared for the possibility that he might need to use it at any moment.

"Who are you?" he asked. This wasn't Hamish.

The newcomer turned slowly to face them. A hood framed his face and shadows rested in the hollows of his eyes. Nothing else about him was distinct.

"You don't have to linger there," the man said.

Gavin glanced over toward Gaspar, who stood fixed in place, saying nothing. Imogen didn't move either. Could this be his employer? He wouldn't have expected Hamish to bring the employer out here.

He took a step but wasn't able to take anything more. It seemed as if he'd stepped into deep mud or quicksand. It formed some sort of strange thickness around him.

The El'aras dagger started to glow.

Sorcery.

The newcomer pulled back his hood. He had close-cropped gray hair and a face that was lean, almost gaunt, with a faint trace of a beard covering his cheeks. He could've been like anyone else in Yoran were it not for the power Gavin could feel radiating off of him. Strangely enough, he was all too aware of that power.

Gavin had been around people with magic before. It was one of the things that Tristan had made sure of. He'd known that Gavin would be exposed to sorcery and wanted him to be learn how to counter it. Mostly that involved a skillfully thrown knife or an arrow shot from a distance, and he'd learned to avoid the effects of many spells. He also had to hone and focus his core reserves of power. It was because of this training that he could feel the power pressing upon him now.

"You will see you cannot go any further," the man said. "I apologize for the steps I was required to take to call you out here, but you can understand why I wouldn't want to be seen quite so openly within Yoran."

"Are you my employer?"

"Your employer?"

"Aren't you the one who's been sending Hamish?"

It was a strange feeling being able to speak but also being unable to move. In the time that he'd trained with Tristan, Gavin had experienced others who had various magical abilities with some component of power, though never a true sorcerer. Sorcery was rare, regardless of where in the world he lived. The Sorcerer's Society claimed anyone with the ability. Encountering it now in such close proximity and feeling the direct effects of the magic were unpleasant.

It was also terrifying. Gavin could feel that power up against him, rubbing across his skin. It seemed almost as if it were moving, almost as if it actually *were* quicksand pulling him under.

"As much as I have to admit being curious as to who this Hamish is, I am not that man."

"And who instructed us to come here?" Gavin asked. If not Hamish, then the encounter in the market had been coincidence? He had a hard time believing that.

"Why, I did."

He glanced over at Gaspar and Imogen before turning his attention to the edge of the trees. That had to be where Wrenlow was, though given the strength of the power that must be pushing upon Wrenlow, Gavin suspected that his partner wasn't even able to talk. As far as he could tell, neither could Gaspar nor Imogen.

"Why?"

"I didn't expect you to bring so many friends. The stories I have of the great Gavin Lorren would suggest he generally works alone. The Chain Breaker, I believe."

Gavin tensed. Tristan was the only one who ever *really* called him that. "If you've heard any stories about me, then you know that's not quite true."

The sorcerer chuckled. His dark eyes seemed to harden, and as he stared at Gavin, there was something almost crazed behind them. It unsettled Gavin in a way that very little did.

"I suppose you're right. You and your friend Wrenlow have traveled together most recently, but before that, I understand that you were independent."

"Not entirely independent."

"No, I suppose all who trained with the great Master Tristan have limited independence."

Even Hamish didn't seem to have this level of knowledge about him. Hamish had been able to discover things about Gavin within Yoran, but that was a simple matter of trailing him and acquiring intelligence. Gavin and Wrenlow had intentionally hidden the information this man knew from outside eyes. Part of that came from how he'd moved from place to place, but part of it had been his own desire to suppress anyone from getting too close to him and risking those around him being in danger.

"What do you want?" Gavin asked.

"I want to hire your services."

"I'm already under contract."

"I'm aware that you are. It was that contract that drew me to you."

Gavin frowned. "If you have so much power, why can't you simply take care of this?"

"An excellent question, and under other circumstances, I'd argue that I would. But my particular talents"—he spread his hands out, and the quicksand magic started to slide even more—"are such that they would attract the wrong kind of attention within Yoran."

Using magic in Yoran was the kind of attention Gavin was concerned about. There were those within the city who were able to combat magic users, which had kept Yoran safe.

"What's the job?"

Imogen's eyes bulged, as if she were straining to say something. The magic that held and constricted her prevented her from being able to do anything.

The sorcerer grinned as he watched her, then turned his attention back to Gavin. He spread his hands out to either side. "What have you heard about the sorcerer known as the Apostle?"

*Another sorcerer?*

Gavin shook his head. "Am I supposed to recognize that name?"

"I only thought that in your time within Yoran, you would have come across it, but unfortunately…"

Gavin looked behind the sorcerer at Gaspar's face, which appeared troubled by this. For whatever reason, Gaspar didn't care for the mention of the name.

"What do you want done with the Apostle?" Gavin asked.

"Why, I want the Apostle removed."

"Removed?"

"Indeed. I thought the great Gavin Lorren—apprentice to Master Tristan, son of Odian, and bearer of an El'aras dagger—would be capable of such a feat."

Everything inside of him went cold. This man was mentioning facts that should not have been known. Even Tristan hadn't known who his father was. It had taken Gavin years to uncover that secret, years that he'd spent searching for information about his heritage.

The sorcerer had made mention of the time that Gavin had spent looking for that information. By then, he'd been separated from Tristan for years and was operating independently until he'd finally met up with Wrenlow.

"I see that I have your attention," the man said, his voice taking on a dangerous pitch.

Gavin was unable to take his eyes off of him and unable to think of anything that he could say or do. "Who are you?"

"Someone you would do well to heed."

"I've already told you that I've been employed by someone else."

"Just because you've taken one job doesn't mean that you cannot take another." He flashed a smile, and with a twist of his wrist, Wrenlow was dragged out from the corner of the forest, floating above the ground, everything in his body stiff and tense. With another twist, Wrenlow bent over and cried out.

"You see, you will *want* to work with me."

"Because otherwise you're going to hurt my friends?"

"I know that you care about Wrenlow. Much like you cared about Jessica. A shame what happened to her."

Anger threatened to build within Gavin. "Was that you?"

"Why would I harm you if I wanted to hire you?" There was something strange about the way he said it with his mouth pressed into a sour line. "No, it has nothing to do with what happened there. But seeing as how you reacted after losing her, I can only imagine how you would feel if it were to happen to someone else you care about. This time, you will be forced to watch." With another flick of his wrist, Imogen was dragged over next to Wrenlow. She stared straight ahead, her jaw set in a tight expression. The sorcerer twisted his hand again, bending Imogen over at the waist so that her forehead practically touched her toes. It was a wonder that she didn't scream or cry out, but Gavin had seen how strong Imogen was. She let out a soft whimper.

*Damn this sorcerer.*

"Enough," Gavin said.

"Good. Now I have your attention." With another wave of his hand, both collapsed to the ground. Tears streamed down Wrenlow's cheeks. Imogen's face had gone pale, all of the blood seemingly draining out of it.

"What do you need me to do?"

"I thought I was clear. I need you to remove the Apostle."

"Or what?"

"Or? Haven't you seen what I'm willing to do?"

"I've seen it, but I want to know what else you intend to do. Why can't you remove the Apostle yourself? I know you claim you aren't able to operate within Yoran because of the restrictions on magic use, but there's something else to this."

"Perhaps there is. It doesn't matter. All that should matter to you is that I will be watching. Perhaps even listening."

He smiled as a faint voice trailed into Gavin's ear through the enchantment. He resisted the temptation to grab for it, pull it away. He stared at the sorcerer.

*Who the hell was he?*

"What's my payment?"

"You would seek to bargain with me?"

"Generally, when I'm hired for a job, there's payment involved. Seeing as how you're threatening my friends, I would suggest a fee commensurate with the risks that undoubtedly are involved in this."

The sorcerer surprised him by smiling slightly. "I must

say that I am intrigued by your stubbornness. I wouldn't have expected you to have quite the spine you do, though the son of Odian should, shouldn't he?"

Gavin glared at him. There would be questions, mostly from Wrenlow. Imogen knew enough and seemed to have a bright enough mind to ask the right questions. Wrenlow might be able to dig around a little bit, but he wasn't the one Gavin was concerned about.

Gaspar would certainly look into his heritage. Gavin knew so little about the old thief, other than the fact that he was as well-connected as anyone within Yoran. It was possible—maybe even probable—that he would know others within the city that Gavin would have to be concerned about as well. Gaspar might know others who would provide him the answers he sought. The only protection he had was that the name Odian wasn't well-known in these lands. It had taken him an extensive period of time to search for it and find what he wanted to know.

"Let's just say that you will be handsomely rewarded." The sorcerer reached into his pocket. Gavin tensed, bracing for another wave of magic, but it didn't come. Instead, the man pulled out a leather pouch and flung it toward him. It jingled loudly as it fell to the ground, and a few golden coins spilled out. "Consider that a prepayment. If you do the job I ask of you, you will receive tenfold that amount."

Gavin's gaze lingered on the coins falling out of the pouch. He knew better than to be drawn in by the promise of considerable pay, but others might not be that way. He glanced over at Gaspar, who was eyeing the contents of the pouch almost hungrily. Wrenlow did as well. The only one who did not was Imogen. Gavin wondered if that was because she understood that with an offer of payment like this, there was always some hidden catch.

"How long?"

"How long?" the sorcerer repeated.

"To do the job. Usually when I'm hired, there's a timeline. I figure you have something in mind, otherwise you wouldn't have called us out here."

"You're mistaken, Gavin Lorren."

Gavin didn't care for the way the man kept saying his name, but he was powerless to prevent him from doing so.

"I didn't call them out here. I called you. You brought them into this."

Gavin stared at him. "How long?"

"You have a week to remove the Apostle."

"And then what?"

"And then you will begin to lose friends."

With that, a haze started to build around the sorcerer, a fog of energy, and he disappeared. The magic that was holding them faded.

Gavin leaned down, grabbing for the contents of the pouch and stuffing the coins back inside. The others were looking over at him, but it was Gaspar who troubled him the most.

"You know him, don't you?" Gavin asked, straightening and putting the coin pouch into his pocket. "You know the Apostle."

Gaspar shook his head. "I don't know him. I don't know that anyone within Yoran knows him, other than by reputation. He's a sorcerer who came to Yoran not long ago and quickly gained a reputation. He's dangerous. Powerful. And if you intend to go after him, then you're putting yourself into considerable danger."

Gavin looked at the two still sitting on the ground, trying to get themselves up. "I don't know that I have much of a choice."

"That's what I'm afraid of. Between this, your other job, and the El'aras, I don't care for what you've brought upon the Dragon."

Gavin sighed. He would've argued and said he hadn't brought anything upon the Dragon, but that wasn't true. Whatever had happened was because of him. Whatever was *going* to happen would be because of him.

"Come on, then," he said, looking down at the other two before offering a hand in helping them to their feet. "I think it's time for us to get to work. We have an Apostle to kill, Hamish's target to find, and the El'aras to stay ahead of."

He didn't know which one of those was going to be the most difficult, but they all seemed impossible.

## CHAPTER ELEVEN

The building rising up in front of him was enormous. It was easily the largest building in all of Yoran, and it towered above Gavin. He stared as he tried to take in the various turrets, the wall that linked them together, and the light glowing within their windows. It was near dusk, late enough that lanterns were already starting to be lit within the palace, but still early enough that the streets were busy. Gavin chose this time to scout so he didn't draw extra attention to himself. Otherwise, he would run that risk if he were to come any later.

"It's impressive," he whispered.

"It is," replied Wrenlow. "The Captain has the most luxurious palace in all of the city."

That was an understatement. Whereas there were plenty of other manor houses that were impressive, this one stood above the rest, something even greater and more impressive than any others.

"How did he acquire it?" Gavin asked.

"There are stories about him, though I don't know how many of them are real. The Captain came to Yoran about thirty years ago and quickly acquired wealth. Some say he had money even before he came, but in the time he's been in Yoran, he's become even wealthier. He's put most of it into building this palace—at least that's how it seems."

It was more than just the palace. From what Gavin could tell, it looked fortified, a barricade to possible invasion. It reminded him of some of the fortresses found along the southern border, many of them centuries old. They were built of stout stone with enchantments running through them that linked the stone and made it even stronger. Maybe there were similar enchantments here.

"We don't even know if the Apostle is going to be inside the palace," Gavin said.

"We don't know that he is, but the Captain is the only one in the city with the cache to protect a sorcerer. And with what Gaspar said—"

Gavin started to laugh, cutting off his friend. People near him on the street glanced over, looking at him as if he were mad. He supposed it might look that way. "Now you want to listen to Gaspar?"

"He does have good intelligence," Wrenlow said reluctantly.

"He's always had good intelligence. You just didn't want to listen before."

"You know that's not entirely true."

Gavin smirked, thinking that it was a shame his partner wouldn't be able to see it. "Tell yourself whatever you need in order to sleep well at night."

"I'm going to sleep a lot better when you get back here."

"I'm not breaking in. This is just a simple scouting trip."

"A scouting trip. Right. Why do I have the feeling it isn't going to be a 'simple' anything."

Gavin started to retort when the gate to the palace opened. He lingered for a moment and watched as a golden-haired woman stepped out, trailed by five soldiers all dressed in light chain mail, swords sheathed at their sides. They marched rigidly, though only the lead soldier looked around him. He was the one to be concerned about. The others followed orders.

*Who was this woman visiting the Captain—and why would someone like her need such protection?*

"She's gorgeous," he whispered.

"Who?"

"This woman."

There was something compelling about her, and Gavin was drawn toward her. She was dressed in a sky-blue cloak that covered a pale yellow gown. As she turned and glanced in his direction briefly, he noticed eyes that matched her cloak. They seemed to take him in, swallowing him for a moment, before she turned and looked in the opposite direction.

"Jessica is lying injured, and you're already drawn to another woman?"

"Jessica would understand," Gavin said before catching himself. "Hell, I think she'd be interested."

The gate to the palace closed again, and he hesitated before trailing the woman. He didn't bother to get too close. There were too many guards around her. Whoever she was, she had money, otherwise she wouldn't have nearly as many guards as what she had surrounding her now.

Maybe she was the Captain's mistress. Gavin couldn't even blame the man. She was incredibly striking, an almost impossible beauty unlike any he'd seen.

He hesitated, heading toward the woman before casting a glance behind him. Maybe this was a mistake. He shouldn't be lingering here too long. It would be better for him to return to scouting the palace, but he'd been there for the better part of a few hours and hadn't come up with anything other than an understanding that it was well fortified. He would've expected nothing less given who they were dealing with. The fact that they knew the Captain to be incredibly well-connected—and wealthy—made them anticipate that he'd have the financial wherewithal to afford the best security in all of Yoran.

"What are you doing?" Wrenlow asked from the other side of the enchantment.

Gavin was tempted to mute it and keep Wrenlow from

shouting in his ear. If only there was some way to adjust the volume, but he didn't know how. Given the magical nature of the enchantments, he suspected it was possible but hadn't uncovered the secret.

"I'm just curious," he said, heading along the street a little bit further.

He couldn't take his eyes off the woman, but the five guards around her also drew his attention.

*Who had the Captain been visiting with?*

Maybe *she* was the Apostle. She was young, or at least it seemed that way from a distance. Youth didn't mean she couldn't be a sorcerer, though it *did* make it less likely. The Apostle was rumored to be incredibly powerful, and a sorcerer's power only increased in time.

Still, it made sense to him that the Captain would be with the Apostle. Someone like that might need a heavy guard in Yoran to keep from revealing their magic. Five soldiers constituted a heavy guard, certainly more than the average merchant would require.

"You should save your curiosity for later. I'm sure I can figure out who some beautiful woman coming out of the Captain's palace is."

"Fortress," he mumbled, turning down the side street where the woman and her guard turned.

In his head, he started doing the numbers. The Apostle was rumored to have come within the last year. Plus she was too young to be a powerful sorcerer. None of it added up.

"What was that?" Wrenlow asked.

In the distance, he made out the movement of the guards. "It was a fortress, not a palace. Too well fortified be anything else."

"Does it really matter?"

"Well, if I'm going to break into a palace, I think there's a different technique to it than if I intended to break into a fortress. With a fortress, I have to worry about fighting my way in."

"Isn't that what you do?"

"Sometimes, but sometimes I need to sneak."

He slipped along the side of the street and pulled himself up a low-hanging roof. From there, he leaned forward over the street and peered down, watching for the guards and the woman. Even if she wasn't the Apostle, maybe she could help him figure out who it was.

"What has your curiosity shown you?" Wrenlow asked.

"Just a hunch."

"I don't like that."

"It's worked in the past."

"It's also ended up with you getting attacked in the past."

Gavin chuckled softly. "Just trust me."

As he continued looking over the edge of the rooftop, he caught sight of the woman and her guard heading in his direction. He'd figured as much. There wasn't much along the street otherwise.

He suddenly started to slide, and he braced himself, trying to keep himself from falling off. The movement drew the guard's attention.

*Oh, shit.*

He scrambled back onto the rooftop, but he could already tell they were aware of him. He moved, shifting forward just a little bit to get to a place where he could hide, but there wasn't anywhere for him to go. He rolled off to the side and dropped down to the street.

Gavin flashed a wide smile. It was likely that it would draw even more attention, but it was the only thing he could think of doing. The guards rushed forward, surrounding the woman.

He raised his hands up. "No worries here, friends. I just wanted to—"

One of the guards darted forward, sword already unsheathed. Gavin growled. He ignored Wrenlow's voice in his ear and reached for the man's hand as he slipped toward Gavin. He grabbed the guard's wrist and twisted off to the side, slamming the soldier back up against the wall and driving him away.

He backed up, eyeing everything carefully. "You didn't give me a chance to finish. I just wanted to take a look at this beauty I see before me."

"What are you doing?" Wrenlow asked.

"Improvising," he whispered.

"Are you sure you should? I mean, she *did* just come from the Captain's palace."

"No," Gavin muttered.

The four remaining guards started toward him. He quickly surveyed them to come up with a plan of attack. He could turn and run, but there was a curiosity within him.

That and a stubborn streak. After fighting the El'aras, facing five traditional guards seemed a challenge he could handle.

He shook his head as they came toward him. "You don't need to do this, friends. All I wanted was to—"

"We aren't your friends," one of them grunted.

With that, two of them surged forward. Compared to the El'aras, they moved almost slowly. He twisted to the side, grabbing the wrist of the first attacker and swinging him around. The guard tripped over the soldier that'd already been dropped. Gavin jumped and flipped in the air, kicking the other soldier in the head as he twisted and sending him staggering backward.

It left two guards. One of them moved forward, though he did so a little bit more cautiously.

"Like I said, all I wanted was to—"

Gavin again didn't get the chance to finish. It was frustrating. All he wanted to do was tell them how he wanted to talk to the woman. Nothing more than a simple chat. Certainly not ogle her.

He twisted and tried to reach for the man's wrist the way he had the others, but this one was more skilled. Or lucky. Either way, it didn't matter. The guard slipped forward with his sword, and it almost cut through Gavin's cloak.

Gavin reached for one of his knives before deciding against it. With a flurry of wrist movements characteristic of the Sudo style of fighting, he swatted the sword down. He smiled as he watched the frustration on his attacker's face. He continued driving forward and coaxed the man into lowering his blade.

The guard did so slowly, barely enough to drop it, and then Gavin kicked a heel up into the man's belly and watched him crumple. Movement behind him made Gavin spin, and he kicked to again knock down the other two attackers who had started to get up. He was careful he didn't strike too hard—or too violently. It wasn't his goal to kill them.

It left him with only one of the soldiers. The crest on his left upper chest signified rank. Not just a soldier. The leader.

"You might need to talk to your men. All I wanted was to—"

The remaining soldier charged forward. His moves were unnaturally fast. Gavin frowned, backing away to survey the attacker. After the El'aras, everybody had him on edge. If this woman was the Apostle, he wouldn't be surprised if she had some skilled swordsman guarding her.

He watched as the lead soldier came toward him with movements that were deliberate, controlled, and tight. Gavin was prepared for anything—other than what happened.

As the soldier moved, his sword started to glow, and Gavin's breath caught.

*El'aras.*

He'd seen it before. Not just an El'aras, but one who

carried a sword. He didn't think this was the same man, but the timing was too suspect.

One-on-one, with anyone else, he expected he would've overmatched them. His trained ensured that. Against an El'aras with a sword, he was the one who was overmatched. Gavin didn't have any misconceptions about that fact.

He glanced at the woman, who watched him with a coolly neutral expression, and flicked his gaze back to the El'aras. If she were El'aras, too, then it was possible she *was* the Apostle. Not a sorcerer, but still powerful with magic. If he had to bring her in…

"I think I found the Apostle," he whispered.

"Did you? Then see what you can do so you can—"

Gavin couldn't wait for Wrenlow to finish.

The El'aras moved forward. Gavin tried to be prepared so he could deflect the next attack. His plan shifted from victory to mere survival. The idea of escaping was far more appealing to him than it had been before.

Gavin slipped his El'aras dagger out of his belt. The other man eyed it for a moment, his gaze dark and angry, and then he attacked. He fought with a rapid sort of activity that was a flurry of violence and tightly controlled movement. Gavin had to back away.

Through it all, the beautiful woman watched. He wanted *some* sort of reaction out of her. He would need to take a risk.

He kicked off the ground and flipped, trying to twist up and over the El'aras. He barely avoided the blade.

While in the air, he swept down with the dagger, brushing the blade off the side. He landed next to the woman.

"You—" he started to say, but the attacker rushed toward him so quickly that Gavin stumbled over his own feet as he backpedaled. He rotated again and darted forward, and from there he slipped to the side, out of the way of the El'aras.

Time to move. He glanced along the street and started to run, footsteps trailing behind him. For a moment, Gavin debated whether to fight, but instead he raced forward until he was able to blend into the crowd on the street. As he slipped away, he looked behind him.

The El'aras was there, standing at the entrance to the street. He blocked anyone else from coming, and others that came near gave him a cursory glance before heading onward.

Who was this woman?

"Are you still there?" Wrenlow yelled in his ear.

"I'm here," he said.

"Dammit, Gavin. You went silent. I thought something had happened to you."

"Something *has* happened to me. I think I found the El'aras who attacked us the night before."

"What?"

"And I think I found the one responsible for hurting Jessica."

He didn't know if this El'aras was the same one responsible for hurting Jessica.

*But how common could an El'aras sword actually be?*

He *had* recognized the fighting style, but maybe it was just the same style and not the same man.

He reached an alley and paused. He waited, looking across the street, but the El'aras didn't return. Slowing his breathing, he turned back toward the fortress, determined to get answers. The Captain obviously had them. It was time for him to take a riskier gamble, but that involved him heading into the fortress.

"Just come back," Wrenlow said. "We can figure this out once you're back here."

"What's there to figure out? The El'aras are involved in whatever this is. So is the Captain. And I need to know what's going on with the Apostle."

The only problem was that he wasn't sure what that would involve. He made his way to the fortress and approached the wall, but then hesitated. Wrenlow was right. This was a dangerous time, and they needed to be more careful than ever. What they needed was information. He would have to wait—but not for much longer.

## CHAPTER TWELVE

Gavin pushed open the door to the room. Jessica lay awake, staring up at the ceiling with her chestnut hair pooled around her head. Her breathing was easier than it had been before. She rolled her head over to look at him, a hint of a smile coming to her face, her deep blue eyes watching him.

"You don't have to look at me like that," she said.

He shook his head. "Look at you like what?"

"Like you fear that I won't pull through this."

Gavin stepped into the room. A candle burned on the table, and her belongings piled up on either side. A washbasin filled with water was set on a small table next to the bed. The sheets had been peeled back and soaked with sweat as she'd recovered. He had changed her out of her bloodied clothes and into clean ones, but she had soaked through them as well.

He pulled the chair over to the bed and took a seat on it. "How do you feel?"

"About how I look, I suppose."

"I think you look great," he said, forcing a smile.

She reached for him, taking his hand before smacking it with the other. "We don't lie to each other, Gavin. I know I look like shit."

He chuckled. "I'm glad you didn't die."

"You and me both." She glanced to the door. "And the Dragon?"

"It's shut for now. At least until you can recover well enough to run it."

Jessica breathed out and winced as she did, reaching for her stomach. The effects of the poison had gone, but the wound to her belly hadn't fully healed. That would take time. "It's going to be a while before I can get on my feet to run the tavern again. There are a few of my girls who could handle it."

"Gaspar thought the same, but Imogen wouldn't let him."

A hint of a smile curled her lips. "Wouldn't she?"

"Why do you smile like that?"

Jessica sniffed. "That's not my secret to share. I suppose if Imogen doesn't want the tavern to open, then it won't. We can wait until I'm back on my feet. Hopefully, it won't be that much longer."

Gavin nodded. "Probably not. You've been looking better every day."

"I told you not to lie to me," she said.

"Fine. You look terrible, and I don't know how long it will take for you to fully recover. Is that what you want to hear?"

"That's better. Have you figured out who did this to me?"

He nodded slowly. He knew that it was El'aras, but he still didn't understand everything involved. More than that, he didn't know what it was going to take to find this Apostle. "It's going to be difficult."

"For you, or for me?"

"Mostly for me. I think the hardest part for you is over," he said.

"I hope so." She closed her eyes. "Why is it going to be difficult for you?"

"I have to find someone who shouldn't even be in the city."

She opened one eye, glancing at him. "What kind of person?"

He shook his head.

"Gavin?"

"A sorcerer."

She sucked in a breath and then coughed, wincing as she did. "Damn. There shouldn't be any sorcerers in the city. The treaty—"

"I know all about the treaty," Gavin said. "And I know there shouldn't be sorcerers here. Gaspar has said the same thing."

"You've been working with Gaspar?"

"He won't leave me alone. Ever since you got hurt, he's forced himself upon me."

She started to smile. "I didn't think you'd be into that sort of thing."

"Jessica…"

"Trust him, Gavin. He's a good man." Her eyes closed again, and she started breathing slowly and steadily.

He watched her sleep for a few moments before getting to his feet, looking around the room. Most of his things were in the room. Gavin was settled in this city in a way that he hadn't been in quite a long time. Seeing Jessica hurt, and knowing that it was because of him, made it difficult for him.

Which was all the more reason that he needed to deal with this. He wanted revenge. He wanted to finish these jobs. And he wanted to ensure that those responsible for what happened to Jessica were dealt with. She deserved that.

"Be careful," she said as he reached the door, her voice weak.

He glanced back, and she was already back asleep.

When he made his way down into the tavern, Gaspar was the only person there. He nodded to Gavin, and they headed out, pulling the door to the Dragon closed behind them. They made their way through the streets, neither of them saying anything. They had already agreed on what they needed to do and where they needed to go. Gavin hadn't been entirely sure whether Gaspar would come with him or argue about this, but the man had come willingly and had said nothing more. They walked through the center of the city and by a market long since closed for the day. The moonlight bounced off the cobblestones, and they passed a few other taverns before heading toward the manor house.

Gavin walked along the street, glancing over at Gaspar. This section of the city had nicer homes, and they were spaced far enough apart that there was green lawn between them, unlike in other parts of the city where the homes were crammed together. Most had massive walls surrounding them, creating an almost impenetrable barrier that prevented anyone from getting too close. He tried to approach as carefully as he could, ignoring the occasional person they passed on the street. He had strategically worn a long cloak that covered his simple shirt and pants, much like Gaspar did. Otherwise, it would be much more obvious that neither of them belonged here.

It wasn't the first time he'd been out of the tavern with Gaspar, but it was the first time they'd stayed in the city. He noted the way Gaspar took everything in, his gaze sweeping quickly before turning in a different direction. Gaspar was on edge, though Gavin wasn't sure he'd ever seen the man not on edge.

"Where was it?" Gaspar asked. His voice was rough, and he looked up at the buildings nearby.

"That one," Gavin said, pointing to the manor house. He tried to do so as nonchalantly as possible, but it was difficult without drawing too much attention.

Gaspar made a casual turn, looking as if he made no intention of heading where he was actually going to be heading. They weaved along the street, and when Gaspar reached the corner where the manor house was, he paused and turned away from it.

Gavin stayed with him. He could learn from the old thief. Tristan had taught him about sneaking along streets and trying to remain hidden, but Gaspar made a living doing so. There was an element of stealth involved in the kind of work Gavin did, but that wasn't what Tristan had trained him for. He'd wanted Gavin to be prepared to end a fight if he were to get into one—to hurt and to kill if necessary.

Gavin looked back at the manor house. He'd been here a few times since that night, and each time that he'd come, there'd been no further activity. The house had been completely abandoned.

"You still don't know anything about the target?" Gaspar asked.

"Nothing other than this location. And that it was a woman."

Gaspar glanced over. "Makes you wonder, though."

"Wonder about what?"

"About whether your target is the same woman you encountered the other day." When Gavin didn't say anything, Gaspar pushed on. "Why would she have been at the Captain's home?"

Gavin had since doubted the woman was the Apostle. The sorcerer who'd hired him had claimed the Apostle was another sorcerer, and Gavin suspected the woman to be El'aras.

"I don't know," he said. He lingered for a moment before turning.

"You aren't going to stay and keep looking?" Gaspar asked.

He'd caught up to Gavin, though he'd done so with such a casual movement that it looked almost as if he were unconcerned about reaching him. Gavin had to acknowledge that the other man was far more skilled with navigating through the city than he would've expected.

"Did you see anything there?" Gavin asked.

"You didn't give me long to look."

"You don't need long to know that there's nothing taking place." He flicked his gaze over. "They abandoned it."

"That makes you wonder too."

"Why?"

"Seems like it's not the kind of place you would simply abandon. The only reason to do that would be if you were afraid you were discovered."

"She *was* discovered. I was there."

"You think they would be concerned if it was only you?"

Gavin frowned, glancing back at the manor house. "I did cut through them fairly easily."

"Did you?"

"Enough to give them a second thought."

"Makes you wonder," Gaspar said again.

Gavin nodded slowly. If it was all about just getting to the woman, then he couldn't help but wonder what else there might be. Whoever had hired him had known he was efficient but not necessarily stealthy.

"They wanted her to know they were after her," Gavin said.

"Obviously."

"Why though?"

"Like I said, it makes you wonder."

"That they wanted me to fail?"

"What do you think?" Gaspar asked.

"Honestly? I don't really know what to think. Not anymore. It could be that this is only tied to the job, but—"

"But you wonder if it's more than that."

Gavin sighed. "I think I have to." He paused and looked along the street again, then finally turned his attention back toward where he'd been coming from. "I need to find Hamish."

"What makes you think this time will be any different?"

"You're going to be with me this time," Gavin said.

Gaspar grunted. "What makes you think I'm going to be any more useful to you than going alone? You have that friend of yours always listening in."

It was the first time Gaspar had made it known he was aware of Wrenlow and his enchantment. Gavin thought that Wrenlow had hidden their communication, that he had proven that he was only scouting for them, but maybe Gaspar had overheard conversations.

"What makes you think that?"

Gaspar grunted again. "Don't take my age for ignorance, boy. I've been around enough people to know things aren't always quite the way they seem. You start to notice patterns, and patterns start to raise questions. In your case, with the two of you always whispering about, it made me wonder." He looked over, and there was a knowing expression in his eyes. "Not sure how you do it and not sure it matters. You want to keep it to yourself, that's your prerogative. All I'm saying is that you and that other kid have a way of talking."

There wasn't anything worrying about the way Gaspar said it. Either he wasn't concerned about the possibility that Gavin and Wrenlow had a magical enhancement, or he was hiding it. Regardless, Gavin wasn't sure that it mattered.

"Well?" Gaspar asked.

"Well what?" Gavin slipped along the shadows, moving closer to the house so he could get a better view.

Gaspar followed him. "Are we going to find this employer of yours?"

"As I said, we don't know where to look."

"We found him once before."

Gavin looked over at Gaspar and frowned. It might be easier to do this without the thief. "We knew he was going to the market. Not anything else beyond that."

"And he's found you other times," Gaspar said.

"Always when he had messages to send me."

"How do you get back to him when you have messages?"

"Usually I don't," Gavin said, shrugging.

"How do you tell him when the job is done?"

"He always seems to know. I've never had to reach out to him."

"Makes you wonder." Gaspar looked over to the manor house, studying it for a long moment.

"How should that make me wonder?"

"Are you always this dense?"

"Not usually," Gavin said.

"If he knows when a job is done and tells you that he has someone close to those you've been targeting, why do you think that should be?"

"I've made it a policy not to think about that."

"Because of the killing."

"It's not only killing." Lately there had been too much of that. "Besides, it's not for me to decide."

"You take all the jobs they offer?"

Gavin glanced over before shaking his head. "Not all of them."

"What makes some of them worthy of your skills?" There was something almost sarcastic about the way Gaspar said it, though nothing in his expression suggested he was being sarcastic. It made it even more annoying.

"That's where Wrenlow comes in. He looks into the background of those we've been targeting."

"And this one?" Gaspar asked, nodding toward the manor house in the distance.

"Smuggler."

"Are you sure about that?"

Gavin nodded. "As far as Wrenlow could tell. They're known to move people in and out of the city."

"People smuggler," Gaspar said. "Slaver, more likely."

"Probably."

"Now I see why you were willing to take the job."

"Not all of them have been like that," Gavin said.

"What about the others? Anything tie them together?"

Gavin and Wrenlow hadn't looked for connections between the jobs, but perhaps they should have. Given how all the jobs had come from Hamish, and therefore from the employer that Gavin still didn't know, he should've questioned.

"I'll look into it," Wrenlow said on the other side of the enchantment.

Gavin nodded, frowning to himself.

"What did he say?" Gaspar asked.

"Did you hear him?"

"No, but from the way you looked at me, I suspected he must have responded."

"He said he was going to look into it."

"You want me to look into it too?"

"I wouldn't want you to get more involved than you need to."

"I've already told you, after what they did to Jessica, I'm involved. I'm willing to do what's needed in order to take care of this. Once this is over, though, I can't make the same promises."

"I know."

"No, boy, you don't."

Gavin just shook his head. "We'll look into the connections they might have. If we find anything, I can let you know."

"When I find something first, I'll let you know. You can tell your friend that."

"You just did."

They stopped at a street corner, and Gaspar continued to look around. He had an intensity to the way he searched. Gavin found himself fascinated by the other man. Gavin wasn't sure what it was, only that there was something intriguing about Gaspar. Maybe it was just the intensity he had, or maybe it was something else. Either way, Gavin couldn't help but watch him.

"What do you know about the El'aras?" Gaspar asked.

Gavin glanced over at the thief, who gave no impression of paying any attention to him, but he had the distinct sensation that Gaspar was completely aware of everything happening. "What would you like to know?"

"Seeing as how I have no experience with them, other than at the Dragon, I thought you might be able to share with me."

"They aren't from here," Gavin said.

Gaspar grunted. "That's an understatement if I ever heard one."

"They have particular talents."

This time, Gaspar turned to him, looking at him and

meeting his gaze. "By talents, I take it you mean enchantments. Sorcery."

"Not sorcery. The El'aras have something different. Pure magic."

"The same as the man we faced in the forest?"

"It's not the same. Not really. Sorcerers use magic they summon, controlling it to do various works of art. El'aras have power within them. They're born with it. Even the least powerful of the El'aras has what you and I would consider magic."

Silence fell between them, and Gaspar continued sweeping his gaze along the street. There were others out, though not so many that they had to worry about keeping their words muted.

"How is it you know so much about them?"

Gavin hesitated. He didn't know Gaspar well enough to tell him the truth. For that matter, he didn't know anyone well enough to tell them the truth. Instead, he shared with Gaspar the lie he shared with everyone. "I was trained to be able to deal with them."

"This mysterious mentor of yours."

"He's not so mysterious."

"What happened to him?" Gaspar asked.

"He was killed."

"You weren't able to protect him?"

Gavin turned away, looking along the street. Movement near the house where they'd just been caught his eye. "Something like that," he said softly.

He hurried back to the manor house. Gavin didn't

need to look over to know that Gaspar followed. His training allowed him to be aware of the man's presence at the edge of his vision. When they reached the manor house, they spread out. Gaspar seemed to know what they needed to do, and he moved off to the side.

There wasn't any movement near the manor house now.

*What had I seen?*

There was no doubt in his mind there had been something, only now that they were near, he didn't see anything at all.

"Can you tell anything?" Gaspar asked.

Gavin shook his head. "It's dark. My vision isn't as good at night."

"No one's is, boy."

Gavin leaned on the building across the street from the manor house, staring outward. He didn't see anything, but as he remained there, he searched for any sign of the movement he was certain he'd seen.

He was willing to wait. If it came down to learning more about this job, learning more about Hamish, and even learning more about the sorcerer who'd hired them, then Gavin was willing to do it.

"You've been quiet," Wrenlow said through the enchantment.

"As far as I can tell, there was movement for the first time near the manor house, and I don't really know what to make of it."

"Movement as in your target has returned?"

"I doubt it," Gavin replied. "The house has been empty ever since that night. There aren't any guards, and without any guards there, I have a hard time believing she's back."

"Maybe somebody else came to see if you finished the job," Wrenlow said.

"The only person who's ever come to see if I finish jobs is Hamish," he said.

"That you know of," Gaspar said.

Gavin frowned. It was true. He wasn't entirely sure that Hamish was the only person who had come. It was possible that others had, though he'd suspect that they were employed the same way Hamish was employed, which was to suggest that they were a part of something different. A network. He needed to better understand that network if he intended to discover who his employer was.

Gavin reached one of the bells trees near the fence. He hesitated there for a moment, then quickly scaled the tree until he got into the upper branches and reached the wall. He jumped over the wall and looked around the inside of the yard. There was much less chaos now than there had been before.

Gaspar jumped over the wall, landing next to him. The other man was far more limber than what Gavin would've expected given his age.

"Didn't want you to think that I wasn't going to come with you," Gaspar said.

"You don't have to do this. If something happens—"

"If something happens, I figure it would be best if I'm

here with you. Given what happened the last time you were here—"

"The last time I was here, I managed to escape on my own."

"You escaped… but look at what followed you."

Gavin shook his head. "They didn't follow me. The El'aras were here."

"You sure about that?"

Gavin wasn't entirely sure. He moved through the grounds instead of answering. Now that he was here and there was nobody else to be concerned about, he moved more openly. He probably should've done this sooner, but he'd been concerned about the possibility of his target's return.

"Have you seen what's inside the house?" Gaspar's voice was barely more than a breath of wind, but somehow it carried to Gavin.

"My target wasn't there by the time I got inside."

"Because you took too long."

"First you criticize the kinds of jobs I take, and now you're criticizing how I do them?"

"If you're going to do a job, you might as well do it right."

"You sound like Tristan," Gavin muttered.

"Who's Tristan?"

"Only a pain in my ass."

He crept from tree to tree, being careful to avoid the leaves of the bells trees. Gaspar seemed to know to do the same, avoiding them as they hurried toward the house.

When they finally reached the house, a shadow cast by the bright moonlight spread out over the lawn and gave them a little more space to hide. Gavin leaned against the building and listened, but there wasn't any additional sign of movement.

Gaspar nodded toward the door, and Gavin motioned for him to take the lead. This part was more up the thief's alley. When Gaspar reached the door, he tested the handle and found it locked. He grabbed something from his pocket and stuck it into the lock before popping it open. The speed with which he picked the lock astounded Gavin. Gaspar pushed the door open and stood off to the side. Gavin crept forward. This was his part of the job.

Stepping into the darkness, he took a moment to allow his eyes to adjust. Shadows covered everything. He crept forward and found himself in a massive foyer with statues that created dark pools near the walls, almost as if there were people standing there. Gavin reached for his dagger, unsheathed it, and held it out. There was a part of him that was concerned that the El'aras dagger might start to glow, and if it did, he would turn and run. There was no point staying in a darkened house with magic. Thankfully, the blade stayed dark.

He and Gaspar moved carefully along the hallway, and the old thief made almost no sound as he moved alongside Gavin. They reached the first door, and Gaspar tested it, pushing it open just a crack and poking his head inside. He closed the door and shook his head slightly.

They stopped at the next door, and much like the first,

Gaspar was the one to look inside. When he was satisfied that there was nothing inside, he pulled the door closed again and shook his head.

They made their way through the hall, repeating this several times. At the last room, Gaspar poked his head in, then pushed the door open wider. Gavin stepped inside and was greeted by the room where he'd dove into the window. Gaspar pointed to the window, and Gavin nodded.

"I didn't have much of a choice," he whispered.

"You wanted to make as much noise as possible?"

"Sometimes."

Gaspar chuckled. "Not much of a thief, are you?"

"I've never been a thief. My jobs pay."

"So do mine. And fewer people die."

Gaspar stepped out into the hallway and made his way down to the end, where he paused at the staircase. Gavin nodded. "That was where I was supposed to go," he whispered.

"What was up there?"

"The target."

"But not when you came."

"Not when I came."

Gavin hurried up the stairs, trying to be as quiet as he could. His feet sounded too loud against the steps, and he climbed as quickly as he could. At the top of the stairs, he hesitated as he looked along the hall.

"What is it?" Gaspar whispered.

"Nothing, I guess."

Gaspar pushed against him. "What is it, boy?"

"Stop calling me that. It's Gavin," he mumbled.

Gaspar flashed a brief smile. "What is it, *Gavin*?" That wasn't much better, at least not the way he said it.

Gavin shook his head. "I'm not entirely sure. Something is troubling me. Thought I saw movement up here."

"You're jumping at shadows. I've seen it with others before. Especially when you've run into trouble."

Gavin frowned to himself.

*Was that all it was?*

He couldn't deny he was a little bit jumpier than he usually was on jobs, but he felt something instinctively. He'd come to trust that feeling, and if it was telling him that something was off, then something was off.

He moved slowly and made sure to stay ahead of Gaspar. The old thief might be skilled and perfectly equipped for all of this, but there was something about this job that had Gavin troubled, and he wasn't going to let Gaspar be the one to take the lead here.

When he reached the next door, he settled his hand on it, focusing on the energy within him. This time, rather than doing it because he needed the strength, he did it because he wanted the reassurance that he was prepared for whatever was on the other side of the door.

"What are you doing?" Gaspar whispered.

"Just waiting," Gavin said.

"Wait when we're safe."

Gavin pushed the door open. Nothing.

Gaspar swept in and hurriedly began to survey the

inside of the room. He had a practiced way of going about it. As he navigated through the room, he went from spot to spot, looking at a table, then a desk, then a bookshelf. With each of them, his eyes hurriedly scanned everything before moving on.

"I don't see anything here," Gaspar whispered.

"I don't either," Gavin said.

"Are you sure you saw something?"

"I'm sure."

Gavin stood in the center of the room, looking all around. His way of searching was different than Gaspar's. As he looked, he tried to find anything that gave him the instinctive sense that something was off. That same instinct now told him to unsheathe the El'aras dagger.

It was glowing.

"Gaspar," he whispered.

The other man was sorting through a wardrobe at the far end of the room.

Gavin turned slowly, holding the dagger out from him, moving carefully.

"Gaspar," he whispered again.

"What is it, boy?"

"Look!"

Gaspar straightened and turned. His gaze drifted to the dagger, his eyes widening. "What does that mean?"

"It means there's magic near us."

"I take it that's not you?"

Gavin frowned. "I can't use magic."

Gaspar just shrugged. "Can or can't, doesn't matter at

this point. I just wanted to make sure that it wasn't you. If this is something we need to be concerned about, then—"

A thump came from below them. The El'aras dagger started to glow even more brightly. There was someone out there.

*How had Gaspar and I missed them?*

Gavin moved toward the door. "We don't want to be caught here with some magic user," he whispered.

"You've taken them on before," Gaspar said.

"We don't know how many there are. It's better to get away."

"I didn't take you for the kind to be afraid."

"Then you didn't take me for a sensible man."

Gavin hurried to the window and jammed the dagger underneath the frame, popping the window open. Once open, a hint of a breeze gusted in. It carried with it the fragrance of the garden; a mixture of flowers along with the bells trees. There was a slightly spicy, almost pungent smell to them. He crawled out onto the window ledge and stood for a moment.

Gaspar joined him and looked down. "It's a bit of a jump," the old thief said.

"I wasn't suggesting we jump."

"No? You'd have us climb down?"

"I thought that might be a little bit more practical."

"Nothing about this is practical," Gaspar said.

Gavin started to work his way down and was hanging by his fingertips when the door to the room they'd been in creaked open. He hesitated a moment, then dropped.

The drop was just down to the main level, but when he struck the ground, he felt a jolt up his leg. He rolled off to the side as pain shot through him, and he ignored it as he had been trained to do.

Gaspar came crashing down alongside him, landing nearby. Gavin glanced over to see him getting up and looking no worse for wear. They backed up against the house. Gavin unsheathed the dagger once again to check it, and it continued to glow the way it had before. Whatever was inside was the source of the magic.

And they needed answers.

He glanced at the door and slipped along the wall, hesitating barely a moment before he went back inside the house.

"What are you doing?" Gaspar asked. "I thought you were the sensible one."

"Head back to the Dragon. I'm going to do something not so sensible."

## CHAPTER THIRTEEN

Gavin ducked back into the house. Everything was quiet, and having come into the house as many times as he had, he felt a strange comfort here he knew he shouldn't. This place was dangerous to him.

*I had nearly died once, been caught a second time, and now I was coming back on his own?*

This was a mistake.

The air was stale and still, and he crept slowly through the house, his feet moving silently on the carpet running along the hallway. The glowing dagger guided him. At least he didn't have to worry about his failing eyesight.

"Gavin?"

Wrenlow's voice drifted in through the earpiece, and Gavin hesitated. Now wasn't a good time for him to be distracted. He tapped on the earpiece, silencing Wrenlow. He hated doing that. There weren't too many jobs where he silenced his friend, but with the unknown ahead of him, he had to.

Whoever was in the house was on the second level. Gavin moved quickly up the hall and toward the stairs, then padded as quietly as he could to the second level. The whole time, the dagger continued to glow, the indication of magic pressing out from it.

His heart hammered, and he forced himself to slow it down. It required him to focus on that core energy, that part of him where he could focus his strength. Tristan would be annoyed with him. This technique was only supposed to be for times when he needed to fight well, not when he needed to sneak through a house after some sort of magic user.

Gavin almost smiled at the thought. Anything that would annoy Tristan was something he was certainly going to do. It had been that way ever since he'd trained with his mentor.

When he reached the second level, he hesitated. He held the dagger out, using the glowing light coming off of it. He started forward, and when he reached the door at the end of the hall, he paused with his hand on it.

This time, he felt something. He wasn't entirely sure what it was he felt, only that he could tell there was something on the other side of the door. A creak behind him caught his attention. The person inside wasn't alone.

He had to act quickly. Gavin pushed open the door, rolled inside, and popped up.

The room was empty.

*How? It couldn't be.*

He swept the glowing dagger around and still came up with nothing. Another sound came from outside. Gavin hurried to the window and looked down. There was movement out in the yard.

He felt something behind him and spun. The door was still closed, and the surge of light coming off the dagger suggested there was considerable magic.

*But where was it?*

It seemed to be getting brighter.

Gavin stayed in place, turning in a steady circle. There was no further creaking out in the hallway. He tried to control his breathing, knowing that was the key to slowing his heart. He embraced the power of his core, ready for anything. This was the job.

He swept his gaze around, looking at everything with as much focus as he could. There was a faint shimmer in the air, different than what he'd seen only moments before. He started toward it, holding the El'aras dagger out until he reached it. Tentatively, he pressed the dagger forward.

The shimmer faded.

And he was thrown back.

Gavin rolled, reacting quickly by swinging the dagger up and around. There was nothing there. He jumped to his feet, flipping into the air and preparing to kick, but he didn't see anything as he spun in place.

*Something* was here. He'd felt it. Whatever was here was concealed magically.

The door to the room opened and Gavin lunged, slamming his shoulder into it. The only thing that mattered was keeping whatever was in the room with him. He turned in place.

There. The shimmer again.

He hurried toward it; this time prepared for what he might face. When he swiped at it, he could feel something changing. The shimmer shifted for a moment, and then power exploded at him again.

Gavin was tossed back the same way as he had been before, but he was more prepared for it this time. He rolled with the energy and scrambled back to his feet. They were attacking him, but they weren't harming him. Somehow, whatever was taking place was blasting him back, but it wasn't hurting him. He didn't think they wanted to—or they couldn't. Either answer left him with more questions.

Immediately, he looked for that shimmer again. There was little doubt in his mind that there would be other ones as well. As Gavin started toward the one he could see, he felt something shifting in the room and something changing in the distance. He held onto that sense of energy and hurried toward the shimmer. He sliced at it again, twisting when he did. When the explosion came, it blasted where he'd been, not where he was. By moving out of the way, he was able to keep himself from getting thrown back by the violence of it.

But then, Gavin wasn't even sure he was the real target. He turned again and found the shimmer once more. This time, he sliced through it, dropping low and springing back up. When the explosion happened, he swiped the dagger through it. Everything faded.

The woman he'd seen leaving the Captain's fortress appeared in front of him.

Gavin darted forward, jamming the dagger against her neck. "You. What are you doing here?"

She eyed him; her expression completely calm. She didn't seem to mind that she was trapped there with him, which suggested there was someone else here. Gavin positioned himself so his back was to the wall, the woman in front of him. He kept the dagger pressed underneath her chin.

"This is my home," she said.

He blinked.

*Her home? So she* had *been the target.*

He could end this now, finish what Hamish wanted, and deal with only the sorcerer. But something made him pause. Maybe it was that he'd seen her in the street and saw how beautiful she was. Or that she was tied to the El'aras—the same El'aras who had almost killed Jessica.

"Sorry," he said as he started to move the dagger forward.

Everything seemed to stop.

It wasn't that Gavin hesitated, it was more the dagger that hesitated. As he tried to shove it forward, to stab it into her neck and end this, he couldn't. Something pushed against him, resisting him.

The dagger took on a blazing white light. The power

that pulsed out of it felt enormous. Magic. That was what was holding him back.

He needed one of his other knives. As he reached for it, magic wrapped around him and immobilized him.

Here he'd thought she didn't have power like the sorcerer. She stepped away from Gavin and turned to face him. The same cool, composed expression crossed her eyes. He strained against the power holding him, everything within him trembling.

Either she was El'aras or she was a sorcerer. Maybe she was both Hamish's target *and* the Apostle.

"I would ask why you came after me, but I suspect it's in your nature," she said, her voice calm.

There was something about her that he should've noticed before, something that confirmed one of his theories. It explained her beauty. The calm expression in her eyes. Her magic. "El'aras," he whispered.

She tipped her head to the side gently, and it gave her an even more beautiful expression.

*What had Hamish been thinking, giving me a job like this? He must've known.*

It explained why Hamish wanted him, but why would Hamish want one of the El'aras dead?

"You have come here twice," she said softly.

"It's just a job," he said.

"Who hired you?"

"I don't know. I know only an intermediary."

"Interesting."

She stayed a pace away from him, close enough that if

he were free, he could lunge at her, drive the dagger into her chest, and then be on with it. Only he doubted that it would be an easy thing for him to free himself from here.

"Who are you?" Gavin asked. "Are you the Apostle?"

If so, maybe he *could* take care of more than one job, though that was counting on him somehow finding a way free of the magical bands that were holding him. There was nothing in her gaze that suggested she recognized the name. Not the Apostle then.

He tensed, focusing on the energy within him to see if he might be able to break free. Something trembled. Gavin struggled to push through the magic holding him.

The dagger was magic as well, so in his mind, it seemed that if anything would be able to carve through this magic holding onto him, it would be the dagger. As he held onto the dagger, trying to cut through what he was feeling, he didn't detect anything changing. There was the pressure against him, the resistance making it difficult for him to move, but nothing more than that.

She watched him. "You won't be able to break free of this. Only another El'aras would be able to cut through this, and only if they were in control of their power." She smiled, and rather than making her look beautiful, there was something terrible and deadly about it. "Tell me who hired you."

"All I know is a name. Hamish."

"Hamish?"

Gavin nodded. "You know him? He likes to dress a bit ostentatiously, but I don't get the sense that he's the one you want to know about. His employer hired me. I don't really know what they're after, only that—"

The bands started to constrict even more, and he couldn't breathe. He focused on the core energy within him to withstand what she was doing to him.

"You will find that I don't take well to people coming into my home."

"You're not even supposed to be within the city," he said, the words difficult to get out as the constriction around his chest made everything painful.

She leaned toward him, breathing in. When she did, he could almost feel her, even though she stayed a few steps away from him. "Neither are you," she said.

He had to concentrate his strength. He might have only one opportunity.

"How do I find this Hamish?" she asked.

"I don't really know. Hamish usually finds me."

"Is that how you do things here?"

"How would I do them anywhere?"

She leaned in more, and the power continued to constrict around him.

Gavin could no longer take a breath. He didn't have long now. She was suffocating him, but she was doing it with magic. Even the sorcerer hadn't attacked him quite so viciously.

*To die here in Yoran, killed by an El'aras who seemed to be relatively high-ranking... after everything I'd been through?*

He seethed at the thought.

The emotion surprised him.

He'd always known there was a possibility that he might die. The kind of work he did only raised that risk. It was one thing Tristan had always taught him.

*Be prepared for the possibility of your own death.*

Gavin had always been ready. It wasn't that he wanted to embrace death, but as someone trained to bring death even though he might not always need to do it, he'd been ready for it to come for him as well. With his training and skill, he figured that it was unlikely to catch up with him so soon.

His vision started to fade. He focused on that core energy within him, which fed him a little bit of strength but not much. He sagged as the door opened, trying to turn toward it, but he could barely move. Then the bands relaxed around him.

Someone lifted him. "Get up," a gruff voice said.

Gavin looked over. "Gaspar?"

"Never thought a woman would be the reason you got knocked out."

"She's El'aras." And dangerous, he didn't get the chance to say.

The woman lay unconscious on the ground. Gaspar seemed unfazed by everything else that was taking place around him.

"We need to grab her," Gavin said.

"Now you want to take her with us? I thought you said she was El'aras."

"She is. She's also my initial target."

"You don't want to finish her?"

"I don't think I had all the information," Gavin said. "I've never known the El'aras to be slavers. They're many things: dangerous, deadly, magic users. But slavers?"

He got to his feet, taking in a harsh breath. With each moment, the pain that had been constricting around him started to fade, and he could breathe more easily. He tried to take in one more deep breath but struggled.

Gaspar looked over at him. "Are you sure this is smart?"

"Not at all. It's probably a terrible idea, but if Hamish wanted her dead, I need to know why before I finish the job."

"Is that how you do all of your jobs?"

"Enough of them."

Gaspar studied him for a long moment, and there was a question within his eyes. Finally, he headed toward a chest near the wall.

"What are you doing?" Gavin asked.

"I saw some rope when I was here before." He reached into the chest and pulled out a long length of rope, then quickly started to wrap it around the woman's wrists and ankles. "Are you going to stand there, or are you going to help me?"

Gavin didn't think he'd be much help. Her wrists and ankles were tied before he could do anything. The type of knot used would pull more tightly the more she struggled.

Gavin lifted her, carried her toward the window, and looked out. "There were others out in the yard."

"That's what I came to tell you. There were five, all moving quickly. I noticed two with daggers like yours."

"Which means the others are probably El'aras too," Gavin said.

"Makes you wonder."

"What will make me wonder?"

"Who she is to be so well protected here," Gaspar replied.

"I'm less concerned about why she's so well protected and more concerned about why she's even in the city."

"See?"

"See what?"

"I told you it would make you wonder."

Gavin shook his head. "I don't think we can jump down from the window. Not with her."

"Not if you want to keep her alive anyway."

"For now."

"What happens when you find out that she's just as awful as you were concerned about in the beginning?"

Gavin looked down at her just as she started to stir.

Gaspar slammed the hilt of his knife against her temple. She stopped moving. "Figured we better keep her quiet," he said.

"Not only that, but we need to keep her from using her magic. I don't know if you felt anything when you came in here, but she had me pretty tightly controlled."

"What?"

"There were bands of power around me," Gavin said. "I couldn't move."

"You were crawling toward her when I came in."

"I was?"

"She was facing you, trying to…" Gaspar shook his head. "It doesn't really matter. At this point, all that matters is that we see if we can't get out of here. As far as I can tell, we're going to have to go down. What do you think?"

"Down means fighting our way out."

"Here," Gaspar said, reaching for the woman. "You're more a fighter than me."

Gavin worried about whether the old man would be able to support her weight. Surprisingly, Gaspar flipped her over his shoulder and stood waiting.

Gavin took hold of the El'aras dagger that had fallen to the ground and started toward the door. The blade glowed with a weak light.

There was still magic here, but it was at least far enough away he couldn't feel the full influence of it. Gavin entered the hall, pausing and listening. He focused on the energy within him, concentrating the reserves of strength he had, holding onto his core as he'd been taught to do. He could feel that energy building within him, trying to give him the strength he was going to need. When he started down the hall, he did so on light feet.

The dagger glowed a little bit more brightly. He didn't know how many El'aras there'd be, but he had to be ready. If they could hide themselves the way this woman had, he'd have to be careful. He had to be prepared.

Gavin moved quickly and glanced back to make sure

Gaspar was still with him. The old thief kept pace and didn't seem to struggle with carrying the woman.

"We don't have all night, boy," Gaspar said.

Gavin grunted and turned at the landing before hurrying down. Gaspar stayed with him. At the bottom of the stairs, he found the first guard and darted forward, stabbing the man with his dagger. The man crashed down to the floor, and Gavin rolled him over. He didn't appear to be El'aras. The markings along his face suggested that he was from Sumter.

"What is it?" Gaspar asked.

"Someone else who shouldn't be here," Gavin whispered.

"Why?"

"Sumter. The tattoos are distinctive. They're too far away."

Gaspar squinted as he looked at the fallen man. "Think she hired him?"

Gavin shook his head. "If she's El'aras, then she'd have other El'aras with her."

"What about the men you were attacked by in the street?"

"At least one of them was El'aras. The others..."

*Could the others have been El'aras as well?*

He didn't think so. He'd incapacitated them far too easily for that to be the case.

"Come on," he said.

The blade still glowed. Whatever else they were going to have to face, there was still magic ahead of them.

Gavin hurried along the hall.

Something jumped.

He swung the dagger and twisted, kicking quickly. The force of both blows slammed into the attacker and caught him off guard, tossing him back. Gavin moved off to the side, rolled forward, and drove the dagger into his chest. Once the man went still, Gavin studied his face as well. Another one from Sumter. It was strange that, so far, he didn't see any El'aras. That didn't necessarily mean they weren't here. Given what he'd encountered with this woman already, he suspected El'aras would be guarding her.

He moved forward. When they neared the door, three shapes caught his attention.

"Give me a minute," he said.

"We may not have a minute," Gaspar replied.

"Well, that's what I need." He took a deep breath, focusing on his reserves of power, deciding that now was as good a time as any to use what he had left. Once he was outside of the manor house, back on the street, he could finally relax. But for now, he had to hold onto that energy.

Power flooded into him, and he darted forward. The nearest attacker was quick, though maybe not El'aras-quick. Gavin thrust his dagger into the belly and carved to the side. He turned and dropped down, sweeping his leg around. He hooked it and jerked the next person down. He spun with his fist, driving it into the man's forehead. Then he rolled, twisted around, and drove his elbow into the midsection of the third attacker. Gavin jumped to his feet and brought his knee up, connecting with that same person's chin. The guard collapsed.

When it was done, he turned and smiled at Gaspar.

There were two men behind the thief. One of them had a glowing blade, though there was something about the El'aras that seemed unusual.

"Gaspar?"

"I'm aware of them, boy."

"I need you to take one small step toward me," Gavin said.

"How do you expect to get past?"

"Just trust me."

Gaspar locked eyes with him for a moment, and then Gavin jumped. By holding onto that core and concentrated energy within him, he was able to jump far higher than he normally could. He flipped over Gaspar, landing between him and the other two attackers. He brought down the one whose sword wasn't glowing, carving through his thigh and then stomping quickly to keep him from moving.

It left only the El'aras, who he recognized as the one he'd faced in the street—though he didn't know if it was the same one who'd attacked Jessica.

"Hand her over, and your death will be quick," the El'aras said.

"I'm afraid I can't do that," Gavin said.

He darted forward. The El'aras was quick, skilled, but in the small confines of the hallway, the longer sword was at a disadvantage to the dagger.

Gavin twisted and swept his dagger around to block the first sword thrust. Then there was another, but he blocked that as well. He deflected each one that came at him. Still, he was forced back.

The swordsman was more skilled than Gavin, but skill wasn't always the most crucial factor, especially not in a hallway like this. He moved forward so that he could get to the El'aras, who blocked each slash of the dagger.

Each time Gavin thought he could get closer to the El'aras, he was deflected. He moved as quickly as he could but wasn't fast enough. He was forced back again and again.

"Come on, boy," Gaspar said.

Gavin glanced back briefly enough to see Gaspar standing in the doorway, holding the woman over his shoulder.

"Go," Gavin said.

"What about you?"

"I'll buy you time. Get to—"

He didn't have the chance to finish. The sword came whistling toward him, and he had to drop, rolling so he didn't take a blade to the neck. He kicked, his boot connecting with the man's knee and dropping him. Gavin lunged and grabbed the El'aras, slamming him to the ground.

The guard was strong, but Gavin had trained for years, and he was stronger. More than that, he had tapped into his core reserves. The power wasn't infinite and would eventually fade, and he'd begin to fail. But for now, by holding onto that power, he could draw on what he needed to get free.

He continued slamming the El'aras against the ground. The man started to lose consciousness. Gavin brought the dagger around, but in a surge of strength, the El'aras wrapped his leg around Gavin's chest and pushed him away.

Gavin still had the El'aras dagger, and he grabbed the sword that was nearby.

The El'aras watched him. "You will suffer if you harm her."

"Who is she?"

"She is the Risen Shard."

Gavin frowned. "That doesn't sound very kind."

The El'aras glared at him. "You will—"

Gavin darted forward, twisting in a Sudo-style kick, and he caught the El'aras in the chest, then in the shin, then in the forehead. The man collapsed without another word. Gavin brought the dagger up to remove this El'aras as a threat, when a shout from the manor yard caught his attention.

"Another time," he whispered. He scrambled away and hurried into the yard.

Five men faced Gaspar. He had a short-bladed knife in hand, but with the woman on his shoulder, he wasn't able to do anything. Gavin raced forward and jumped over Gaspar, landing in front of him. He spun while holding onto the dagger and the sword in a deadly flurry of movements.

If there was one thing that Tristan had trained him to do, it was to be a master of all fighting styles. That included the sword. He didn't need to use it often, but when he did, he didn't doubt his skill. He carved through two men before they had even realized he was there. By the time he got to the remaining three, they backed away warily, watching him.

*No. Watching the blades.*

They were still glowing, which meant there was still someone using magic nearby.

*Maybe it was the woman.*

He thought she was unconscious, but with the kind of power she had, it was possible she used magic even while incapacitated.

Gavin jammed the blade into one of the attackers, then turned and reached the next one. He stabbed the dagger into the man's side and sliced upward. Then there was only one remaining. Gavin darted toward him, but the man turned and ran, disappearing into the darkness. He wanted to give chase, but there was no time. It was better for them to get out of here.

He glanced at the other fallen attackers. They didn't all have the same sun-kissed skin as those who'd lived in Sumter their entire lives, but all of them had the markings.

*What was going on?*

He'd gotten himself involved in something, and now he had to figure out how to get out of it. Somehow, this woman was at the heart of it all.

They hurried through the manor house grounds and reached the wall. Gavin helped Gaspar up first while holding onto the woman, then he passed her up and over to Gaspar. When they landed on the other side of the wall, Gavin looked around.

"This has been fun," Gaspar said.

"Has it?" Gavin asked.

"Probably more for you than for me, but I must say I'm left with more questions than I had before." He looked at Gavin with a strange expression in his eyes.

"Don't blame me. Blame her."

"I'm thinking both of you share some blame."

Gavin held Gaspar's gaze for a moment before shaking his head. "Let's get back to the Dragon before Wrenlow gets too angry with me for having silenced him."

"Why would you do that?"

"I don't need him shouting in my ear while I'm dying."

Gaspar barked out a laugh. They started off and blended into a crowd. Gavin looked at the dagger and the sword, and both of the blades continued to glow.

He couldn't shake the troubled feeling it gave him.

CHAPTER FOURTEEN

A fire crackled in the hearth of the Roasted Dragon, giving a warmth to the room that Gavin didn't feel. Two lanterns provided light from the opposite wall, though shadows still drifted around and filled the inside of the room. Those lanterns cast a pale light on the woman. She was bound, her wrists and ankles tied to the chair, and the dagger Gavin held was angled toward her. He sat in the chair opposite her, watching.

"I can see why you didn't want to hurt her," Wrenlow said.

"It's not like that," Gavin said.

"Still, I can see why."

Gavin shook his head. "Anyway," he muttered.

"Anyway? That's all you're going to give me?"

"I don't know if you deserve anything more than that."

"You silenced me. That wasn't the deal," Wrenlow said.

"You keep in communication with me. That way I know you aren't hurt."

"In this case, I didn't need you chattering in my ear."

"Will the two of you stop?" Gaspar asked, dragging a chair over and taking a seat next to Gavin.

He looked over at the thief. The dark lines around his eyes were deeper than they had been. He looked tired—as tired as Gavin felt. By the time they'd reached the Dragon, Gavin was exhausted from holding onto the strength, that power of his core, for too long. He needed to replenish his stores, to rest. Even if it was for only a little while, he needed to recover.

The inside of the Dragon was quiet. It was nothing like it'd been before Jessica had been hurt. There'd been a vibrancy then, a sense of activity, a life. It was almost as if when she'd been hurt, the tavern had been hurt with her.

"We need to question her," Gaspar said.

"Why do you think I wanted to bring her with me?" Gavin asked.

"The same reason your kid suggested."

"I'm not a kid," Wrenlow said, looking indignantly at Gaspar.

"To me you are," he said.

"I think the entire city is a kid compared to you," Gavin said.

Gaspar grunted. "Maybe. What's going to happen when she comes completely around and starts to wrap that power around you again?"

"We just have to be ready for it."

"Ready?"

"I don't really know. I don't have any special protections against magic."

Gaspar watched him for a moment. "You don't?"

"No. Do you?" Gavin asked.

"No, but I suppose if I needed to find them, I could get them."

"Considering that you were with us when we were forced into a job by a sorcerer, I would've expected you to decide that was necessary by now."

"Possibly," Gaspar said.

Gavin could only shake his head. "Possibly."

The woman started to move, twisting in place, and Gavin turned his attention to her. Her chin was tilted slightly toward him, and she had a pale complexion and long golden hair. Power seemed to radiate from her, and yet he couldn't move. She was incredible. Though Jessica rested upstairs, still recovering, he thought she'd understand his inability to take his eyes off this woman. He rarely saw someone this beautiful.

*If it turns out she's a slaver, would I still be unwilling to harm her?*

The woman opened her eyes. The dagger started to glow more brightly.

"Don't," Gavin said. "If you use magic on any of us, we'll stick a knife in you."

"Where am I?" she asked.

"You're with us," he said, smiling broadly and sweeping his hands around him. "You're alive. You should be thankful for that."

"Thankful?"

"Maybe not thankful exactly, but you're alive. Isn't that enough?"

The woman continued glaring at him, and her gaze drifted from Gavin to Gaspar and finally to Wrenlow.

Maybe Wrenlow shouldn't have been there. He looked away, and Gavin could only shake his head. If she was going to use magic on any of them, it was most certainly going to be Wrenlow, especially now.

"Who are you?" Gavin asked, sliding his chair forward and holding onto the El'aras dagger. "Your guard—husband?—called you the Risen Shard."

"Because I am," she said.

"What is that?"

"Does it matter?"

"Not to me, but I'm looking for a reason not to kill you, so I figure it's in your best interest to tell me as much as you can."

"And if I don't give you that reason?"

"I suppose I'm going have to finish my job."

"The one Hamish hired you for."

"As I told you back at the house, Hamish wasn't the one who hired me. I don't know who my employer is, only that it goes through an intermediary. Who do you think has a reason to want you dead?"

"Many people," she said softly.

"I'm sure. Especially if you wrap everybody in power the way you did with me."

"You did have a dagger to my neck."

"I did," Gavin said, smiling. "Give me a name. I'm not going to call you Risen Shard."

"Anna," she said.

"Just Anna?"

The woman nodded. "That's all you need."

Gavin glanced at the others. Wrenlow might be able to use this information when questioning his contacts. If not, maybe Gaspar would be able to find something. They were already looking into the title "Risen Shard," searching for anything to explain who she was and why she'd been targeted. Gavin wasn't optimistic that they would find anything.

"The El'aras aren't supposed to be in Yoran," he said.

"And yet we are," she said.

"Why did you attack me here?"

She looked around the inside of the tavern before settling her gaze back on him. "I have never been here before."

"Your people have. They attacked me."

"Did they?"

"There were five El'aras that attacked here. A friend of mine nearly died. I know what I saw," he said.

She tipped her head back, eyeing him. "Do you?"

Gavin growled, sliding his chair closer to her. "You do realize what kind of person I am, don't you?"

"Perhaps even better than you do," she said softly.

"Who within Yoran would want you dead?"

"That's a different question, with a different answer."

"That's the same question I asked before."

"It's not. Not really," Wrenlow said. Gavin looked over at him, arching a brow, and Wrenlow shrugged. "Well, it's not. You asked her who wants her dead. She told you that many people do. And now you asked her about who in the city wants her dead. You got more specific."

"Thank you," Gavin muttered.

"Your friend is correct," she said.

"That doesn't mean I have to like it."

"Enough," Gaspar said, twisting in his chair so he could face her. "We need to know who in Yoran wants you dead." There was a violence within his eyes, something that raged just beneath the surface.

Gavin understood. Gaspar was still angry about what had happened with Jessica.

"I don't know," Anna replied. "There shouldn't be many who even know I'm here."

"Why not?"

"Because my presence has been hidden intentionally."

"You're hiding out here?" Gavin asked.

Anna looked over at him, and she tipped her head in a slight nod. "Hiding. Staying safe. Or, I *had* been staying safe, until you found me."

"Well, I didn't really have to work all that hard. Hamish was the one who found you and guided me to you. So if you thought you were safe here, I'm afraid you were wrong."

"I haven't been seen many places," she said. "And I've been wrong many times."

Gavin could only shake his head. "You might be more trouble than you're worth."

"Perhaps."

Gavin leaned back, watching her. There was something about how much she irritated him that he couldn't help but enjoy at the same time. She was powerful, and most of the time, he hated being around those who were more powerful than him. If there was one lesson he'd learned incredibly well from Tristan, it was to avoid those who might be more powerful than him.

"Listen," he said. "We could've killed you back at your house, but we didn't. I want to know what's going on so I can better understand."

"Better understand so you can decide whether to kill me?" she asked.

"Yes," Gavin said.

"Is that how you do your jobs?"

"Sometimes. Especially when I have troublesome targets like you."

Wrenlow gasped, and Gavin ignored him. The dagger continued to glow, and he didn't even know if there'd be any way for him to do anything to her. He'd already seen how she could push back any power he might try to use against her. With her connection to magic, she might be able to stop the knife from getting too close.

"Why would Sumter be involved in attacking you?" He watched her, looking for spark of recognition, but there was nothing.

"I don't know," she said.

Gavin sighed. Despite his best intentions, he believed her. "Tell me why you're in the city." He flipped the dagger and slipped it into the sheath. He crossed his arms over his chest, watching her.

She regarded him. "I came to the city to hide. Isn't that why so many people come to Yoran?"

"Yes," Gaspar said softly.

"I thought I'd be safe. I should've been safe. That I wasn't suggests I was betrayed."

"Betrayed? Why would anyone betray you?"

"Because I am the Risen Shard."

"What does that mean?"

"What do you know about the El'aras?" she asked. She leaned back and watched him. He'd thought she'd been cool, almost far too calm, but that wasn't what he saw from her at all. The more he looked, the easier it was for Gavin to recognize there was something else in her eyes that he hadn't seen before. Maybe it was a hint of fear, but he wasn't sure about that. No, what he saw was uncertainty. She was powerful, yes, but she was also helpless. It was a strange dichotomy.

"I've had some dealings with them," Gavin said.

"I suppose you have. You don't fear facing one like so many would."

"I don't fear."

"All men fear."

Gavin nodded. "I guess. I've trained not to fear. Is that better?"

"Does it make you better?" she asked.

"It makes it so I'm more efficient."

"Is that all you're after? Efficiency?"

"You were telling us about the El'aras," Gavin said.

"We were talking about fear," she said.

"*You* were talking about fear." He shifted in his chair. He could feel Gaspar looking at him, almost as if there was a question in the old thief's eyes—one Gavin was determined to ignore.

"I am of the Yassir El'aras. We live beyond the forest that surrounds Yoran. In the old growth and a place of much power."

"How can anyone live there?" Wrenlow asked, leaning forward in his chair. "I've heard it's so dark that no light gets in. The trees are so tall the sun never strikes the ground."

"You can see the sun when you climb to the top of the trees," Anna said.

"You can climb to the top of the trees?"

"Hundreds of feet above the ground," she said, her voice taking on an airy, wispy quality. "That's where my home is. The city buried within the forest. It's a place of incredible beauty."

"I'm aware of the Yassir El'aras," Gavin said as he thought of what Cyran had told him of the different types of El'aras, along with which of them had a treaty with Yoran.

"I suspected you were. Within the forest, the city of Asaindar can be found. It's nothing like your cities. It's beautiful and blends into the trees. Life in a way that we were meant to be."

He leaned toward her. "You still haven't explained anything. You need to give me a reason to keep you alive."

"You asked me what being the Risen Shard means." She smiled, and he couldn't help but feel a pang within him, almost as if there was something pulling upon him. "If you give me a moment, I'll tell you what you want to know."

Gavin sighed. There was no point continuing to push her, not like this. And he *had* asked her.

*If she was willing to share more about who she was, how could I not wait to see what I could uncover?*

He'd never had the opportunity to speak to one of the El'aras quite like this. He'd experienced them before and had suffered because of them, but never had he the opportunity to sit with one and ask questions. Perhaps that was what he needed to do now. They could all have their curiosity sated.

"What's it like in the forest?" Wrenlow asked.

"It is beautiful, unlike anything you could even imagine," she said.

"I've seen incredible beauty. Sometimes what you think is beautiful is actually deadly," Gaspar said.

"You could be describing Asaindar," Anna replied. "It is beautiful, but it can be deadly as well."

"Why deadly?" Wrenlow asked, his gaze flicking to the far side of the room.

Gavin followed the direction of his gaze to Imogen, who was leaning against the wall, silent as ever. There was something in her posture that made him think that she'd be capable in a fight. Perhaps it was the slight tension within her, though it might be something more.

"Because not all view the city in the same way. Some see us as a threat," she said.

"Because of what you've done over the years," Gavin said.

"What we have done?"

"I've seen the lands in the south. I've seen the destruction the El'aras have caused."

"Not the Yassir El'aras."

"Are you different than other El'aras?" asked Wrenlow.

She glared at them. "Others are more violent."

"Don't get her started," Gavin said.

Wrenlow looked at him. "We want the opportunity to know more about her, don't we? Isn't that why you brought her here? Because you didn't know whether or not you should complete the job? Until you know, then we should learn as much as we can about her."

"The kid's right," Gaspar said.

"I'm not saying he's not right," Gavin muttered.

Anna shook her head. "The Yassir El'aras have never attacked your people."

Gavin grunted. "You attacked me."

"Did we?"

"I was here."

She leaned toward Gavin, and there was a darkness as she smiled. "What do you think you saw?" she whispered.

"I saw one of your El'aras with this dagger," he said, holding it up. "I saw them come after my people."

"Can you blame them, if it were true?" she asked. "If you came after me, how can I be blamed for coming after you?"

Gaspar started laughing. Gavin swung his gaze over and looked at the other man, who shrugged. "She's not wrong," he said. "I mean, you did go after her to kill her."

"Because I was told she was a slaver."

"You were told?" Anna said.

Gavin glanced over to Wrenlow, who had paled. "My sources suggested you were a slaver. Does that make you feel better?" Gavin asked.

Anna watched him. "Regardless of what you believe, it wasn't my El'aras who came after you." She twitched her wrists, and the rope around both her wrists and ankles suddenly disappeared.

Gavin scrambled to his feet, holding the El'aras dagger out. He didn't know if it would even make a difference at this point. If she had enough control over her magic to free herself, even the dagger might not make a difference for him.

She stared at him as Gaspar got slowly to his feet, reaching toward his knife.

*What was a knife going to do against somebody with magic? For that matter, what did I even have that could fight against her magic?*

It was a wonder that he had the dagger, but even with it, he wasn't going to be able to do much to slow her. She'd already proved that she was fully capable of overwhelming him even when he had the dagger.

Gavin glanced over at Gaspar. "I thought you had her bound."

"The binding would've worked on anyone else," he said.

"Anybody but someone like her," Gavin said. Not that he could've done any better than Gaspar did. With her ability, and seeing how easy it was for her to break free, he didn't know if there was anything he would've been able to do. It was a wonder they'd managed to incapacitate her as they had.

She stood, looking at them with a serene expression on her face. With a wave of her hand, Gaspar's hand darted down toward the ground, dropping the knife harmlessly. Wrenlow cried out, and Gavin looked over to see him standing rigidly, his own knife clattering to the ground.

The only weapon she wasn't dropping was the El'aras dagger. Gavin didn't know if that had more to do with the fact that it was an El'aras blade or whether it was because she was taking her time, turning her attention to him last. Regardless, as she looked at him, he could feel something within her gaze, some weight that lingered there.

"You are going to do something for me," she said.

"What exactly do you think I'm going to do for you? I think we both know what the situation is."

She smiled, and there was a darkness within her smile. Despite that, there was still something almost beautiful in it. Gavin shook those thoughts away. He couldn't think of her in that way. He needed to think about her as the dangerous woman she was, not the beautiful El'aras who stood before him.

The hand holding the El'aras dagger started to lower. It was an invisible pressure pushing on him, and as much as he tried to resist and keep the blade pointed at her, it dropped slowly. He was tired from everything that had happened throughout the night. He didn't even have his residual stores of energy to access. The only thing he had was what little strength he had left.

The El'aras dagger continued to glow, and there was something about the blade that took on the energy around him. Gavin fought against what she was doing, trying to hold onto the dagger, wanting to keep it pointed outward. There was a struggle, but it wasn't much of one. She was strong—stronger than him.

As he held onto the blade, she watched him. Amusement glittered on her face, and she waited as he held the dagger out, still resisting her. It took him a moment to realize what she was doing. She was waiting for him to grow weaker by exerting himself. She wanted him to overdo it. Rather than fighting, Gavin dropped his arm to the side, clutching the El'aras dagger as tightly as he could.

She smiled at him. "Good. This will go much easier for you if you don't fight."

"What will?"

The door to the Dragon thundered open, and Gavin looked up. A familiar face stepped into the tavern: the El'aras he'd left unconscious within the manor house.

## CHAPTER FIFTEEN

Gavin tried to step forward, but Anna maintained a squeezing grip of magic around him. Whatever power she held onto kept him from doing anything, so he stopped struggling and instead prepared to try a different tactic. He just didn't know what it would be.

"Did they harm you?" the El'aras asked, striding over toward her. He kept one hand on his El'aras sword, the blade glowing softly. He held the other outward, almost as if he were holding onto a shield Gavin couldn't see.

"Do you really think they are capable of harming me, Thomas?"

Thomas flicked his gaze from Wrenlow to Gaspar, then finally settled it on Gavin. It lingered there the longest, something almost knowing in his eyes. "It's possible. You know what has nearly happened since we've been in this city."

"I know what's happened, not what's nearly happened. And what's happened has involved a betrayal."

Thomas turned toward her and ignored the others. He slammed his free hand up to his chest, bowing at the waist. "You have my blade, my—"

Anna tapped him on the shoulder, shaking her head slightly.

Gavin frowned as he looked at her. Something didn't quite make sense here. He was surprised to realize that he could move again though. He quickly shifted with the dagger and held it up.

Anna glanced over at him. She attempted to squeeze him with a magical band again, but he swung the dagger once and danced back near Gaspar.

"What do you think you're doing, boy?" Gaspar asked.

"I'm going to resist whatever she intends to do to us."

"If she wanted to hurt us, she would've done that by now. She wants something from you."

Gavin hesitated. The man was right. Given how much power she'd already displayed, if she'd wanted to harm him, it wouldn't have taken much for her to do so—just her power to constrict him. She might've even been able to suffocate him. That she hadn't suggested that either she needed for them to live or she had no interest in actually hurting them. He relaxed and backed away. He continued to grip the dagger, looking at Thomas, then letting his gaze drift to her.

"Is he right?" Gavin asked. "Do you want something from us?"

"I want to know who hired you," Anna replied.

"I'm afraid I'm at just as much of a loss as you are."

"You have some way of getting to your employer, don't you?"

"Only when the job is done," Gavin said.

"Fine."

"Fine?"

"You will complete the job. When it's done, then you will have your employer come."

Gavin frowned, glancing over at Gaspar and then Wrenlow. "I'm afraid you don't quite understand what the nature of the job entailed."

"Don't I? You were hired to eliminate me." She stood with her arms crossed in front of her. "You aren't the first, but you did get closer than most." Thomas paled slightly, and he shot Gavin a look filled with anger. "I think that says something about you, but it also says something about the one who employed you."

"What does that say about them?" he asked.

"It suggests they believed you'd be able to get to me."

"I have a reputation."

"I'm sure you do, Gavin Lorren."

She said his name with a strange familiarity, and his last name in particular rolled off her tongue, the accent even correct. Few said that part right. Not even the sorcerer had.

*How had she learned it?*

Gavin tensed. "What do you want from me?"

"Nothing from you," she said.

He smiled. "You want something from me. Not just from whoever employed me."

"I think I will take your employer."

"In order to get to them, I have to prove you died."

"You don't think you can?"

"I think it'll be a little bit difficult to prove in this situation."

"Perhaps." She looked at Thomas and nodded to him. His jaw clenched for a moment, and then he slipped his sword into his sheath. She turned back to Gavin and said, "You will find your employer."

"What do I get out of it?"

She cocked her head, studying him. "Why, you get to live."

Gavin started to laugh.

"I fail to see why that amuses you."

"It's only that you're the second person in as many days who's promised to let me live if I complete their assignment. You'll forgive me if I'm feeling a little bit less than enthused about such offers." Gavin held onto the El'aras dagger but kept it pointed at the floor. He still had the other sword he'd taken off Thomas, though somewhere the El'aras soldier had come up with another. "With the kind of work I do, I usually get paid."

"You don't think your life is a worthy payment?" Anna asked.

"Mine is," Gaspar said.

"Quiet," Gavin said. He turned back to Anna. "Maybe it

is, but I think there's something else you might be able to offer me."

"What is that?"

"I need your help finding someone in the city."

"That isn't the kind of thing I'm well equipped for," she said.

"I'm not asking you to do anything unpleasant." Though, if she were willing to do it, then perhaps it would be easier on him. "All I need is a location. With your contacts, you'd be able to find this for me."

"What contacts do you think I have?"

"I saw you coming out of the Captain's home."

She stared at him.

"Which makes me think you're at least somewhat well-connected within the city. Perhaps you don't want to use those connections, but I'm going to need you to."

"And if I refuse?"

"I don't think you're going to refuse," Gavin said.

"What makes you think that?"

"Because you want to know who my employer is." Silence hung between them. Gavin stared at her, trying to gauge her reaction.

Finally, Anna offered a hint of a smile. "I might be able to uncover something for you."

"Good. I'm looking for a sorcerer who goes by the name of the Apostle." Neither she nor Thomas reacted in recognition of the name, the title, or anything. "Do you know anything about the Apostle?"

She shook her head. "I do not. Why?"

"Another job I was offered."

"The same job that had terms similar to what I offered you?"

Gavin smiled tightly. "Possibly. And I know that they're powerful, and rumor tells me they haven't been in the city all that long. Since you're cozy with the Captain—"

"He provides certain protections within the city I have benefited from," she said.

"Good. Then you'll help me with this job."

She studied him a moment. "And am I to take it that you negotiated for similar terms as you did with me?"

He smiled again. "You may assume all you want."

She shook her head. "You are playing a dangerous game, Gavin Lorren."

"It's the only game I know," he said.

Anna held his gaze for a long moment before turning and nodding to Thomas. They strode across the Dragon to the doorway. She turned back to him, watching him. "I will find what I can of this Apostle. I will meet with you in two days, at which point you will confirm my demise with your employer."

With that, she strode out of the Dragon, leaving Gavin to exhale slowly.

"What was that about?" Gaspar asked.

"That was about me trying to see if we can't find a way to get more information about this Apostle."

"You're going to pit one job against another? You really are a fool, aren't you?"

"I don't know any other way to go about this. We have two employers with magic who are trying to corral us to work on their behalf."

"There isn't any 'we' here," Gaspar said.

"You got involved."

"Not by choice." Gaspar limped toward the back of the tavern and disappeared up the stairs.

Gavin sat there for a long moment before getting to his feet. He headed to the kitchen and poured himself a mug of ale. He walked back out into the main room, took a seat, and propped his feet up.

It just wasn't the same without Jessica and the music and the activity that he was used to in the Dragon. Tipping back the mug, he sipped it slowly, savoring the flavor. It wasn't the best ale he'd ever had, though it was far from the worst. There was one thing Jessica had prided herself on, and that was the quality of her food and her drink.

Wrenlow pulled a chair out and sat across from him. "I don't like this," he said.

"I don't like it either."

"What're the odds of having two magical beings come after us in Yoran at the same time?"

"Not good," Gavin said between drinks. He wiped his arm across his mouth before setting the ale back down.

"I'm serious."

Gavin tipped back his drink, swallowed it quickly, and set the mug back down on the table in front of him. "I'm serious too. I don't think the odds of any of this are good, which is what troubles me."

"Why?"

"There's a reason we're in Yoran."

"Because the jobs guided us here," Wrenlow said.

Gavin looked up. He was drained, but it seemed as if he were just about to make some sort of connection he needed. "The jobs guided us, but it was something more than that. *We* were guided. Something else brought us here."

"What're you getting at?"

Gavin didn't answer. Instead, he stood and walked to the kitchen to pour himself another mug of ale. He returned to his seat across from Wrenlow, who hadn't moved. He was still leaning forward and resting his elbows on his knees, watching Gavin with a worried look in his eyes. "I'm not really getting at anything. I guess what I'm saying is that we've been in Yoran for a few months now."

"We have," Wrenlow said.

"Before that, we were in Jessup."

"And before that, we were in Tial and then Unahf and—"

"I remember," Gavin said.

They didn't stay too long in those cities, though that was partly because the jobs had dried up. None of the cities were nearly as large as Yoran. In a city like this, situated on the northern border, it was easier to find more work. Because of the sheer size of Yoran, with several hundred thousand people living within its borders, there was an almost endless supply of jobs. The key was finding the right employer, but once they'd reached Yoran, the employer had sought him out almost immediately. Gavin hadn't had any difficulty finding work.

It was almost too easy. He'd known from the beginning that things didn't feel quite right, but the jobs had been the kind he'd almost been meant to take. It was like they'd been crafted for him, knowing that he didn't take just any job or target. He needed a reason.

Tristan had always tried to work that out of him, wanting him to lose that side of himself, but Gavin had failed. It was one of the few times he'd disappointed Tristan during his training.

He closed his eyes, sleep almost claiming him as he remembered the first time he'd disappointed Tristan. There was a target in the riverside village of Carp. The man couldn't have been more than his mid-twenties, with dark black hair, a mischievous smile, and a confident walk. Gavin had slipped along the rocks, moving quickly.

"You see your target?" Tristan had asked.

Gavin remembered looking out at the target, already calculating the various ways he could take him out. A drowning would be the cleanest, but it'd be the most difficult for him.

"You want it to look like an accident or to be obvious?" he'd asked his mentor.

"A good question, and any employer should specify.

Some prefer not to be involved, whereas others want to send a message."

"What kind of message?"

"The kind suggesting that those who oppose them will find a similar fate."

Gavin had drifted forward and moved casually, though he'd stayed near the small buildings that lined the river. He'd kept the target in sight, which wasn't difficult. The man hadn't been moving that quickly, and Gavin still hadn't felt completely comfortable with this.

"What did he do?" he had asked.

"What do you mean?"

"The target. What did he do?"

"You ask that question each time," Tristan had said.

"Most times you answer."

"You know you have to stop asking."

"I don't want to," Gavin had said. "I want to know what he did."

"Why would that change anything? A job is a job. That's what you're being trained for. You need to be prepared for the types of jobs you'll be asked to do."

Tristan had brought back his hand, and Gavin had twisted, ducking underneath the blow.

He'd expected a satisfied smile of Tristan, but it never came. Most of the time, when they were training, Tristan had offered him that reassurance when he'd done something well. In this case, there had been nothing but disappointment in his mentor's eyes.

"You ask about what a target did, but all that should matter to you is what the client is willing to pay."

Gavin could only stare and shake his head. "No."

"No? That's the nature of the job," Tristan had said.

"Then I don't want the job."

"You know what happens if you leave."

"I know… but I still want to know," Gavin had said.

Tristan had watched him, and the disappointment had never left his face. "You're training for a job. You won't be able to serve if you fail me here."

"I'm not trying to fail you. I'm just trying to understand. Don't you think I'm going to do a better job if I understand the reason behind what you offer?"

Gavin had watched the target move along the street and hadn't paid any attention to Tristan.

The blow had come out of nowhere. It had struck him in the face, knocking him down.

They had been standing between a pair of buildings, and he'd been trapped. He'd tried to raise his hand to deflect the next attack, but Tristan had been quick. More than that, he'd been the one to train Gavin and teach him all of his fighting techniques. He was a master of all of them and used that to his advantage. Tristan had pummeled Gavin and knocked him to the ground, beating him until everything had started to go black.

"You don't get to question!"

That was the only thing that had lingered in his mind as he'd passed out.

Gavin shook himself from the memory, and he looked at his mug of ale.

"What is it?" Wrenlow asked.

"It's nothing," Gavin said, tipping back the mug and drinking.

"Something is troubling you."

"Maybe it's just an overactive imagination." He glanced toward the door, nodding. "Get some rest. I don't know when we're going to need to move again, but if we have to make it look like Anna's dead, it's going to be a complicated assignment."

"What about the Apostle?" Wrenlow asked. "I have my feelers out on that, but I haven't been able to find anything so far."

"I suspect we aren't going to find anything."

"Why?"

Gavin got to his feet, the chair he'd been sitting in tipping back and clattering to the ground far too loudly. He lifted it and swung it back into place before setting the mug of ale on the table. "Because I think we were meant to ask Anna."

He strode toward the door, pausing there for a moment with his hand on the doorframe before stepping out into the darkness.

Wrenlow's voice sounded in his ear. "What're you doing? Where are you going? Don't you need rest?"

Gavin resisted the urge to tell him he did. He was exhausted, and after having used his core strength, he didn't really have all that much energy remaining. He needed to rest, if only so that he could fully recuperate. Instead, he wanted to be out in the night. To be alone.

"I'll be fine. Get yourself some rest. We can talk in the morning."

"Gavin—"

He tapped on the enchantment. As he walked through the city, he let the darkness and the quiet surround him. It was late enough that there weren't many people out, and in the solitude of the night, he was able to find a sense of peace. He hurried along the streets, enjoying the quiet.

There was something about stalking through the city at night that he found particularly comforting. After a while, he ended up on the street with the manor house. He didn't know if he'd done so intentionally or if his subconscious had drawn him there. Either way, there was no movement inside.

*Why had Anna returned there?*

She had disappeared into hiding because they'd targeted her, but something had brought her back. That seemed significant to him, though he wasn't entirely sure why. As he stared at the house, he remembered that she'd been in the upper room where he'd gone. Not only that—he had intervened before she'd found anything.

He made his way to the manor, and when he reached the outside wall, he lingered for a moment to listen. There was no sound of movement. In the darkness, he couldn't see much and resisted the urge to pull out the El'aras dagger. He climbed over and crept through the yard toward the house.

Gavin hesitated. The bodies of the Sumter attackers were gone.

*Had Thomas removed them?*

He tested the door of the house, which was still unlocked. He hurried through the hall and up the stairs, padding as quietly as he could until he reached the second level. Once there, he lingered for a moment before heading straight to the room where he'd found Anna.

*Why had she been here?*

He stepped into the room and closed the door behind him. Only then did he unsheathe the El'aras dagger. Thankfully, there was no glow from it.

He paused in front of the chest where Gaspar had found the rope. He sorted through the belongings inside but didn't find anything valuable. There was a cloak, a blanket, and a dress. Probably all Anna's.

He paused another moment and then started to flip through the wardrobe. This held only dresses, and there was nothing in any of them that he thought would be valuable. Perhaps to one of the El'aras, but not to him.

Gavin paused and moved back to the center of the room.

*Why had she returned? I know that's significant... but how?*

As his eyes struggled to adjust to the darkness, he couldn't make anything out other than shadows in the room. He was tempted to find a lantern, but that ran the risk of attracting attention. Maybe the El'aras dagger could help him find something. It was magical, and if there was anything here valuable to someone like Anna, it would be something equally magical.

He started to circle the room. As he did, he pointed the dagger at the walls and everything within the room while moving slowly, deliberately. He made an entire pass, but nothing caused the dagger to react. Not that he expected anything to change. It would've been too much good luck for that to be the case.

Gavin closed his eyes, holding the dagger out from him. It was almost as if he could sense something through his closed eyes, and he swung in a steady circle. As he did, there was a point where he began to feel a hint of resistance. He didn't know if it was his imagination or not, but it felt somewhat like when Anna had caught the dagger. Maybe it *wasn't* his imagination.

He moved toward the resistance, and when he opened his eyes, he found the dagger pointed at a stretch of empty wall. He walked to it and stood in front of it. "This?" he whispered to the dagger.

*What am I doing?*

He shouldn't be talking, and certainly not to the dagger. If he wanted to talk to somebody, Wrenlow would certainly be willing to speak to him. All he had to do was turn on the enchantment, and his friend would be there. He might be sleeping, but Gavin was certain Wrenlow would wake up if he was needed.

He closed his eyes again, focusing on the wall. He turned the dagger, twisting it in place. As before, there came the sense of resistance, and this time he was certain he hadn't imagined it. He opened his eyes, brought the dagger up, and pressed the blade into the wall. It was simple wooden paneling, and the El'aras blade went right through it like butter.

Gavin peeled back the paneling and froze. There was something within the wall—an access panel he'd overlooked. He reached in and pulled out a metal box suspended in the wall, then returned to the center of the room and popped open the box.

His eyes widened. Inside was what looked to be a fragment of crystal. It glowed softly, reminding him of the El'aras sword and dagger when there was magic around. He glanced over at the dagger, but it remained dark.

*What was this?*

The sound of creaking wood elsewhere in the home alerted him that he might not be alone. Gavin hesitated for a moment before turning to the door. It wasn't worth it for him to linger here. Gathering the metal box and the dagger, he considered going toward the stairs, but he wasn't about to risk getting caught if somebody was down there. Not with the crystal fragment and not until he knew what it was. If nothing else, it might be his safety net.

He tucked the box under his arm and turned toward the window. He paused for a moment, listening for the sound of movement around him. When he was satisfied there was no additional creaking, he almost turned toward the stairs again. Again there came a faint sound, little more than a scraping.

Gavin crawled out the window, hanging on the ledge for a moment before dropping. Since he'd done it before, he knew to roll, and he landed less awkwardly than he had the last time. He popped up to his feet and hurried across the yard by slipping between the bells trees.

He paused once he reached the wall. As he lingered there for a moment, he watched the window where he'd just been. A figure appeared in the window. Someone had returned.

The El'aras dagger didn't glow, so whoever was there wasn't magically connected, but the timing was suspect.

*Why would they have come at the same time I had? Had they been following me?*

It troubled him. The coincidence was too much. For that matter, the coincidences lately had all been too much. He scrambled up the wall and dropped down on the other side into the street, then hurried into the darkness of night.

## CHAPTER SIXTEEN

Gavin lingered on the outskirts of the city, pacing along the street, though trying not to look as if he were. He was tired. There'd been no chance for him to rest, but he needed sleep. Everything within his body seemed to cry out for it.

*Where was Cyran?*

The fact that he wasn't at home was surprising. Dawn had started to break, and with it would be daylight. All Gavin needed was some rest.

He remembered when he'd lost his friend one other time. Tristan had given him the assignment of finding Cyran, and it had been the only time Gavin had intentionally failed. He'd known that Cyran and several of the other students had snuck out from the compound, though he didn't know why. Even though he was friends with Cyran, he was never close with the others. It was difficult for him.

Tristan had demanded Gavin find them. He knew the punishment for failure would be severe, but once he realized why they'd left, he hadn't cared what happened to him.

Bristol and Horace, two of the younger trainees, were with Cyran. Both had been injured, though Cyran was not. Despite his denials, he'd been favored by Tristan for many reasons, not the least of which was his incredibly bright mind. The trainees' injuries likely came from their sparring, though Bristol had burn marks along her jaw and her hands. When Gavin had found them, he'd believed that it had been an accident, though there were times when he wondered otherwise. He knew firsthand just how often Tristan could use violence as a motivator. None of them had wanted to return with him, at least not until they had a chance to recover. They'd known they wouldn't have that opportunity with Tristan watching.

Gavin had left them alone to heal. The beating he'd received had been severe, though by that time in his training, he'd long ago learned how to withstand pain. Handling the beating for that punishment had not been difficult.

Cyran had never thanked him. Gavin didn't know if Cyran understood just what he'd done for him, though the looks that Bristol and Horace gave him suggested that they were aware of what he'd done and what it'd meant. Gavin's naturally rapid healing had helped conceal the full extent of his own injuries for his failings, and considering that he didn't want to ever share with others what he went through, he didn't explain to them what Tristan had done to him.

Gavin pushed those thoughts away. Memories of that time kept coming to him, more often now than was useful. He needed to focus, which meant that he had to remove all external influences, and that included memories of his own training.

He clutched the metal trunk under his arm, trying to keep it covered by his cloak. The El'aras dagger was sheathed, as were his other knives, and he paced along the street. Thankfully, it was not all that busy at this time of the morning. There wasn't anyone here who seemed to pay any attention to the fact that he'd been pacing here. Gavin hadn't even been mixing up his movements, not the way Tristan had taught him. He knew better than that, but his mind was not only tired but distracted.

Finally, he caught sight of smoke drifting out from the chimney.

*Had he been there the whole time?*

It didn't matter. He needed his old friend's help.

Hurrying forward, Gavin reached the door and raised his hand to knock right as the door opened. Cyran jerked his head back and reached for something under his traveling cloak. When he realized who was there, he quickly calmed himself and smoothed his hands down the front of his cloak.

"Gavin, you startled me."

"I wasn't trying to. I was coming to you for help." Gavin looked beyond Cyran, but he didn't see anything inside the home. He glanced over his shoulder, along the street. "Where are you going at this time of the morning?"

"Nowhere." Cyran took a step back and motioned for Gavin to come in. "Who needs healing now?"

"No one. Well, maybe me."

"What happened?"

"Nothing other than extreme exhaustion."

Cyran looked at him for a long moment with a determined expression in his eyes, then he turned and hurried to his kitchen. He returned a minute later with a steaming mug in hand and offered it to his guest. Gavin nodded his thanks and took a tentative sip. The drink had a bitter taste, but he immediately felt a jolt of energy coursing through him.

"What is it?"

"Just something to keep you going."

"Is this something that Tristan taught you?"

"Do you think he taught me everything I know?"

Gavin looked around the inside of the home. Jars rested on the counter, some of which looked as if they'd been moved around recently. He was struck by the clutter. Cyran had always been neat and organized when working with Tristan. While studying poisons, it was essential to keep completely organized, mostly so that the poisons didn't get contaminated. Gavin had learned that secret himself, knowing that were he to make a mistake, it might be his life that was forfeit. Though he didn't know nearly as much about poisons as Cyran, he'd been forced to study them to the point where he could identify many, if not most, of the ones that Tristan used.

The rest of the home didn't appear nearly as cluttered. There were two chairs near the hearth, though there was no fire in it. He frowned.

*Hadn't there been smoke drifting from the chimney?*

He glanced over at Cyran, who was resting in one of the chairs, waiting for an answer.

"No," Gavin said. "The same way that he didn't teach me everything I know."

Cyran chuckled. "Maybe not, but you *were* always his favorite."

"It didn't always feel like that. He didn't have any problem abusing me when it served his purposes."

"You were never abused. Not the way that some of us were."

Gavin took a seat in the chair near the hearth. As he sipped the tea, he inhaled the fragrance within it, letting it fill his lungs. "You weren't abused. I took the brunt of most of that."

"We were all abused, Gavin," Cyran said. "You took the physical abuse. The rest of us… well, we took a different kind. Some of it wasn't as bad as others, but you can be called stupid only so many times before you begin to believe it."

"Stupid? You were always one of his brightest."

"That's not what he told me. And he made sure he told others how they were his favorite; how they were far more talented than me."

"He forced me to fight others. If I didn't win, I wasn't strong enough."

"You always won." Cyran rested his forearms on his legs, leaning forward and studying him. "I always marveled at that. Even when you went up against some of the larger kids, you came out of it better."

"Better? I can't tell you how many bones I broke," Gavin said.

"Bones heal."

"What doesn't heal?"

Cyran shook his head. "There are some things that don't improve with medicines."

"That's why you left," Gavin said.

"We all did. You took longer than the rest of us, but we all left."

Gavin took another sip of the tea. He really was starting to feel better, almost as if he could *feel* his core strength returning. It wasn't the same as what he'd feel with a good night's rest, however long that might be, but it was better than he'd felt in a while.

"How long will this last?" he asked.

"It's an artificial stimulant. It's going to make you feel more energized, but when you crash… I can't tell you that it's going to be pleasant."

"That isn't an answer," Gavin said.

"I suppose not. You're going to hurt."

"How so?"

"You're going to need to sleep. Like, seriously sleep. I know Tristan trained you so you don't need as much as anyone else, but in this case, it's going to make you sleep."

"When all of this is over, I think that might not be a bad idea."

Gavin wasn't accustomed to it, but there was something to be said about a good night's rest. For the most part, he got by on no more than a few hours at a time, and though he could function that way, it didn't mean he felt well.

"What did you need?" Cyran asked.

"Information."

"What kind of information?"

"We were visited by the El'aras last night," Gavin said.

Cyran sat up, shifting in place and looking at him. "The El'aras?"

"We went back to the manor house. Gaspar thought it made sense to go and see if we could uncover anything about who hired me, but all we found were the El'aras." He told Cyran about what had happened, including the fight with the men from Sumter on the way out. Cyran was quiet, watching him pensively. "When all was said and done, we dragged one of the El'aras out and brought her back to the tavern with us."

Cyran leaned forward. "Is she there now?"

Gavin shook his head. "She's gone. She's El'aras, and powerful it seems, so ropes didn't hold her all that well."

Cyran laughed nervously. "They didn't try to kill you?"

"Not this time."

Gavin took a deep breath and drank another sip of tea.

He could feel his energy continuing to return with each one. He focused on the core energy within him, thinking about the power there and whether he could use anything within it to strengthen himself even more. He had never tried to use his core strength to replenish his own stores before, though such a thing should be possible. When he'd tried to use the energy in the past, it always left him incredibly weakened.

He got to his feet, still holding the trunk under his arm. "I don't know what I was hoping for by coming here. I guess I was thinking that you might've uncovered something more about the El'aras, but I know you didn't want to look into it."

Cyran smiled, and he offered a hint of a shrug. "I can keep looking, but you know that I left Tristan with a purpose. Traveled in the South for a while…"

"I know why you left," Gavin said.

"And I have a job here. A life. People I serve."

Gavin looked around Cyran's home. It was sparsely decorated, more workshop than anything else. In that way, it reminded him of Tristan and the kind of places he preferred. He wasn't altogether surprised. His own preferences tended toward Tristan's as well. Partly that came from the years of training—or torment, such as it was.

"I don't need to keep you from whatever you were running off to," Gavin said.

"I wasn't going anywhere."

"You were. When I came, you were heading out."

Cyran smiled tightly. "Maybe I was, but when my

oldest friend—my only friend—comes to visit, I figure I owe it to him to be here for him. Especially considering how much trouble you've gotten me into since you've returned."

Gavin laughed. "I haven't gotten you into any trouble. It wasn't until just recently that I even bothered you."

"It's not a bother. With you, it's never a bother."

Gavin leaned back, finishing off the tea. He turned toward the door. "Don't look too hard with the El'aras. I don't want anything to happen to you."

"I know how to be careful, Gavin," Cyran said.

"I know you do. And I know you aren't going to do anything foolish, but… don't get dragged back into this."

"What makes you think I will?"

Gavin forced a smile. "I know how easy it is to be drawn into this life again. I know how hard it is to leave in the first place. You deserve better. You've always deserved better. That's why I tried to protect you."

Cyran watched him, nodding. "You did what you could."

"I tried, but I never was as successful as I wanted to be."

"I don't think anybody could've been successful against him."

Gavin lingered near the door, watching for a moment. There was something in the way Cyran said it that struck a nerve. "You really hate him, don't you?"

"Don't you?"

"I don't know. I can't deny he made my life miserable,

but he also changed it. Were it not for him, I don't know what would've happened to me."

"Have you ever considered that he was the one responsible for what happened to you?"

"I don't think Tristan was the one who killed my parents. My brother. Everyone else in that home." Gavin said it more forcefully than he intended and shook his head. "I'm sorry, Cyran. I'm tired."

"I understand. And I'm not saying Tristan was the one who killed them, but what if he was responsible for it? Have you ever considered that?"

"Is he responsible for what happened to your family?"

They were all orphans, or they had been until Tristan had taken them in and begun training them. Each of them had been given different assignments based on the skill set Tristan believed them capable of. For the most part, his analysis and assessment of someone's inherent skill were incredibly accurate.

It had been for Gavin. For Cyran too.

"I don't know," Cyran said. "I looked, but I didn't find anything."

"I've been looking," Gavin said.

"I know you have."

"You know that?"

Cyran smiled again. "You've always been looking, Gavin. You aren't so good at hiding your motivation as you would have others believe." He leaned back, crossing his arms over his chest. "Even when you were with us, you didn't hide much."

"I didn't try to," Gavin replied.

"You were always ambitious."

"That was how I didn't take beatings."

"But you were also always willing to do what Tristan wanted of you," Cyran said.

"I wasn't as willing as you would think."

"You were his favorite. I would've expected that, as his favorite, you did everything he asked of you."

Gavin found himself rubbing his jaw where it'd been broken. Tristan had beaten him when he'd failed to take out the target near the river. That had taken him a few weeks to fully recover from. In the time spent healing, he'd been forced to eat only liquids and hadn't seen any of the other students.

It was common for him not to see any of the other students though. Tristan had kept him separated—partly to train him and partly to create a division. Gavin had learned how to understand Tristan's planning and recognize his manipulation. He'd been manipulated his entire life. Still, he didn't hate his mentor.

Gavin shook away those thoughts. "I haven't thought about him this much for years."

"Really?"

"I try not to. If I let myself sink into those old memories, it becomes… difficult."

"I have a hard time *not* thinking about it," Cyran said.

"Even though you got out?"

"Some wounds haven't completely healed."

Gavin held his gaze. "I'm sorry."

"Don't be. You're here. It's... well, it's nice having someone else who understands what we went through."

"It makes it harder though," Gavin said.

"I suppose it does."

"Not that I would change anything. I'm glad you welcomed me to Yoran."

Cyran laughed. "Yoran is a large city. You don't need my welcome."

Gavin took a deep breath. He was feeling a little lightheaded, and the tiredness that had been threatening him started to bubble up. He focused on the core strength within him again. "I should let you go," he said.

"Are you sure?"

"I am. Don't dig too deep on the El'aras."

"You've already said that."

"Have I?"

Cyran nodded. "You have, but you also told me that you're tired, so I suppose that makes sense." He smiled. "You should be careful."

"I was trained for this, you know."

"I know," Cyran whispered.

Gavin pulled the door open, and he headed out into the street. The daylight was unbearably bright, making it difficult for him to focus. His head throbbed.

*Was that because of the sun or something else?*

The strength within him started to fade. With each passing moment, it dissipated more and more.

*How long would I be able to stay awake?*

The tea didn't work as long as he had expected. Maybe

Cyran had lost his touch. Gavin was forced to dive into that core strength again, letting that energy fill him. He maintained his connection to it, using as much of it as he could as he powered through the street.

He wandered and tried to keep his focus, which was difficult to do when it seemed as if the city had changed on him all at one time. The streets became unfamiliar. Gavin staggered, weakness washing over him. He wasn't going to be able to make it.

Something was off.

*Was I sick? Drugged?*

He looked around. It felt as if somebody was following him. Had the El'aras found him? They had poison. He'd seen it with how they used the blades. If they had slipped past him and cut him…

He needed to keep moving. He needed help, and there was only one way to get it. He tapped on the enchantment but heard nothing on the other end.

"Wrenlow?" He whispered his friend's name as he continued along the street, staggering forward. "If you're there, I need your help."

There was nothing but silence.

Gavin stumbled and managed to catch himself before moving forward again. He had a vague sense of where he was in the city and had to hope that he could follow the direction of the sun in order to guide himself back to the Roasted Dragon. He'd been there often enough over the last few months that he should be able to go by instinct.

His mind seemed to be spinning; everything around him moving.

"Wrenlow?" He heard the concern in his own voice. He'd used so much strength and energy to survive over the past few days. He'd been awake for too long, and he'd tapped into his core strength too many times. He knew better than that.

He staggered, dropping to his knees. "Wrenlow?" he said again.

He looked up, noting the position of the sun. It was bright. So impossibly bright. Gavin blinked against it, and he scrambled once again to his feet. He had to call upon all of the strength within him. He had to find that energy to somehow reach the Dragon.

"Wherever you are, Wrenlow, I need your help."

He stumbled again. As he crouched on the cobblestones, he could feel movement near him. He was in danger. He lunged forward, crawling, but he started to drift.

Reach the Dragon. Rest. That was all he needed.

He was tired. So tired.

Movement nearby startled him, and he swung his fist uncontrollably. Tristan would be disappointed. He'd taught Gavin better than that.

This wasn't normal. Had he used too much of himself? This wasn't the first time he'd felt this way, pushed to the edge of his reserves. Maybe he'd done it again. Even when Gavin had been tired during training, Tristan had wanted him to have control over his fighting technique and to be able to use every last bit of energy. If it were going to come down to death or putting every last bit of himself into an attack, Gavin needed to choose the latter.

He could feel that energy within him, that drive to try harder. He had to summon some hidden strength. Even as he tried, he didn't know where he was going to find it.

A familiar voice near him drew his attention.

"Cyran?"

He resisted the urge to kick. If Cyran was there, then he was safe.

Gavin finally drifted off, sleep claiming him.

## CHAPTER SEVENTEEN

"How do you feel?" Tristan asked.

Gavin tried to hold his eyes open, but he was drained. Every part of his being seemed to scream against what was happening to him. He'd been awake for hours—days, really.

*I could barely stay alert, and now Tristan wanted me to find some way to remain awake even longer?*

"How am I supposed to feel?" His words came out slurred, his voice groggy, no different than his mind. He could feel thoughts crawling through his skull. Nothing seemed to work the way it should.

"You have to learn how to fight through this."

Tristan was there, something striking Gavin on the side. Almost as if delayed, pain raced up along his flank, and he pushed it away. If nothing else, he'd learned that lesson well enough to know that he could ignore the pain within him. Tristan had made sure of it. He blinked to try to clear the sleepiness from his eyes and the fog that hung over his mind, but he couldn't.

"How am I supposed to ignore my body's need for sleep?" he asked.

Something else struck him, this time on the other side. Gavin cried out, but that was rewarded with another strike. Any reaction to pain was an invitation for another attack. He knew better. He knew what Tristan would do to him if he gave any sort of response.

"Within us, we all have the innate ability to tap into something more," Tristan replied.

"More?"

Gavin struggled with what his mentor was teaching him. It seemed as if there was a lesson there, but within that lesson he felt nothing but confusion.

"The core part of your being. Your strength. You have it. I've seen that within you, Gavin." With that, Tristan struck him in the gut.

Gavin doubled over, trying to fight the pain off and steady his breathing, neither of which were easy. He panted as he struggled to control all of his emotions, the pain that was rolling through him, and the sense of agony that filled him.

He had to find some way to do so. Even as he attempted to hold onto that emotion and that sense of pain, he could feel something moving near him.

Gavin turned, and when Tristan struck, he blocked.

"Good," Tristan said.

He was little more than a blur, though Gavin doubted

that was actually true. As far as he knew, Tristan was right across from him.

"You need to find the sense of strength within you, and then you can hold onto that. When you learn how to access that core strength, you will find something you can command when everything else is failing you."

"How?"

"I can't tell you how to find *your* core strength. It's different than mine."

Another strike, this time battering at his shoulder. Gavin crumpled and wanted nothing more than to lie there, but he knew better. If he were to stay in place, motionless, another strike would come.

Tristan wouldn't quit until he was beaten. Broken. Even destroyed.

Gavin got up slowly. There was a kick to his side, but he ignored it. He heard laughter.

*Find your core strength.*

He had no idea whether there was any possibility of doing that. He had no idea whether or not he had that within him. Maybe he didn't possess what Tristan believed him to. Only, everything else Tristan had taught him had been accurate. Everything else he'd been working on had served him.

*Why wouldn't this help me as well?*

Gavin tried to dive deep within his sense of self, searching for some awareness or power, but even as he did, he didn't find anything. Movement caught his attention, and he tried to turn and twist, to be ready for the next attack. When Tristan struck, Gavin caught it with his arms and deflected it.

"Better," Tristan said.

"When can I sleep?"

"When you defeat me."

Gavin wanted to tell him that it'd be impossible even if he weren't sleep-deprived, but that answer wasn't going to satisfy Tristan. He knew better, which meant that he was going to have to figure out whatever answer Tristan wanted to hear. Maybe it really was a matter of beating him.

Not that Gavin thought that such a thing was even possible. He had faced Tristan many times using all of the different fighting styles he'd been taught, and never once had he come close to actually defeating him. Now that he was exhausted, there was no hope for him.

*Core strength.*

Those words seemed to reverberate in his mind, a demand made by Tristan. Gavin tried to summon that strength by thinking about what he was asked to do, but he couldn't come up with anything. He felt helpless as he struggled.

Another blow struck him from the side, this time forcing him to roll over. He landed on his back and stared up at the ceiling. The lanterns around him provided a bit of light, though not nearly as much as he would've liked. Gavin was never able to see that well in the dark, and he always complained about the lighting in the room. Tristan preferred the darkness and used it to his advantage.

Maybe this had something to do with Gavin's fear of the dark.

Even as tired as he was, his mind drifted to the sounds of whimpering—the sounds of when his parents had been murdered and taken from him. He'd been so young that he couldn't remember anything else, but the sounds of their deaths stayed with him. He suspected they always would.

Gavin heard Tristan's footsteps on the stone as he approached again. He rolled as he threw his arms out in a blocking pattern, catching Tristan's leg. He twisted his wrist and jerked, not caring whether he was successful. All he cared about was sleep.

He climbed back on his feet and drove his elbow down, slamming into... nothing.

Pain jolted up his arm. Something cracked. He could feel the pain and the agony within the broken bone, and he knew he wasn't going to get out of this without more suffering.

Now that one of his arms was useless, how was he going to be able to defeat Tristan?

Gavin crawled and tried to stand. "I can't beat you. Not like this."

"You only think you can't beat me like this. You need to find it within yourself."

"How?"

"By drawing upon your core strength."

Gavin struggled, wanting nothing more than to prove himself to Tristan. That was all he ever wanted. Tristan demanded obedience and respect, and the price for failing him was too great. He didn't want to fail his mentor. None of the students wanted to.

His left arm hung useless as he got to his feet. There was pain, but he knew how to push it away. He didn't know how badly he was injured, but he'd experienced enough breaks in his training to be familiar with that kind of agony.

He held himself up and looked all around him, trying to clear the fatigue from his mind. For a moment, he was able to. Gavin didn't know if that was only his imagination or not.

*How could I suddenly have such clarity?*

He tried striking again, but this time there wasn't the same strength within him. As he attempted to kick, he couldn't get his body to work how it needed to. He could feel that there was something wrong with him. When he tried to focus his mind, he couldn't feel anything other than a sense of pain. With that pain came panic. Gavin tried to keep moving, but everything within him was screaming and fighting what he was feeling inside.

Tristan attacked again. Gavin could feel the whistle of the wind as it came toward him. He tried to ignore it, focusing instead on the strength within him. That was what Tristan wanted him to do—to find that core energy. But he wasn't even sure how to do that.

*What did it mean?*

He rolled off to the side, trying to avoid the next attack. There was nothing in him.

*So far, I've managed to survive, but for how much longer?*

Gavin struggled, trying to stand again. Pain and fatigue mingled and made everything difficult for him. He strained, wanting nothing more than to get up.

That was what Tristan wanted him to do. If he could get to his feet again, then he might be able to fight back. Gavin struggled. Everything within him throbbed from pain. He could barely move his arm, and the ache of it left him practically trembling.

"You have to find your core," Tristan said.

It sounded so easy, but he strained to figure out how.

Gavin could feel movement near him. He tried to do as Tristan suggested, turning his attention inward. Within himself, there was a little bit of strength from the reserves of energy he still had. He focused on that while thinking about what Tristan had told him, thinking about the power he needed to find.

*If there was energy there, how was I supposed to access it?*

He was tired. So tired. Everything he'd been through screamed against him, struggling to make sense of what was happening. Gavin knew he needed to find some way to get to freedom, to survive this, but with every passing moment, he could feel failure looming.

Somewhere near him, Tristan laughed—a sound Gavin had come to hate. In all their training, the man made a point of taunting him and reminding him of just how little he could do. Tristan had defeated him time and again, and he always showed Gavin just how helpless he was to withstand that kind of attack. He held onto that irritation. Maybe there was something within it that he could use.

Gavin turned toward the movement he detected. When he felt the air around him surge, he jumped. There was something deep within him that demanded he jump, and he held onto that feeling. By focusing on that power, he turned and spun in the air to find the right position. When he landed, pain jolted up his arm, but he ignored it.

He swept his leg, kicking where he'd detected the sense. He swung his fist at the same time. The combination connected, and between the two, he managed to strike. Gavin leapt forward, holding onto the pain and the rage, and he let himself be filled with that anger. When his fist connected, he turned and rolled off to the side.

"Enough," Tristan said.

Gavin got up, and he took a deep breath.

Tristan nodded. "Better."

"That's all I get?"

"What more do you need?"

"I want to be told I'm doing well."

Tristan came close enough that Gavin could see him despite the blood and tears in his eyes. He struggled to maintain focus. Up close like this, not only could he see his mentor, but he could smell him too. Most of the time, Tristan smelled of pine, along with a sweet undercurrent that Gavin had never identified. This time, the pine seemed almost pungent and practically overwhelmed him. The sweetness was absent.

"If you want to be told that you're doing well, then you

need to do well. I'm not going to give out praise just because you want it," Tristan said, then turned away from him.

Suddenly, he spun back around while sweeping his leg. Gavin darted back, bringing his knee up in a partial block, but he attacked at the same time. He used his good arm, swinging his fist, but Tristan was prepared for that.

What he wasn't prepared for was Gavin swinging his injured arm and shoulder toward him. It throbbed as it slammed into Tristan's jaw, but he knocked the man down.

Gavin pounced. He landed on top of Tristan, and with his good arm, he started to punch. Up close like this, he could feel the strength within Tristan. He pulled on that energy, calling on it, and he pummeled. He used everything within him to fight. He punched over and over, and with each one, he could feel something within him exploding with strength he didn't know he had.

"Enough," Tristan said again.

Gavin slowly climbed off. He'd thought he was tired before, but the exhaustion that washed over him now was unlike that. He panted, the pain making it difficult to focus on anything other than the steadiness of his breaths.

"What did you feel?" Tristan asked.

Somehow, he didn't seem to be harmed. Gavin thought he'd pummeled him to the point where he should've been injured in some way, but there was no evidence that anything had happened to him.

"Anger."

"Of course you felt anger. What else did you feel?" Tristan asked.

"I don't know. What was I supposed to feel?"

"Where did that strength come from?"

Gavin leaned forward, resting his hands on his thighs. "I don't have any strength."

"I would disagree. Look at how you suddenly were able to attack when you didn't have anything left before. You had strength. Where did it come from?"

Gavin didn't know.

"Find that place," Tristan continued. "That's your core. That's what I want you to learn to reach into. When you can master that, you will find that you can be stronger than you ever believed. When you can understand the nature of that core power within yourself, then you will be unstoppable."

"Unstoppable?"

Tristan watched him. "More than you could ever know." He slipped an arm around Gavin, guiding him forward. "Come. We will get you healed, and then you will rest. You might find that you need to sleep for longer than you are used to sleeping, but after what you did today and the success you had, I would say that you earned it."

"Is that praise?"

"I told you that you would get praise when you did well."

Gavin smiled. Praise from Tristan was rare, and when he got it, he valued it. He cherished that praise, holding onto the sense that he'd done well. He slept for days.

When he came back around, something was different. Tristan forced him to reach into that core power again and again, and Gavin found it easier to do each time.

The memory started to fade, and Gavin opened his eyes. He quickly assessed himself for injuries, but there didn't appear to be any. Whatever had happened had left him unharmed, just fatigued.

He sat up and looked around. The room was dark, and he jumped up, realizing that he was in a small room. He spun in place, trying to get a sense of where he was.

The El'aras dagger rested on a chair near the bed.

*His* bed.

The Dragon.

He had been brought back.

*How?*

Gavin slipped into his clothes. As he strapped on his belt, he made sure his knives were in place, then flipped the dagger into the belt as well. He pulled his cloak over his shoulders and looked around the rest of the room for anything else but didn't see anything. There was only Jessica's belongings. A brush. A hairpin. Nothing else. It was almost as if she'd never been with him, and as he stood there and looked at everything in the room, he couldn't help but wonder if perhaps it would've been better for her had she not.

Gavin pushed those thoughts out of mind. He opened the door and headed down into the tavern. He felt a sense of movement behind him and spun around.

Wrenlow approached, dressed in a loose-fitting jacket

and pants. He studied Gavin, worry wrinkling his youthful face. He scratched his chin where a beard had started to grow, though not nearly as much as what Gavin knew Wrenlow wanted. He always wanted to look older and had been that way ever since they'd met.

"Gavin? You should still be sleeping."

"I think I've slept enough."

"You haven't. I've seen you like that before. Usually you need days to recover."

"I don't know that we have days. With what's going on, and the El'aras, and with Hamish, and the sorcerer"—Wrenlow took a step toward him, resting his hand on Gavin's arm—"you still need to rest."

"I'm fine."

"Are you sure?" There was a look of real concern on Wrenlow's face.

Gavin nodded. "I'm sure. How did I get back here?"

"What do you remember?"

"I remember my energy fading. I had focused myself for so long and so hard that I'd pushed too far. I knew I had, and when I went and saw Cyran—"

"Your poisoner friend?"

"I'm not so sure he wants to be called a poisoner anymore. He's made a point of trying to be more respectable."

"You don't think that poisoning is respectable?" Wrenlow asked, smiling.

"It's not so much what I think, it's what he thinks. Regardless, he's tried to become more respectable... well, I guess more." Gavin shook his head, trying to think through what happened. He could barely remember being at Cyran's house. He'd been given something that had built up his energy. "Anyway, as I was leaving his home, my strength started to fade, and that's why I called you." He looked up, frowning at Wrenlow. "How did you find me?"

"I almost didn't. The sound through your enchantment made it difficult, but there was a particular call that told me where you were."

"A call?"

"You were near the central market," Wrenlow said.

The central market was not at all where he should've been going, which seemed unusual. Even when he was exhausted, even wiped as he was, Gavin would've expected he could maintain some sense of focus. In the past when he'd been as tired, he'd been able to use his core strength in order to find his way. Then again, it'd been a long time since he'd pushed himself that hard. There hadn't been the need.

"I had something with me," Gavin said.

"You had the dagger. I made sure to bring it." Wrenlow glanced down at Gavin's waist. "You have it."

"Not the dagger. There was a metal box. I found it in the manor house—"

"I thought there wasn't anything in the house."

"I went back. After I left here, I went back and found something in the wall. It was a…" Gavin wasn't entirely sure how to describe what it was, only that it'd likely be

El'aras-made, especially because it was in Anna's home. He might be able to use it or trade it, but only if he could figure out what it was and what it might be worth. "Anyway, I found something."

"You didn't have anything with you. You were lying on the ground. People were almost trampling you."

"What?" He could've sworn he'd heard a voice near him. That voice had seemed to know him, and there was something familiar within it.

*Could I have been mistaken?*

Gavin didn't think he was. He remembered the way that voice had called him, the way it sounded, and the way that it seemingly told him it was going to help.

"That wasn't you?" he asked Wrenlow.

"What do you mean?"

"I…" Gavin sagged. He tried to reach for his reserves of power, but even as he did, something about it was off. Strange. He attempted to dive within it, searching for a way to replenish himself, but he couldn't. He stumbled, and Wrenlow caught him and helped him back to his feet.

"Gavin? I told you that you needed to sleep."

"Something is wrong."

"You're exhausted. You've been going hard for the last few days."

Gavin tried diving into that reserve of power once more. With even a little bit of sleep, it should've been replenished. He was familiar enough with this process that he knew it should be there.

Instead, there was nothing.

He tried to draw himself up, but he didn't have the strength to do so and slumped to the ground. Wrenlow leaned over him. Gavin looked up at his friend, and a worried thought came to him.

*What if Cyran had done something to me?*

CHAPTER EIGHTEEN

When Gavin came back around, he slowly opened his eyes. There had been no dreams, nothing of his training, and nothing of his past. That might be for the best.

He looked over at Jessica sleeping next to him, as she had been doing since her injury. She'd survived but wasn't strong enough yet to make it down to the tavern. Gavin didn't know when she would be fully recovered, but he hoped it would be soon. For now, he was thankful she lived. He ran his fingers through her hair before sitting all the way up and scooting to the edge of the bed.

Wrenlow had left him fully dressed, and Gavin leaned over to collect the rest of his things. He reached for his knives but changed his mind and grabbed the El'aras dagger instead. Once he pulled it free, he ran his hand along the blade. The writing there was not familiar to him, though perhaps it should be.

Gavin took a few slow breaths.

*Why was I suddenly thinking about my training so much?*

It had been years. Most of the time, he was aware of it more as a distant thought, but never quite so acutely. In this case, he found himself thinking back on Tristan almost daily. Maybe that was simply because he was here in Yoran and had been spending time around Cyran.

Gavin held onto the El'aras dagger as he got to his feet. He stumbled and caught himself. Hesitating for a moment, he reached for the reserves of power within him, but as he did, he could feel that something was still off. Even after resting more, he still hadn't replenished his strength.

He looked back at the bed. Maybe he hadn't been sleeping enough. He certainly had been sleep-deprived lately, and it wasn't unthinkable that he could merely be exhausted, but the idea that this was just the result of fatigue surprised him.

He stumbled into the hall and made his way down to the main room of the Dragon. He stopped there.

The sight of Anna stopped him in his tracks.

She radiated a regal appearance, her deep green wool cloak draped over her shoulders making her seem even more impressive. She swept her gaze around the room before settling on Gavin. Thomas was with her, wearing a matching cloak, though his was shifted off to the side so that he had easy access to his sword. Ever the soldier, his eyes darted from side to side constantly, looking for threats that might appear at any moment.

They sat across from Gaspar and Wrenlow, with Imogen standing and listening in the background. She was frowning, and when he stepped into the room, she gently shook her head at him. He didn't know her nearly as well. He knew her to have a quick mind, which was the reason that Gaspar valued her as he did.

"There he is." Anna turned to him, smiling widely. The El'aras dagger started to glow, and he felt ridiculous as he held it out.

"Gavin?" Wrenlow watched him and then jumped to his feet, coming over to stand next to him. "Is everything—"

"Fine," Gavin mumbled.

He felt like his mind was in a fog, but he had to fight through it. He knew he could. His experience with that energy told him that he could reach for that core part of himself, but he was going to have to dive deep in order to do so. Maybe he'd extinguished all of his reserves, and what he really needed was more sleep than he was getting.

Then again, if that's what he needed, he would've expected his body to have simply slept. When he'd exhausted himself in the past, waking hadn't been an option for him. This time, Gavin had continued to wake, but there was something wrong each time. Something off.

Wrenlow guided him over to a chair, helping him to sit.

"Are you ready to meet with your employer?" Anna asked.

"Is it time for that?"

She frowned at him. "We talked about two days. Have you not made preparations?"

*Two days? Could I really have slept that long?*

If so, he would've expected more core recovery than what he'd experienced.

Something was terribly wrong.

He looked over to Wrenlow, holding his gaze. "I've been trying to find answers," he said carefully.

"You look as if you've been sleeping," Anna said.

"No." Gavin straightened, holding onto the El'aras dagger and trying to force his strength through him. For a moment, he had clarity and saw everything around him with a different light. It was brief, like a flash of energy. And when it faded, he was left with nothing.

He struggled, trying to reach for it, but it wasn't there. "I've been—"

Anna reached across the table and grabbed him. The others started to reach for weapons, but Thomas held his El'aras sword out. Anna pulled Gavin by the hand, stretching him across the table.

"What're you doing?" he asked.

"Quiet," she whispered.

The dagger glowed, and she made no attempt to take it from him. He realized that, in the time he'd known her, she'd never tried to retrieve the dagger from him. It was almost as if she didn't care about it. Strange, especially considering how much he'd come to value the El'aras dagger.

He'd possessed high-quality weapons before, but

nothing quite like it. The El'aras sword was useful, but it wasn't nearly as easy to hide as a dagger. The longer weapon was beneficial against someone like Thomas, but then again, Gavin didn't often find himself in a sword fight with a sword master like the one sitting before him.

A strange warmth washed through him. "What are you doing?" he asked Anna.

"I am testing you."

"Testing me for what?"

"Quiet," she said again.

She held onto his wrists, and the sense of power continued to wash over him. Gavin could do nothing other than stay still. He tried to pull away, but each time he did, she squeezed more tightly around his wrist and kept him from moving. Even if he were fully recovered, he wasn't sure he'd have enough energy to withdraw from her grip. Anna had incredible strength—one of the many special traits the El'aras possessed.

After a moment, she released his wrists and leaned back. She flicked her gaze over to Thomas. "I need sh'rasn."

Thomas frowned for a moment before nodding. With that, he sheathed his sword, spun, and darted out of the Dragon.

Gavin turned and stared at the closed door. His mind felt like it was still in a fog, and he tried to work through what had just taken place. "Where did he go?"

"Why don't you tell me what you've been doing over the last few days?" she said.

She knew. She must've followed him when he'd gone into her home, and she must've known that he'd found something there. Maybe Anna was responsible for this all happening to him.

"What do you want to know?" he asked.

"You haven't been doing what you claimed."

"Maybe not."

"And you've been sleeping," she said.

"Maybe." Gavin sat back and crossed his arms, trying to hold onto the El'aras dagger as he did. "I've been tired."

"I imagine."

"What's that supposed to mean?"

"What have you been doing?" she asked.

"Why don't you tell me what you were hiding in that house?"

She frowned. "Hiding?"

Gavin nodded. Gaspar was watching him. "You went back, despite knowing there was a threat to you. And you went back with help, but there was another threat to you. Not me that time." He'd been trying to work through what the Sumter attackers were about, and it was the only thing he could come up with. They had been there because of Anna, though not because they were working for her.

They had been there to attack her.

"You went back to the room where I found you," he said.

"Perhaps I did. It was sentimental."

"There wasn't anything there that would be sentimental to you. Besides, I don't know the El'aras to be a sentimental people."

"You might be surprised," she whispered.

"I can tell you what I found when I went back: some clothing and the rope we used to bind your wrists and ankles." Her brow furrowed as he said this, her face darkening for a moment. "Nothing else, and certainly nothing that would warrant your return. If there was anything there you needed for sentimental purposes, you would've sent Thomas."

Even though his mind worked in a fog, that moment of clarity had been enough for him. Her presence had to be the key to why she went back.

Gavin glanced over at Wrenlow. "When you get a chance, I want you to look into Thomas."

"You might find that to be difficult," Anna said.

"Probably." He took a deep breath and closed his eyes, trying to focus on pulling the threads together. "You went back because there was something there you needed. And you were there when I went back alone."

"What?" Wrenlow asked.

"There was someone there," Gavin said. "I didn't see them, but I heard them coming up the stairs."

"Are you sure about that?" she asked.

"Pretty sure. There was someone there. And then when I left, I saw a shadowed form in the window."

"What did you find?"

"Nothing," he lied.

She watched him. "What did you find?" she asked again.

There was a heat and an intensity to her voice, almost as if there was a command that he could not ignore. Gavin met her gaze, and there was a desire within him to ignore her request, but at the same time, he didn't know if he could.

"What was in the metal box?" he asked her.

Gaspar turned to look at Gavin. "What box?"

"There was a box within the wall." Gavin held onto Anna's gaze as he said it, waiting for her reaction, but there wasn't any.

"How did you find it?"

"It was hidden, but this helped." Gavin held up the El'aras dagger.

"The dagger?" Wrenlow asked.

"Yes. Somehow, the dagger guided me in finding this strange box in the wall. And then I was able to carve the box out of the wall because of it."

"You should've left it there," Anna said.

"What is it?"

"That is the Shard."

Gavin frowned, staring at her. "The what?"

"That is the reason I'm here. It was to remain hidden. *I* was to remain hidden."

"I'm sorry about that," he said.

"You should not be. Your employer should be."

"What does that mean?"

"It means we have gone to great lengths to mask my presence here," said Anna.

"There hasn't been much masking as far as I could tell."

"Really? I have been in the city for five years, and this was the first time anyone has made any attempt to come after me. Something changed."

"What is the Shard?" Wrenlow asked.

"It is an item of great power to my people."

"Why do you have it?"

"Because I am the Risen Shard."

"I still don't know what that means," Gavin said.

She smiled at him. "Good."

She leaned back, studying him. There was a moment of silence, and in that moment, a sense of power flowed from her and streaked toward Gavin. He could feel the energy she used, the power she pushed upon him that constricted around him.

"Stop," he said. "Whatever you're doing, stop."

She frowned. "I'm not doing anything." She got to her feet and glanced down at the dagger, her eyes widening. "We need to move."

Gavin looked up at her. "Why? Because you want to find this Shard? I don't know what happened to it, but I don't have it now. When I was coming back to the Dragon, I collapsed."

"It doesn't matter. We need to move."

"Or what?"

"Or we die."

Gaspar jumped to his feet, reaching for his knife.

Wrenlow scrambled, and Imogen pulled a narrow blade from a sheath beneath her cloak, standing ready.

Gavin held onto the El'aras dagger and stood still as he stared ahead. He couldn't focus. Everything within him still seemed off, and as much as he tried to maintain a sense of focus on what was taking place around him, he couldn't. He knew he needed to do something different, but his mind wasn't working the way it needed to. He looked over at Wrenlow. "I'm going to need your help."

"With what?"

"With everything. I…" He sagged, and Wrenlow caught him. He slipped an arm underneath Gavin and helped him to stand.

Gaspar frowned. "What is wrong with you?"

"I used too much of my core strength," Gavin said. Either that or he'd been poisoned. *If that were the case, then how had it happened—and when?*

"You used too much of your *what?*"

"My core strength. It's a training technique I learned. I can focus my reserves of energy, but it sometimes uses too much."

"How long will it take you to recover?" Gaspar asked.

"Usually I do by now, so the fact I haven't is a little bit surprising," he said. Anna watched him, an unreadable expression in her eyes. Gavin frowned. "Why are you suddenly concerned?" he asked her.

"What do you feel?"

"I told you already."

"And now?"

Gavin focused on the sense within him, but he didn't notice anything. This was partly because his core reserves were gone, but also partly because the pressure of magic she'd been wrapping around him had eased.

"You're not holding power on me anymore," he said.

"I wasn't doing that before either."

"If it wasn't you, then who was it?" He turned in place. The El'aras dagger continued to glow, and when he looked over at Anna, she shook her head.

It wasn't her. And if it wasn't her, there was another magic user here.

*Could it be the sorcerer?*

They still hadn't seen anything from him, though Gavin hadn't done much to accomplish his job. He'd been threatened, but the sorcerer had also given him a week to complete the task. It wasn't even close to the deadline. This probably wasn't the sorcerer then.

*What about the Apostle?*

Gavin couldn't think through it. He started to sag again, his strength fading. "Something is definitely wrong," he mumbled.

"Stay with him," Anna said. She headed toward the door, and the El'aras dagger glowed more brightly.

"What are you doing?" Gavin asked.

"I'm waiting for Thomas to return."

"If there's someone else using magic here, I'm starting to think we need to move."

She nodded. "We definitely need to, which is what I

said earlier, but you aren't in any condition to leave. Not until Thomas arrives."

"I know he's a skilled fighter, but I'm not without my own abilities."

"You are while you are restricted."

Gavin shook his head, smiling. He tried to take a step forward, but again his strength was fading. There wasn't much he was going to be able to do.

She was right. He was restricted, though it had to be more than just the depletion of his core reserves. Something else had happened, though he had no idea what that might be. All he could tell was that he was failing.

He looked at Wrenlow and Gaspar, but neither were watching him. Both were paying attention to Anna, who leaned forward against the door. As she pressed her hands to its surface, her hair took on a faint sheen, almost as if it were glowing.

Gavin's eyes widened in surprise, and he wasn't sure if what he was seeing was real. His mind certainly wasn't in any place to determine that, and given how tired he was and how he could barely stand, it was possible that what he was seeing wasn't accurate.

*If it was, then how was she glowing like that?*

The only things that glowed were magical enchantments—not people.

"We need to go," Gavin said, glancing at Gaspar. "I don't know what's going on, but if she's concerned, then we need to be concerned."

"Don't you think we should stay with her?" Wrenlow asked.

"Do you *want* to stay with her?"

"I don't know. It depends on what's coming."

"I think the boy's right," said Gaspar.

"Thank you," Wrenlow said.

Gaspar grunted. "You're the kid. He's the boy," he said, motioning to Gavin. "I don't know if we can trust her. Not sure what she's going to do or what she's even doing now, but I don't know that we want to be here to find out. I certainly don't."

Gavin looked over at Anna. With whatever power she was holding onto, he couldn't help but feel as if they were in danger because of it. He nodded to Gaspar, and the old thief guided them away from the door, away from Anna, and toward the kitchen.

"Are you sure we should be doing this?" Wrenlow whispered.

"I don't know," Gavin muttered. "All I know is that I don't want to be too wrapped up in whatever the El'aras are doing. And with her," he said, nodding toward Anna, "I really don't know if I want to be a part of it."

"You could've fooled me," Gaspar said.

"What's that supposed to mean?"

"I saw the way you were looking at her."

"She's El'aras. How else am I supposed to look at her?" Gavin asked.

"Not like a lost puppy chasing after his mama."

Inside the kitchen, the darkness was almost absolute.

Gavin held out the El'aras dagger and used it to guide them. He stumbled, making too much noise, but Gaspar was there and propped him up.

"Keep him on his feet," Gaspar snapped at Wrenlow.

"I'm doing what I can," Wrenlow said. "He's heavy."

"I'm not *that* heavy," Gavin mumbled.

"Maybe not. I'm just…" Wrenlow looked past him, exasperation in his eyes. "Can you help?"

"What do you think I'm doing? It's not like I'm doing this on purpose."

Together, they hurried through the kitchen, moving into open space. When they reached the far side of the kitchen, Gaspar hesitated near the door. He raised a hand for them to stop and motioned to his lips to indicate silence.

Gavin could take only slow breaths. Something was terribly wrong. Every time he tried to tap into a greater strength, that core energy he knew he should have, something blocked him.

*Had I really been poisoned? When could that have happened, though?*

Maybe he'd been injured during one of the attacks. Everything had happened so quickly that he hadn't really paid much attention to it. It was possible someone had cut his skin with a knife without him knowing.

He looked over at Gaspar. The man was fuzzy, something about him difficult for Gavin to even make out.

Gaspar looked back at him. "Stand straight," he barked.

"I'm trying."

"You need to try more. I don't know what's going to happen on the other side of the building, but I have a feeling we're going to need that fighting ability of yours."

Gavin swallowed. He could do that. For Wrenlow, he would do that. Maybe even for Gaspar, who'd been working with him and trying to help.

"Where's Imogen?" he mumbled.

"She went ahead," Gaspar said.

"Are you sure that's safe?"

"Imogen will be fine."

"With the El'aras, you don't know—"

"I know."

Gavin just nodded. There wasn't anything else to say. He took a deep breath and began to focus on the energy deep within him. That was the key. That was what Gaspar wanted. What they needed. By holding onto that strength, he could find something deep within him. He *had* to find it.

Unless it really was gone.

Old lessons came to him about ignoring all distractions, including those of his own body. They were lessons Tristan had made sure he learned—and learned well. Tristan had wanted Gavin to know how to draw upon power, to be able to reach for strength, and to use it in a way that would allow him to dig deep within himself. Gavin could do that now.

He *had* to do that now.

He could feel that there was energy inside. Faint, but definitely there. He grasped for it, reaching for the stores of energy he knew were within him. Then he pulled on it.

He nodded to Gaspar. There was so little strength remaining within him. Not enough he could rely on it too long, but enough he might be able to survive.

They stepped out of the building into an alley next to the Dragon. From here, Gavin could see the street in front of them. There was no movement—nothing to suggest there was anything dangerous coming—though he'd seen the concern in Anna's eyes. He didn't know her well, but he recognized fear. Fear from one of the El'aras was enough that he knew to be concerned by it too.

Gaspar looked around. "What now—"

Movement came behind them.

Adrenaline rushed through Gavin as he pushed Gaspar out of the way and dove forward, thrusting the El'aras dagger into an oncoming attacker. He'd felt somebody, though he wasn't entirely sure who they were. He spun, adding everything he could to overwhelm the attackers. He tried drawing upon strength, but there didn't seem to be anything more for him.

Gavin caught sight of a little movement and twisted around. Fatigue nearly overwhelmed him as he drove his fist outward. There was no real power left within him. Everything he was doing was by instinct and nothing more.

He brought his fist around and crashed into something. Then he dropped his shoulder and stabbed with the dagger. It met resistance.

Gavin staggered forward. Somewhere behind him, he heard a shout. It seemed to be calling his name, but he ignored it. He stumbled and found himself out in the open. Everything around him was a blur, as if there were a haze around him.

He took a deep breath, trying to reach into that core strength again. He could feel energy buried within him, and he dove toward it. He called upon that power, and it bubbled up within him. Then he used it.

It was the only thing he could think of doing. By holding onto that and taking every last bit of energy he had, he could overpower whatever came at him.

Movement around him told him he was surrounded. Gavin darted toward one person and stabbed with the dagger. He couldn't see anything other than an outline of a shape.

*Could these be El'aras? Why would the El'aras be attacking now?*

It didn't make any sense, but a lot of what had been happening to him didn't make much sense. He found another reserve of strength, and he blinked, clearing his vision.

Dark cloaks and tattoos. He would swear on his life that these were Sumter attackers. It didn't mean they weren't skilled. Men from Sumter were always skilled sword fighters, but they weren't nearly as deadly as the El'aras. Which meant he had time.

He darted toward the first attacker and stumbled. While falling, he managed to twist and bring his dagger up. The fighting style was crude, and certainly nothing Tristan would be proud of, but maybe that didn't matter. All that mattered was that he continued to fight.

Gavin swung again, and this time, there was more movement near him. His eyes wouldn't focus, making everything dark, and he stumbled forward once more. He could feel a presence nearby, and he swiped with the dagger. The next Sumter attacker fell. He spun again and took down another.

How many were there? He thought about what he'd seen in the manor house. If there were that many attackers, it might be more than what he could handle in his current state.

He had to embrace a different fighting style. Normally, Gavin mixed together all of the different techniques he'd been trained in, but in this case, perhaps that was a mistake. He didn't have enough strength to shift between them, but there was one style that would be somewhat fluid and somewhat rough that he could use. Tristan had called it the Drunken Justan style, supposedly named after the man who'd taught it to him, though Gavin suspected it had another name.

As one of the Sumter attackers came toward him, Gavin fell to the ground. He stumbled slightly while doing so, but this time the fall was intentional. The key to this fighting style was that every stumble had a purpose. When he twisted, he brought the dagger around and slashed across the man's thigh. Then he spun back around, toppling over him.

Gathering himself, he got to his feet. This fighting style fit him today. He staggered forward again, stumbling, and then crashed into the next attacker. He brought the dagger around, jamming it into their back.

He took a deep breath, trying to find more of that source of energy within him. There had to be something there. It would be the last of his strength. He didn't have much hope of being able to do much more, but if it bought Wrenlow and Gaspar time, it would be worth it.

He threw himself toward the next man. As a sword came toward him, he twisted, his arms flopping. He brought a dagger into this man's side, carving through him.

Gavin crashed to the ground. He tried to get up, but someone was there, heading toward him.

He blinked, and there were five—no, *seven*—Sumter attackers.

Too many for him.

CHAPTER NINETEEN

A light came toward him. For a moment, he wondered if it was Anna and her glowing hair, but this had a different shape. The glow was all he saw.

It wasn't Anna. It was Thomas.

The El'aras sword master's blade worked in a quick blaze, carving through the Sumter attackers. He then looked down at Gavin, his face little more than a blur. "Get up."

"I'm afraid that I'm spent."

"Get up."

There was something like the steel Gavin had often heard in Tristan's voice in Thomas's now. He scrambled, trying to get himself moving, but his body didn't react the way it should've. He looked up, feeling stupid.

"I can't."

Thomas grabbed him, jerking him to his feet. Gavin leaned there for a moment, wobbling in place. Suddenly,

Gaspar and Wrenlow were there, and they put their arms around his waist, guiding him. They were away from the street, he noted. The blurriness that surrounded him began to increase, making it difficult for him to see anything.

"What's wrong with him?" Wrenlow asked.

"Poison," Gavin said. "El'aras."

"This is not El'aras."

*It was Anna. She was here?*

He smiled at her, though he felt foolish as he did so.

"If it's not El'aras, then what is it?" He tried to keep his eyes open, but he couldn't. It was as if everything in him had failed. As much as he wanted to stay awake, the fatigue was too much. "I need to get to Cyran. He makes a tea that can help."

If there was anyone who would be able to help him, it would be Cyran. Only, Gavin didn't know if he'd be able to stay awake long enough to reach him.

"What kind of tea?" Anna asked as she stood in front of him. She was glowing more brightly than she had before.

He reached for her hair.

*What made it glow like that?*

He'd been around other El'aras during his travels, and he'd never seen any who had hair quite like that.

"I don't know," he said. "Something that restored me. Gave me energy."

"Do you have it?"

"What do I have?" Gavin felt as if he were floating.

"The Shard."

"Lost it. I was coming back to the Dragon with it. I thought I'd ask you about it, but..."

She was silent for a moment. Were they still moving? Gavin couldn't tell, but he thought they were. If they were moving, then he wanted to stop. He wanted to sit. Sleep.

"Let me rest," he said. "I need to restore my core. Then I can help you."

"You won't be of any use to us like this. Drink." Anna handed him something. It was cold—almost too cold. He started to push it away, but she took his hands and forced them toward his mouth.

"Drink. Don't argue."

"What is it?"

"Sh'rasn."

The liquid hit his lips, and he nearly cried out. There was a burst of cold that surged along his lips, down his throat, and into his tongue. He tried to ignore it, but it was painful. Tristan had taught him to suppress pain. Gavin had trained for years to perfect that. Even now, he could hide the sense of pain, but there was something about *this* that made it difficult.

"Swallow," she commanded.

Gavin didn't have a choice. The liquid worked its way down. He tried to fight and cough, but Anna continued to run her hand along his throat, keeping him from doing anything else. The pain worked through him.

"What did you do to him?" Wrenlow's voice sounded distant, as if he were asking the question from across a room.

*Where am I? Where are we all?*

There was darkness around him, though a hint of the glow coming off of Anna's hair made it so that he could see some. He tried to blink to clear his vision, but it didn't do anything.

"The sh'rasn will help," she said.

"With what?" Gavin managed to ask.

"With the separation."

"I just need to recover."

"You need more than that." She stayed in front of him, then tipped the mug to his lips again. This time, Gavin didn't fight. There was no point in doing so. He swallowed, letting the liquid roll down his throat. "This is more than what is normally used, but I suspect you've pushed harder than most would have."

"Are you sure about this?" Thomas asked. He was nearby—near enough that Gavin could feel him. The sword he carried continued to glow, though its intensity wasn't nearly as much as what he saw from Anna's hair.

"It's necessary if we want the Shard," she replied.

"He doesn't have it."

"No, but he can get it. Can't you?" she asked, watching Gavin.

He shook his head. "I don't know where it is. Told you, when I was coming to the Dragon, I stumbled. It was with me until then…"

He coughed, trying to clear his throat, but something else happened: His vision started to improve. The pain within him didn't ease, but that didn't matter. Gavin could ignore the pain. He looked at Anna. Now that he could see a little bit better, he could make out the glow of her hair—and the concern on her face. Was she worried about him?

"Most people struggle with the sh'rasn more than this," she said.

"Struggle how?" Gavin asked.

"Pain, mostly. I would've expected you to scream."

"I've experienced quite a bit of pain in my days."

"Really? That is… unfortunate."

She handed him the mug, and this time Gavin took another drink on his own. When the cold hit his lips and washed along his tongue and throat, he swallowed quickly. Whatever this liquid was happened to be helping. He breathed in, and energy began to return to him.

Thomas watched with suspicion in his eyes. Gaspar and Wrenlow were on the opposite side of what appeared to be a narrow alley. There was darkness around him, though the glow coming from Anna's hair and Thomas's sword helped him see.

He looked around. "Where's the dagger?"

"That's your first question?" Wrenlow asked.

"I've got a lot of questions. I need the dagger if I'm going to protect myself."

"He does need it," Anna said, turning to Thomas.

Thomas glared at Gavin, then pulled the dagger from a hidden sheath. He handed it hilt first and took a quick step back.

"How do you feel?" she asked.

"Better. What did you do to me?"

"It's not a matter of what I did to you, it's a matter of what had already been done to you. I simply countered it. It was a nasty bit of poisoning. I wouldn't expect to see it in Yoran, but with the way you were acting…"

"What do you mean, 'a nasty bit of poisoning'?"

"The kind you experienced is one that's well-known to the El'aras. You were treated with the same thing."

"It wasn't on your blade?" he asked, nodding to Thomas.

"I wouldn't dare use that," Thomas said, disgust filling him.

"What about the Sumter attackers?"

"I doubt that any of them would have the means to concoct it. Whatever was done to you required the proper concentration, especially seeing as how potent it was."

There was only one explanation.

Gavin took a deep breath. He was feeling better, and what was more, the core reserves of his strength were starting to return. He could feel that energy within him and thought he might even be able to draw on it if necessary. It was more than what he'd felt in quite some time. He hadn't realized just how much he'd been missing until now. Now that he could feel it, he recognized that power and the way he needed to call upon it.

He looked over at Wrenlow and Gaspar before turning his attention to Anna. "Unfortunately, I think I know what happened to me—and to your Shard."

*Could Cyran really have done this?*

Gavin had gone to him for help, and not only had he

been betrayed, he'd been poisoned as well. It didn't make sense that his oldest friend would do that to him. He couldn't believe it, but he didn't have any other explanation.

Everything started to come together in pieces, though none of it made sense.

*How could Cyran have been the one?*

Other theories formed, ideas that made even less sense.

*Cyran couldn't be...*

Gavin shook that thought away and took a deep breath, nodding toward the mug. "How much can I have?"

"There is a limit to how much the El'aras can tolerate. Mostly, it's a matter of the pain."

He tipped back the contents of the mug and swallowed it in one gulp. The pain that flared within him was incredible, and he tried to tamp it down and ignore it. Even as he attempted to do so, he struggled.

Gavin collapsed.

"What did you do?" Wrenlow asked Anna.

"This is on him," she said.

Gavin looked up and saw that she had an arm restraining Wrenlow. Pain continued to work through him, which he fought to ignore. He took a deep breath, holding onto the energy within him, trying to push back that pain and agony. He had no choice but to do so.

Finally, it started to ease and fade away. Getting back to his feet, he took another deep breath and found more of what he needed—that energy and that strength.

He looked over at Thomas. "We might need your blade."

"We?"

"If you want to get your Shard back, it's going to have to be a 'we.'" Gavin looked over at Gaspar, adding, "And I might need your thieving skills."

"Why?"

"Cyran was one of Tristan's best students. He didn't always see it that way, but he had one of the brightest minds. I'd always relied upon the fact that he was on my side. I hadn't considered that he might be working against me."

Even now, Gavin had a hard time coming to terms with it—but everything fit. More than that, a different suspicion had started to form. The jobs had always seemed so perfect for him, almost as if they'd been tailored to him.

Because they had been.

He should've been more suspicious before now, but he'd simply taken the jobs and was willing to do the work. It had been a long time since he'd questioned this.

Tristan would've been disappointed in him.

"If Cyran is responsible for what happened to me, I suspect he's the one who also took the Shard. He's probably even our employer," he said, glancing at Wrenlow.

And he would've been the one responsible for Sumter. He'd mentioned traveling in the South, and there *were* the items Gavin had seen in the house.

Wrenlow's eyes widened. "Why would your friend do that?"

"I don't know. But I intend to find out."

He started down the alley, and when he reached the end of it, there was movement along the street. It was late enough in the day that he stepped out without worrying about anyone else. He *did* need to know whether Jessica was safe from the attack.

"What about the Sumter attackers?" Wrenlow asked.

"That has to be Cyran too," Gavin said.

He didn't have a lot of experience with Sumter, only that they were skilled swordsmen from the South. They were probably working for Cyran, but he had to wonder if perhaps there was something else to that, especially since he felt as if he understood so little.

He hurried through the streets. Now that his energy had returned, it was easier for him to make his way, and the others kept pace with him. Gavin glanced over to see Anna and Thomas staying with him.

"You don't have to come with us," he said to her.

"I intend to reclaim the Shard," she said.

"Even if it means putting yourself in danger?"

"For the Shard, I will."

Yoran was large, and it took a while for them to navigate to the edge of the city. When they reached the central market, Gavin hesitated. This was where he'd collapsed. This was where Wrenlow had found him. He'd been going in the wrong direction from the Dragon. It was a wonder Wrenlow had found him. He had to thank him, but later.

Moving onward, he weaved through the street until he reached Cyran's home. There was no smoke rising from the chimney as there had been before. He paused on the street, glancing at the others. "This is his shop. His home."

Anna closed her eyes, and when she opened them, she shook her head. "There is no one here."

Thomas moved forward, and he slammed his sword into the door, prying it open.

The door exploded, tossing Gavin, Wrenlow, and Gaspar back. Anna reacted, holding her hands out and twisting her wrists slightly. Something curved around Thomas, who looked frozen.

Gavin got to his feet and helped the other two up. He turned and watched Anna and Thomas, who stood in the doorway. Neither of them looked harmed, though Thomas frowned as he stared inside, sniffing.

"An interesting precaution," Thomas said.

"Dangerous, as well," Anna replied. "He would have to have control over it to have placed it."

Gavin walked over to them. "What are you going on about?"

"Your friend. He has skillful sorcery."

"I don't think Cyran is a sorcerer."

"What we just experienced would suggest otherwise."

He looked back at Gaspar, and the old thief frowned at him. Gavin knew what he was thinking.

*Was Cyran tied to the sorcerer who had called us out into the forest?*

He paused a moment in the doorway. It felt as if he had

been here only a little while ago, but the home almost seemed empty. There was an air of nothingness, of staleness here. As he breathed it in, he couldn't tell whether it was something that Cyran had done intentionally or whether there was something about this place that had changed.

He headed toward the kitchen. Anna tried to reach for him, but Gavin moved forward, keeping the El'aras dagger out in front of him. If there was other sorcery here, the dagger would alert him.

The kitchen was empty. He pulled open the cupboards, but there was nothing in them. Cyran had cleared out of here.

"He's gone," he whispered.

"He knew you would come," Anna said.

"Either that or he thought I wasn't a threat anymore." He looked up. "If he poisoned me, he must have thought I wasn't going to recover."

"Without the sh'rasn, you would not have."

Cyran had been willing to kill him. Anger started to fill Gavin. All this time, out of all the people he'd known while training with Tristan, Cyran was the one person he never would've believed could do that.

Cyran had gotten out. Worse, if he was now some sort of sorcerer, or at least someone who had magic, then he was going to be far more difficult to remove as a threat.

"The Shard isn't here," Anna said.

She and Thomas headed toward the door, and Gavin held his hand up. "Wait."

"For what? Your friend is no longer here. There is nothing for us to do other than continue our search for the Shard. It must be recovered."

"What if I have a way?"

"How?" Anna asked.

An idea started to form in his head. "If Cyran was the employer, then that means Hamish is still out there. He's the key to this."

Somehow, they would have to find him, though Gavin wasn't at all sure how that would work. When he'd gone looking for Hamish in the past, he'd failed. But he'd done it without the El'aras.

They needed Hamish too. They could use him and get whatever answers they had to in order to find Cyran. Cyran would answer for what he'd done to Gavin.

"You don't know how to reach him," Anna said. "You told me that you didn't have any access to him."

"I don't, but we still have the one thing we were planning before."

"What is that?"

"Your death. The problem is that I think we're going to have to prove it to him."

She watched him for a moment and then closed the door before looking over at Thomas. "For the Shard, I think this will be necessary."

CHAPTER TWENTY

The low-roofed stone building loomed in front of them. It was one of the oldest buildings in the city, designed at a time before Yoran had banished all magic. As Gavin neared, there was a feeling of power coming off of it, a tingle that suggested there was magic still worked into the stone. The stone itself was a dark gray, so different than other stone buildings within the city. It had an angled roof, and though it was a single story, it still seemed to tower over the nearby buildings. There was no sign of any activity along the street. No people, and thankfully no constables. Not that he expected patrols around the morgue, and definitely not at night.

Gaspar followed him in silence, though Gavin wondered if there was anything for Gaspar to even say to him. It was a strange plan, and he no longer knew whether or not it was the right one.

"How is it that you know how to find this place?" Gavin whispered.

Gaspar looked over at him, arching a brow. "I've lived in the city a long time," he said.

"That's not an answer."

"It's all the answer you're going to get."

Gavin laughed. In the darkness and in the night, the laugh sounded strange, almost hollow. He had to be careful. He knew he should be moving more quietly than he was.

*But who would ever think anyone would attempt to break into a place like this?*

He reached the door and tried the lock, and he was surprised to find it was sealed. "Why would they even keep it closed?"

"To keep people like us out," Gaspar said.

"Really?" Gavin asked, arching a brow at him.

"Probably more to keep thieves from coming for their belongings."

"That sounds more likely, and it sounds more like the kind of thing you've done before."

"I've never robbed from the dead," Gaspar said. He looked at Gavin, a flash of anger burning in his eyes.

Gavin raised his hand, trying to ward him off. "I wasn't saying—"

"I know what you're saying. And I'm telling you my answer. It's the only answer."

"You don't have to be so touchy about it."

"There are some things that aren't made light of," Gaspar said.

"If you say so."

"I do."

Gavin stepped off to the side to let him press his hand against the door. Gaspar reached into his pocket and pulled something out from underneath his cloak, which he shoved into the lock, twisting gently. With a soft click, the door opened. They crept inside, and Gavin closed the door behind him. A wave of cold washed over him, causing him to frown.

Gaspar looked over. "Enchantments," he said.

"I thought the city didn't care for magic."

"Enchantments are different. Besides, how do you think they keep the bodies preserved?"

"I don't even know why they would care."

"Do you think the families of the dead want to come and find their loved ones decomposing?" Gaspar shook his head. "Enchantments keep this room and this building cold. It gives them time to make the arrangements."

"For a city that hates magic as much as this one does, I find that interesting."

"You would be surprised about Yoran."

"Other enchantments?"

"More than you would believe," Gaspar whispered.

They walked along the hall. It was empty, but there remained a strange, almost unpleasant sense within the room. Gavin had been responsible for sending plenty of people here. In that case, he supposed he should be curious about it, but he felt only uncertainty.

They reached a door at the end of the hall. Gaspar pressed his hand on it, then twisted the lock before shoving the door open.

There was a man inside. The priest was dressed in a dark gray robe. A silver necklace hung from his neck, likely with a symbol for the Star, the god the people of Yoran followed. He was rotund, filling out his robe, and stood between two tables in the center of the room. He looked up the moment they entered, his pasty face going slack and his eyes widening as he reached into his pocket.

Gaspar froze.

Gavin didn't.

He darted inside, twisting while pulling one of his knives free and heading straight toward the man.

"No!" Gaspar hissed.

Gavin shot a look over his shoulder and spun, flipping his knife and slamming the hilt into the man's forehead. He crumpled to the ground.

Gaspar sighed as he crossed the room to join him. "I thought you were going to kill him."

"Because he deserved it? He's a priest who's making preparations for families. He doesn't deserve to die. What now?"

"Now we find what we need," Gaspar said.

Gavin looked around the inside of the room. Cupboards lined all of the walls. A table rested in the middle of the room, and a naked man lay atop it. The priest that he'd knocked unconscious had been working on this man, but there was nothing else here.

Gavin frowned, turning to Gaspar. "Where do we look?"

"Where do you think? Here. Find a body that you think will work."

Gavin shook his head. "I don't see any bodies here."

"Look in the cupboards. Dammit, boy, do I have to do everything for you?"

"Seeing as how you're far more familiar with this place than I am, maybe you do," Gavin said, a hint of a smile on his face.

Gaspar glared at him.

Gavin went to the cupboards and pulled one of them open. A blast of icy air hit him as a cart with a body on it slid out. He looked at the older man lying on the table. This wouldn't work.

"They don't have anything like this in other cities," he muttered.

"No? What do they do with their dead?"

"Most of the time, they're buried before they reach the point of decomposition."

"In Yoran, the priests of the Star want to have the time to properly prepare for the afterlife. Before this was here, they had to prepare them quickly. It preoccupied most of the priests' time, and they found they were less efficient."

"I didn't realize there was an issue with priestly efficiency."

"Do you think preparing for the afterlife is the only thing the priests do?" Gaspar asked.

"I'll be honest and tell you that I haven't thought a whole lot about anything the priests do."

"Given that you've been responsible for placing some of these people here, I'd think you'd give some thought to it."

Gavin shook his head. "Maybe some, but not much."

He started going through the cupboards, pulling one after another open. Most of the dead were older men and women. They needed somebody who would resemble Anna closely enough for the illusion to hold and to be compelling.

"We aren't going to find anyone," Gavin said.

"Just keep looking."

"I am looking. I'm also noticing that everybody here seems to be of a certain age. That makes it a little difficult for one of the El'aras illusion enchantments to be effective."

"What would you rather do?" Gaspar asked. "Would you rather go hunting through the street to find somebody else to sacrifice for this assignment of yours?"

Gavin frowned, turning to face him. "Is that what you think of me?"

"I'm not entirely sure what to think of you. Isn't that the kind of work you do?"

"I take only specific jobs. Not all involve killing." Enough had though lately. That Cyran had been involved made that less of a coincidence than it once had felt like to him.

"I'm sure you do," Gaspar said, turning his attention back to the cupboards. He opened them quickly, quietly, pulling the cart out long enough to look inside before shoving it back in. Despite his obvious frustration, he managed to work much more quietly than Gavin.

"I do," Gavin said softly.

Gaspar looked up at him. "I've seen men like you come through Yoran before. I've seen men like you stop at the Dragon before. Hotheaded, and more often than not getting involved in things they shouldn't."

"That much is true," Gavin mumbled, opening another cupboard and finding the older man's body unusable.

"Then you come here, and you start spending time with Jessica. Usually, she's a much better judge of character."

"You don't think she is?"

"Usually," Gaspar said.

"And?"

"And it led to her getting hurt. Damn near killed. All because of you." Gaspar looked over, locking eyes with him. "All I'm saying is I don't care for that."

"I don't care for that either," Gavin said.

"Right. Because an assassin like you wants nothing more than killing."

"Not an assassin," Gavin whispered. "And have you seen what I've done since we were attacked?"

"I have, which is the only reason I'm with you here."

"That can't be the only reason."

Gaspar shook his head, pulling open another cupboard and pausing. He stared for a moment before slamming the cart back into the cupboard. "That isn't the only reason." He turned to Gavin. "I haven't decided whether or not you should walk out of here."

"Really?" Gavin shifted toward him.

He was old, but there was something deceptive about his age, along with his skill level. Gavin suspected that the man would pose an interesting challenge if they were to face off. Not that he wanted to fight Gaspar.

He had helped Gavin. Maybe he'd done it because of a desire to protect Jessica, and maybe he'd done it because there'd been no other choice. Either way, they'd worked together.

"Tell me," Gaspar said, looking at Gavin, "what makes you so different?"

Gavin looked around the inside of the building, and he shook his head. "Perhaps nothing. You might be right. I'm not all that different. I've been responsible for putting people here. It's just…"

He opened another cupboard and pulled the cart out. He glanced down, his breath catching. It was a younger woman. She didn't look exactly like Anna, but with her blonde hair and her overall figure, she had a passing resemblance. The wound to her abdomen suggested she'd been stabbed.

Gavin clenched his jaw.

"What is it?" Gaspar asked.

"Nothing."

"It's not nothing. I can see from your expression that there's something."

"Obviously, considering your opinion of me, it doesn't matter," Gavin said.

"You don't even know my opinion of you."

"In the last few moments, you've made it quite clear what you think of me and how you're considering dealing with me."

Gavin pulled the cart out a little further, looking at the woman. She was going to work. *This* was going to work.

"If you think you can overwhelm me, make a go at it, but don't make passing threats," he continued. "I've dealt with enough of those in my time to know better." He looked up and frowned at Gaspar, who stood across from him and said nothing. "If you're going to help me remove the cloud that hangs over the Dragon—and Jessica—then grab an arm and help me carry her."

Gaspar hesitated, watching Gavin for a long moment before shaking his head. "Damn," he whispered.

"What?"

"Still can't get a read on you, boy."

"No? Then stay nearby. Maybe you'll get a better chance to do so."

Gavin slipped an arm underneath one side of the body and waited. Gaspar did the same on the other side, and together they lifted her. She was heavy—heavier than he would've expected.

"That's part of the preparation," Gaspar said. "They ready the body for the afterlife."

"What did they do, inject lead into her?"

"I don't really know. I'm not one of the priests. All I know is that it's part of the process."

Gavin frowned as they dragged her off the cart. He paused to kick the cart back into place and close the cupboard, and when they reached the door, he glanced back.

So much of this room relied upon the dead, much like so much of his life and training prepared him for the dead. It was a strange thing to see, but stranger still that he had a hand in much of it. Perhaps not so much of those here, but in general.

They approached the main door. As they reached it, a shout came from behind.

"Time to hurry," Gavin whispered, and Gaspar grunted in agreement.

They kicked open the door and hurried out into the street, pulling the body along with them. They tried to prop her up so that she was hanging between them, but it would appear strange to anyone who might pass by. Gavin motioned for them to stop.

"We can't drag a naked woman through the street," he said as he slipped his cloak off and threw it around the body.

"Probably not," Gaspar said. "Though, in a place like Yoran, that wouldn't be the strangest thing ever seen."

Gavin chuckled, and they moved as fast as they could, given the awkward situation.

"We can't take her back to the Dragon," Gaspar said.

"I don't have any intention of taking her there. I have a better idea."

"Where?"

"We need to prepare for the meeting."

"I'm not going out there at this time of night," Gaspar said, glancing toward the distant forest. It was just visible along the street, and the darkness swirled around it.

"Are you afraid?" Gavin asked.

"Aren't you?"

"Let's see. A sorcerer attacked us out there. I've been poisoned by my friend—who might also be the one employing me. Then there's the danger that lives within the forest in general. You're damn right I'm afraid." Gavin laughed. "But I still don't think we need to be worried about the forest. At least, not the outskirts. The real danger lies deeper within."

"What real danger? The El'aras?"

Gavin shook his head. "There are things that are more frightening than even the El'aras."

They reached the edge of the forest and paused. Gavin glanced behind him and saw movement coming toward them. He motioned for Gaspar to follow him, and they plunged into the trees.

"Now would be a good time for Anna to come," Gavin whispered.

"*Now* you want one of the El'aras here?"

"She might be helpful in this situation."

"You are a strange boy," Gaspar said.

"You have no idea."

"What happens if this goes wrong?"

Gavin looked over at him but didn't have an answer. Gaspar grunted as he shifted the woman's weight. They were under the canopy of the trees. Gavin tried to figure out how far they had to carry her before they could leave her so they could stop and rest. They had to stay far enough on the outskirts of the forest to ensure that she wouldn't be discovered by animals, but they also had to go deep enough that no one would find her before they returned. Either that, or one of them had to stay with her overnight.

"It's not as if you have the best record with these sorts of things," Gaspar said. "What happens if the body doesn't look enough like the El'aras woman? The sorcerer decides to attack, and the rest of us become targets. What do you do then?"

Gavin took a deep breath and let it out. "I'll do what I have to then."

"What does that mean to you?"

Gavin looked over and held Gaspar's gaze. "I'll do whatever it takes."

"To get yourself to safety?"

"Just myself? Is that what you think of me?"

"I don't know what to think of you. Like I said, I can't get a read on you. Most men like you, most assassins, think only of themselves. That's what I suspect in your case, but maybe not."

"You'll have to wait and find out then," Gavin said.

They carried the woman into the forest and said nothing else. Every so often, Gaspar looked over at him with a question lingering in his eyes, but he didn't ask it. Gavin didn't offer any more information either.

He couldn't shake the heart of the question Gaspar had asked, though.

*What would happen if this went wrong?*

Given what they'd gone through, and given what Gavin had done, it was all too likely that it would go sideways somehow. He just had to prepare for that possibility and prepare for what he might do—only, Gavin wasn't sure what that would be. When it came to Cyran and how complex this situation seemed to be, Gavin simply didn't know.

## CHAPTER TWENTY-ONE

The narrow street in this section of the city was dark, and there was little movement along it. Buildings lined either side of the street; most of them shops long since shuttered. Fading signs didn't catch much of the streetlight or any of the moonlight. No windows glowed in any of the storefronts, though some candles were lit on the upper levels where the shop owners lived.

Gavin stalked forward carefully. Any noise might change what they hoped to accomplish. He needed to be careful, but he also needed to be convincing. He glanced to the far side of the street. Even though he couldn't see Gaspar, Gavin knew he was there, trailing him. The old thief had proven quite adept at navigating through the street without being seen.

There was still no sign of Hamish. It was almost as if he wasn't concerned about completing the job, which, as much as Gavin hated to acknowledge it, might be true. There was the possibility that Hamish had only wanted him to complete a job on Cyran's behalf to keep him preoccupied.

He didn't think that was likely though. More likely was that the job had been intended to remove Anna from the house so that Cyran could go after the Shard. Now that he had the Shard, it was possible that Cyran didn't care what happened to Anna.

Their plan counted on the fact that Cyran *did* care about what happened to Gavin. As far as Cyran knew, he was dead. He hoped to use that to lure Cyran to come after him so he could recover the Shard.

Moving in the darkness like this reminded him of the many nights he'd spent planning jobs and applying what he'd learned through his training with Tristan in his own way. Here he'd begun to believe that Cyran had moved away from that, but instead he'd gone a different way altogether.

There was a shimmer of movement. He stiffened, though he didn't step out of the darkness. The fabric was the most prominent feature, a distinct pale yellow velvet. It swirled outward, creating the appearance that Hamish wore a dress rather than heavy robes. Each time Gavin saw him, he seemed to be dressed even more ridiculous than the last.

*How could a man like that go unnoticed?*

And yet, in the time Gavin had been in Yoran, trying to find Hamish, he'd never managed to hear any word of him. It was almost as if the garish clothing hid him even better. Maybe Gavin needed to try the same strategy and dress the same way.

Hamish wasn't a powerful man, as far as Gavin knew, but he was well-connected. Something kept him safe and tied him to their mutual employer.

*What exactly did Hamish know?*

Gavin needed answers, and he planned to follow Hamish to their employer.

"Do you see anything?" Gavin whispered.

"Nothing. Keep moving," Gaspar said.

With Gaspar now wearing the enchantment, it gave Gavin a different confidence moving on the street. Wrenlow could provide intelligence, but Gaspar could provide information based on direct observation. Gavin wished he had an enchantment that allowed him to speak to both of them simultaneously. Somewhere out in the night, Imogen also stood guard. She and Gaspar would keep an eye on Gavin from afar and would warn him if Cyran appeared.

He started forward, trying to look as casual as he could as he headed toward Hamish. He wasn't surprised when Hamish turned as he approached, almost as if anticipating Gavin's arrival.

"I didn't think you were going to come," Gavin said.

"And I would make the same claim," Hamish said.

"The job is done."

Hamish frowned. "Which job?"

"What do you mean 'which job'? You hired me to

remove the woman as a threat. I finished it." He hesitated, not wanting to get too close.

Hamish watched him, and there was something in his eyes that warned Gavin. "I need proof. Since you drew so much notice at her home, it's difficult for me to obtain the proof I would have otherwise."

"I can show you the body," Gavin said.

Hamish's eyes widened. "You have it?"

"I had to take it from the priests attempting to preserve it." He smiled, resting one hand near the El'aras dagger in case he needed to reach for it. He didn't know what Hamish would do if he did though. "I can lead you to her."

"That won't be necessary," Hamish said.

"You said you needed proof. I can take you to it."

"If you tell me where it is, I will find it. If our employer is satisfied, you will receive your payment."

"How is our employer, anyway?"

Hamish looked over at him, frowning. "The same as always. Wanting anonymity, as you know."

"I'm sure. I just thought I would ask."

"If you're concerned about jobs disappearing, you needn't worry. You have proven yourself. You can be effective, even if you are somewhat careless."

"Careless?" Gavin asked.

"Yes. You have done little to shield your presence. I think that makes you careless. Regardless of whether our employer is satisfied by your work, I am not."

Gavin smiled, meeting Hamish's eyes. "It's a good thing he's the employer and not you."

"He?"

"I assumed. Perhaps she."

Hamish watched him for a moment. "Where is the body?"

"There's a place deep in the forest. It will involve a bit of a walk, but I didn't figure you'd be too upset by that. Sometimes it's nice to get out of the city."

Hamish glared at him. "Where in the forest?"

"Like I said, not far. It won't take you long. There's a trail that leads from the outer edge of the city. All you have to do his head toward Byron Street and veer off of that."

Gavin watched Hamish, looking for any recognition of the name. If the man had been to Cyran's shop on Byron Street, he wasn't giving any indication—not that Gavin really expected Hamish to do so. If nothing else, he'd proven himself incredibly adept at maintaining a neutral expression.

"I'm familiar with the street," Hamish said.

"Good. It winds into the forest. It's not the easiest place to reach, but I figure you won't have much difficulty. I doubt you're all that eager to leave the city though. To be honest, I'm not either. I don't really know what we might encounter there, but…"

"But what?"

"But it was the easiest place to dispose of the body and not deal with the attackers. They were from Sumter. Did you know that?"

Gavin figured it made sense to give Hamish something. He also hoped that by mentioning Sumter, he could find out if Hamish knew anything about it.

Hamish nodded slowly. "There have been rumors of men from Sumter moving through the city. A vile place with equally vile men."

Gavin nodded. "Unfortunately for the constables throughout the city, I've removed quite a few of them. There have been bodies left behind. I don't know that the constables will be pleased with me."

"I can take care of that."

"Our employer has those kinds of contacts?"

"Like I said, I will take care of it."

Gavin nodded again as he continued watching Hamish closely. "If that's the case, then you can find the body about an hour into the forest."

"Why an hour?"

"It took me a while to get away from the Sumter attackers. They chased me, but they chased her as well. It was the strangest thing." Gavin flashed a smile, shrugging. "Regardless, they are a threat no more. And the constables might appreciate that there are fewer Sumter attackers in the city."

Hamish studied him for a long moment. "If the body is there as you say, then you will be reimbursed. If not…"

"If not, I can't take the blame. There are wolves and werin and all sorts of other creatures there. None of that would be my fault."

Hamish stared at him and finally shook his head. "The body. Otherwise you will not be paid." He started to back away, and Gavin made no effort to move. He needed Hamish to see him still standing there.

"He's going," he whispered.

"I see him," Gaspar said.

Gavin followed Hamish at a distance so Hamish didn't think he was being pursued. He found the man hurrying down one of the side streets and used the swish of the bright yellow fabric as his guide. Hamish turned another corner, disappearing from view.

"Gaspar?"

"Still on it."

Maybe this was an assignment Gavin should've done himself, but he'd seen how quickly and quietly Gaspar could move. He was certainly quieter than Gavin, whose training wasn't in stealth and thieving.

He turned a corner and found a sign of Hamish in the distance, much further ahead than he would've expected. Strange, that. It was almost as if Hamish had his own enchantments, though nothing about him had ever suggested he was magically enhanced. Perhaps Gavin should've pulled out the El'aras dagger to check. Instead he'd been more curious about what Hamish would say and how he'd react when he heard where they were sending him.

"Are you able to keep up with him?" Gavin asked.

"Is this what the kid is like for you?"

Gavin started laughing. "Maybe."

"I can see why you get so annoyed with him."

"I don't get annoyed with him. It's more that he just

chirps in my ear the entire time I'm trying to work. I need some quiet when I'm taking on my jobs, though I figured an old-timer like you wouldn't need that. You probably enjoy the conversation, what with you being as lonely as you are. You know, I—"

"Enough," Gaspar said.

Gavin chuckled again. "Which way is he going?"

"The opposite way of where you told him to go."

Gavin hadn't expected Hamish to head straight toward the forest. That wasn't a task to do in the middle of the night. It was one he'd need to do when he had enough rest, daylight, and others with him for support. He doubted Hamish would risk himself by heading into the forest like this.

He turned a corner and didn't see anything. He continued to listen for an update from Gaspar, but there was no sound from the other side of enchantment to suggest he was even there.

*Had he muted it?*

Gavin rounded another corner, and a figure moved in the distance. Small but fast. He started after them.

He thought it was Imogen, though he wasn't entirely sure. As he hurried after her, she moved more quickly than he could keep up with. Maybe he still wasn't fully recovered. He focused on his core strength, and energy flowed through him.

He raced forward after the figure in the distance, who didn't appear to know he was in pursuit. He darted after her and turned another corner.

Hamish was ahead, trying to outrun her. He hurried, but she was even faster. She caught Hamish and stabbed him with her small blade. The man dropped to the ground.

Gavin skidded to a stop as she ran off, disappearing along the street.

*What the hell just happened?*

He reached for the El'aras dagger and found it glowing. He raced forward and paused near Hamish. Blood coated the cobblestones.

*Was the injury fatal?*

He crouched down next to him. "What happened?" he asked Hamish.

The other man looked up at him, his eyes starting to glaze. Gavin frowned and rolled Hamish's head to the side. Wait. Not Hamish. It looked like him, and it was dressed like him, but the nose and the eyes weren't quite right.

*What had Hamish done? More importantly, what had Imogen done?*

He quickly searched the body of the fallen man, looking for anything that might provide any answers. Nothing.

Gavin left him and chased Imogen. As he held onto that core energy, he knew it wouldn't last. He thought he caught sight of her as he darted around a corner. She was turning away, disappearing again.

He paused, tapping on the enchantment. Gaspar *had* to

be there. "Do you know where Imogen went?" He was surprised when he heard an answer.

"Why?" Gaspar said, his voice a little breathless.

"She just killed a Hamish look-alike."

"She just did *what?*"

"There was a man dressed like Hamish," Gavin explained. "The same robes, moving along the street. Imogen slid a blade into his back before running off. I'm curious as to why."

"She wouldn't have done that."

"I was there. I was only a step or two behind her."

"Show me," Gaspar said.

"You're supposed to be after Hamish."

"I'm aware, but he disappeared."

Gavin shook his head.

*What was happening here? They were supposed to tail Hamish, and now they were going to lose him?*

The whole situation troubled him. More than that, it angered him.

He looked at his surroundings. "It was by Tiller Street."

"I'll meet you there."

Gavin raced back toward where he'd seen the Hamish look-alike. The body was gone. Blood still stained the cobblestones, but there was no sign of the man. He lingered there and waited for Gaspar, and he thought he heard the sound of movement but didn't see a sign of the old thief.

Gavin slipped across the street to hide in the shadows.

*Where was Gaspar? What happened to the body Imogen had left?*

He wouldn't have expected someone to come through and remove the body already.

*Was the man still alive?*

He hadn't thought so, but maybe that was possible.

A shadow from along the street caught his attention. "Is that you coming?" he whispered.

"Who else would it be?" Gaspar said.

"I don't know. The body is gone."

"What do you mean that the body is gone?"

"That's exactly what I mean," Gavin said.

He stepped forward and looked across the street, searching for any clue as to where the body had disappeared to. There wasn't even a trail of blood. It was almost as if whoever had been here had simply vanished.

He met Gaspar in the middle of the street and pointed to the pool of blood. Gaspar crouched down and traced his finger through it. "What do you think?"

Gavin shrugged. "I don't know. I'm not accustomed to people who've been stabbed in the back getting up and walking away so easily."

"Who said this was easy?" Gaspar asked.

"Fine. Getting up and walking away at all."

"Are you always so difficult?"

He crouched down next to Gaspar and studied the pool of blood, which seemed to be drying already. Gaspar kept his finger in it and traced something through it, then brought his finger up to his nose.

"It doesn't smell quite right," Gaspar said.

"I'm not so sure what to make of that."

"Nothing more than that it just doesn't smell quite right. What do you think of it?"

"It's blood," Gavin said.

"Sure."

"You don't think so? I saw him get stabbed."

"Are you sure about that?" Gaspar asked.

"I'm pretty sure."

Gaspar smiled at him. "That's not the same. Not at all."

Gavin rolled his eyes. "Are you always this difficult?"

Gaspar stood and wiped his hands on his pants. He looked at the surrounding area. "I know you thought you saw Imogen, but it wasn't her."

"How do you know?"

"Because she was near me. If it was her, she would've had to slip away without me knowing." He shook his head. "That wouldn't be possible."

Gavin sighed. "I don't know what it was then. I was sure I saw Imogen."

"Maybe you saw somebody who looked like her, the same way you saw somebody who looked like Hamish."

Gavin didn't know if that was what it was. Either way, everything about this was strange. Here he thought that he'd been the one to trick Hamish. Maybe it was the other way around.

"We've lost him for tonight, so we might as well get into position for the other part of this," he said.

"I don't know if it's going to work the way you think it will."

Gavin took a deep breath and let it out slowly. "At this point, I'm not sure about anything. Not anymore."

Gaspar grunted. "At least that makes two of us."

## CHAPTER TWENTY-TWO

The forest was quiet around them. Gavin listened to the sounds, and he could hear something making a soft scratching sound in the forest. Gaspar stood across from him on the opposite side of the small clearing and wore the enchantment again.

It was strange to admit, but having Gaspar on the other end of the enchantment was actually helpful. He could not only listen but act—something Wrenlow wasn't able to do.

Gavin knew Wrenlow was disappointed, having to remain at the Dragon and being unable to help. But if all of this went well and they got through it, then Gavin was determined to ask Anna to help with another enchantment.

"How long do you think this will be?" Gaspar asked.

Gavin shook his head. "I don't really know." He looked down at the ground. The body resembled Anna closely enough that it would be worth taking a second look. With the enchantment she'd placed on it, he suspected it would pass even a closer inspection, but he worried about whether the second inspection would involve magic. If so, whoever performed the inspection would likely realize an enchantment had been placed, and they would lose their opportunity.

He was determined to find Cyran. This was his only chance.

"What makes you think he's going to come out here?" Gaspar whispered.

"If Cyran's my employer, he's going to want to know whether or not I lived."

"What makes you think he won't have another way of finding out?"

"If Hamish went to him"—and Gavin was still operating on the assumption that Cyran had hired Hamish, who had then hired him—"then he'll question it. I don't know why, but he wanted me removed as part of this job."

*Why this one, though? Unless he hadn't cared.*

Gavin would've thought that he'd be far more useful to Cyran alive rather than dead because then Cyran could continue to use him for whatever jobs he wanted. For whatever reason, it'd been decided that now was the time to remove him.

A soft whistle pierced the forest. It sounded something like a bird, but the call was not quite right and certainly not one found in the forest normally. That was the whistle they were waiting for. Gavin and Gaspar backed away, moving out of the clearing.

"I think her whistle was a bit too sharp," Gavin said.

"You tell Imogen that."

"I don't think so."

"Are you afraid of her?" Gaspar whispered. There was a hint of mirth in the question.

"Aren't you?"

"Oh, yes. I've known her longer though. My fear comes from the time I've worked with her."

"And mine comes from seeing her stab a man in the back."

"We went over this with her already. You know that wasn't her you saw," Gaspar said.

Gaspar and Imogen had discussed this when she'd returned to the Dragon last night. Gavin had witnessed the exchange and had come to trust that it wasn't her. He didn't understand *what* had happened, only that magic had been involved—and that Imogen hadn't done what he'd feared.

Gavin shrugged. He moved next to a tree and lingered under a branch, staying in the shadows. If only he had an enchantment that would hide him, but those sorts of things were incredibly expensive.

He tapped on his other ear. "Are you ready?"

"I'm watching," Anna whispered.

Her enchantment was a little different and far easier for her to control. She'd created this one, so she could not only control it but also adjust the volume. Gavin wished he could do the same with his.

He flicked his gaze to the treetops. There was no sign of her, though he knew she was there. In his mind, she and Thomas were here for a different reason. He'd seen the enchantment on the door Cyran had placed. If Cyran were to use something explosive like that again, the two El'aras would be the only ones who could withstand it.

Gavin watched through the trees. Another whistle sounded, this one soft and barely more than a chirp.

*North.*

Imogen was following them through the forest. Gavin hadn't been entirely sure whether she was going to be able to, but she was skilled.

"I have to give her credit," he whispered.

"Tell her, not me," said Gaspar.

"I'm telling you so you can tell her, if something happens and I don't make it out of here."

"Do you think it matters then?"

"I don't know. It matters to me."

Gaspar shot him a look in the distance. "You're going to get out of here just fine. I'm the old one, remember?"

"It's pretty hard for me to forget," Gavin said, laughing again.

There was another whistle. *East.* Hamish was weaving through the forest in a roundabout approach.

Gavin twisted, positioning himself so that he was out of sight as the potential approach came, but he didn't see anything.

Another whistle. *South.*

"Something's off," Gaspar said.

Gavin nodded. "That's my concern."

"She's doing her best to track it, but—"

Another whistle. This one was sharp. It signaled concern.

"Go to her," Gavin said.

"You might need my help," said Gaspar.

"And she definitely needs your help. Go to her."

Gaspar frowned before nodding to him. "Let me know if you need anything."

"I thought you didn't like it when I chattered in your ear."

"I don't, but I think—"

Another whistle.

Gaspar spun and headed into the trees without saying anything else, leaving Gavin alone.

"Do you see anything?" he asked Anna through the enchantment.

"There is no presence here other than what we've already uncovered."

"Are you sure of it?"

"If there was movement here in the forest, I would know."

He looked down at the body of the fake Anna. It didn't move, but something about it started to change. A moment passed before he realized what it was: There was a hint of shimmering energy around it.

"Something's here," he whispered.

Gavin tried to be as quiet as he could, not wanting to draw any attention to whoever was here. He glanced down at the El'aras dagger. The blade glowed with a bright light. There was power here, although he didn't need the dagger to know that.

The body started to move—not the kind of movement that indicated someone was dragging it, but the kind of movement that suggested that the body was being reanimated from death.

His breath caught. It looked as if the fake Anna were dancing in some sort of rhythmic death movement. Even knowing that it wasn't Anna, he found this difficult to see. He watched the body as it marched through the forest in strange jerking motions. It strode away from him, leaving him unsettled and hesitant as to what to do next.

He followed the body. "Are you seeing this?"

"There is something that prevents me from seeing anything," Anna whispered.

"It looks like you're walking away."

"Me?"

"Well, not you, but the body."

"You should be cautious," Anna said.

"I didn't think you were concerned about me."

"You are my way of getting the Shard back."

Gavin would've laughed were it not for the dead body rhythmically dancing its way through the forest. He paused at another tree and pressed his head against it, feeling the coolness of the bark. A strange chill washed over him. It came from the body, or at least from watching the body. The feeling left him troubled as the body danced, moving along the ground, feet dragging lifelessly.

*Anna couldn't help, but what about Thomas?*

"Send Thomas," Gavin said.

"What do you think Thomas might do that you cannot?"

Gavin trailed the animated body, tamping down the fear coursing through him. He marveled at the idea that whoever was controlling this could have that much power.

"I'm sure that he can do more than I can when it comes to this," he said.

"When this is over, Gavin Lorren, we will have to have a conversation about just what you are capable of."

He shook his head. He didn't care about any of that, only that she send help. He needed Thomas to help him stop whoever controlled the corpse.

The body moved away while he waited for Thomas, but the El'aras was taking far too long. The minutes ticked by, and Gavin decided to go off on his own. So much for a plan.

A whistle sounded from deeper in the forest, and he hesitated.

*Strange. What did this whistle indicate?*

Before, Imogen had been whistling to signal where Hamish was traveling, but now he had no idea what this one meant. This couldn't be about Hamish.

*Did they need help?*

He tapped on his enchantment. "Gaspar, do you need—"

"Stay back," he heard through the enchantment.

He'd muted it.

But not intentionally.

The voice on the other side of the enchantment sounded like Gaspar, but there was more terror in his voice than Gavin had ever heard before. He glanced around, and the body continued to march quickly through the forest.

He needed Anna. He tapped on the other enchantment and hesitated. The body had stopped.

"Where's Thomas?" he asked.

"He should be coming," she whispered.

The whistle came again. Gavin turned and headed toward it.

As he ran through the forest, he came across Thomas. "Find the body. Follow it. I don't know what they're doing with it, but that will lead you to whoever is controlling it."

"Controlling it?"

Gavin had already started off, but the question made him stop and turn. "Someone is controlling the body. I'm not really sure what's going on. They have magic, which means you're better equipped to stop them."

"Where are you going?"

"Something happened."

The whistle came again. Gavin ran. As he did, he tapped on the enchantment again. "I'm coming, Gaspar."

There was nothing but silence on the other end. He

focused on his core strength again and drew upon the energy within him to race toward the source of the sound. The forest blurred past. He reached where he thought the whistle had come from. There was no sign of Gaspar. There was no sign of Imogen.

The El'aras dagger glowed in his hand, and he realized he could use the light to see what was here, the same way he'd found the Shard. He closed his eyes and turned in place. Unlike when he was inside the manor house, this time he moved with a sense of urgency. As he turned, he felt something slide across him. The resistance.

Gavin opened his eyes and started toward it. He took several steps and then froze.

Imogen hung from one of the trees. She was grabbing the rope around her neck and kicking wildly, a look of desperation in her eyes.

He unsheathed one of the knives he carried. He'd practiced throwing knives in his training, but it'd been quite a while since he'd attempted anything like this. Cutting the rope would take a perfect throw. He had no idea if he'd have the accuracy.

Gavin took a steadying breath and hurled the knife. It whistled through the air and struck the rope, carving through it. Imogen crashed to the ground and rolled to her feet. She raced toward him as she peeled the rope off her neck. From what he could see, aside from being shaken, she was physically unharmed.

"Are you okay? Where's Gaspar?" he asked.

Her breaths were ragged. "Don't know. Dragged away."

"Dragged away? By who?"

"Not a who. A what."

There were all sorts of creatures in the forest, though few ever got close enough to the city to pose much of a danger. They were on the border of El'aras lands, where the creatures tended to be more dangerous.

He closed his eyes, focusing on the El'aras dagger again. Turning slowly, Gavin felt for the resistance that might be in the forest. He didn't feel it where it had been before, which told him that whatever power had been holding onto Imogen had been released. That didn't mean they were out of danger here though. Gavin made a circuit while holding onto the dagger, but he didn't feel anything.

What was going on? Hamish had tried to distract him, which meant Cyran was going to get away—

Cyran.

He opened his eyes. "Come with me."

"Gaspar still needs our help."

"And I think I know where to find him."

Gavin raced through the forest. Imogen kept up, almost as if she were floating.

*Did she have magic of some sort?*

He hadn't seen any signs from her, but he knew she was incredibly talented. Gaspar wouldn't have a magic user around him, especially in a place like Yoran where there was such a suspicion of magic. Then again, Gaspar hadn't seemed all that troubled by Gavin's use of enchantments or by any of the other magical circumstances that had occurred. Maybe he didn't care.

Gavin raced past the clearing where he'd first waited with the body. There was a crackling in his ear, not from Gaspar or from Anna, but almost as if there was some sort of interference with the magical communication.

He followed the trail across the forest floor, which had formed where the corpse's feet had dragged across the ground. The undergrowth had been disturbed, with thorns and leaves and the soft ground itself all creating a path he could easily follow. Gavin swept his gaze back and forth around him, looking for the body.

Then he found it. Thomas faced the corpse with his sword unsheathed as if preparing to fight.

*But why?*

Something was taking place here.

A flicker of movement behind Gavin caught his attention. He noticed Gaspar watching and waiting, an unreadable expression on his face. He remained hidden near a massive tree, the shadows of the forest concealing him.

The El'aras dagger suddenly blazed with bright light. Gavin grabbed Imogen and pulled her to the ground. They rolled so that magic wouldn't strike them, but nothing came.

"What was that about?" she whispered.

He shook his head. "Something's not quite right. I don't know what, only that—"

"You can come out, Gavin. I know you're there."

He recognized Hamish's voice, but that wouldn't have been enough for Thomas and Gaspar to be on edge.

"If you can hear me, let me know in some way," he whispered into both of his enchantments.

"I can hear you quite well," Hamish said.

*Balls.*

Had Hamish been able to hear him through the enchantment all this time? That didn't seem likely. Which meant he had Gaspar's enchantment.

Gavin had to know for sure. He tapped on the one he shared with Anna and whispered, "Is it possible for him to listen in on our conversation?"

"He should not have control over it," Anna said.

Gavin exhaled in relief. "Can you see anything from where you are?"

"Nothing that can help. Thomas is troubled by something."

"I think he's troubled by Hamish, but there's something else too. The dagger is glowing brightly. There's magic here. Considerable magic."

"Then it might be your friend."

He had a hard time thinking that Cyran was that powerful, but what if he was? He held onto the dagger and started forward, moving slowly. Imogen stayed with him. He pulled one of his belt knives out and handed it to her. "At least it's something."

Gavin lingered for a moment. Then he darted forward.

## CHAPTER TWENTY-THREE

The forest around him seemed to have gone completely still. The air hung, waiting in anticipation. There was no sound other than his beating heart and his breathing, which were both far too loud in his ears. He turned and looked for the attacker but found nothing. Something had to be here though. Thomas stood frozen in place before the animated corpse. Hamish's robes billowed around him, though they were the only things that moved.

*Could it be magic?*

Gavin had never known Hamish to have magic, but it was possible he had enchantments.

"Thomas?" he whispered.

"Something is amiss. A danger I have not faced before," Thomas said.

Gavin turned his attention to Hamish. "What are you doing?"

Hamish eyed the El'aras dagger. "An interesting weapon for you to carry."

"I took it from one of my attackers. I thought it might be useful."

"A blade like that would be quite valuable. I suppose our employer might be willing to purchase it from you."

"It's not for sale," Gavin said.

"Everything is for sale."

"Not the dagger."

Hamish stared at him. "You should return to the city."

"I don't think so. I need to know what's going on here."

"What's going on is that I am claiming the body."

Gavin couldn't sense whether Hamish believed the enchantment Anna had placed over it, but he doubted it would hold against someone truly able to use magic. He wasn't completely convinced Hamish was that person. The man might have some control over power, but as far as Gavin could tell, Hamish wasn't the powerful one.

"Where is our employer?" he asked.

"I'm afraid that's not how it works. If you want to keep taking jobs, you will need to maintain a certain distance. That is how he likes to do things."

"Then you're confirming our employer is a man? I've become all too aware of how *he* likes to do things." Gavin held out the dagger and took a step toward Hamish. Something else was still bothering him. He didn't understand the purpose of the Hamish look-alike that had been killed, other than to conceal his departure. Neither did he understand the purpose behind the Imogen look-alike.

There was something behind these deceptions, some key he was still missing.

"I'm tired of doing things without meeting face-to-face with him," he continued. "At this point, I would like to see him. If I'm going to continue taking jobs, I want to know who's employing me. And who's taking my partner's enchantment."

"As you can well understand, he prefers to have a level of anonymity. I believe that in your line of work, you can appreciate the need for anonymity."

Gavin took another step toward him, squeezing the El'aras blade. He could feel resistance coming from the blade, almost as if there was pressure as he moved toward Hamish.

He shook his head. "The time for anonymity is past us. Besides, I need to know who to thank for such perfectly arranged jobs."

Hamish watched him.

"It didn't occur to me at first. I suppose it probably should have. Given everything I'd been through before in other cities, I became selective about the jobs I took. Not many people know that about me. Most have heard of my reputation or have learned of what I can do, and they're willing to hire the name. But they didn't look deeper. In the case of our employer," he said, emphasizing it as he started to put things together, "I never bothered to question why the jobs were always ones I'd take. What did I care? I was in a new city."

As he talked, he glanced over at Thomas, who remained standing with sword in hand. Gavin realized that Thomas couldn't move. Gaspar was likely frozen in place too.

*What about Imogen?*

She had her own unique abilities, though he didn't have any idea what those were. If his hunch about what was taking place now was correct, then it wouldn't even matter.

He focused again on Hamish. "My jobs always came through an intermediary, and this intermediary knew so much about me."

"It has been my role to ensure that our employer knows all the details about you."

Gavin forced a smile and gripped the dagger tighter. "All of the details? I don't think so. There were certain details even Hamish shouldn't have known. Should he, Cyran?"

He stared at Hamish, the curiosity from the previous night's events coming back to him. Hamish's disappearance and the use of doppelgängers for him and Imogen all suggested magical involvement. In the city, there shouldn't have been that many people who had magic, yet he continued to encounter them. He doubted the sorcerer he'd encountered in the forest was responsible for all these occurrences.

*But the Apostle?*

The timing fit, as did the rumors of an incredibly

powerful sorcerer. The El'aras had magic, but they weren't the ones pulling the strings. No. The one responsible for all of this was the person he never knew had magic.

Gavin looked around. "You can show yourself. I might not be as quick as you, but Tristan made sure I could piece through puzzles, same as you."

There was a soft shimmer around Hamish, and suddenly Cyran stood in front of him. The robes that were wrapped around him swirled with color, but even that began to fade.

Cyran watched him, grinning. "It's taken you a long time, Gavin."

Gavin glared at the person he once thought of as his friend. "Like I said, I may not be as quick as you, but eventually I learn."

"Eventually? You wouldn't believe how long I've been waiting for you to uncover the truth, but you continued to fail me. Had you uncovered it sooner, I might've been more willing to spare you. You did make me uncertain with the enchantment you use to communicate. I had to get creative to understand it."

"Creative… is that why you made it look like Hamish died?"

"I needed you to be close enough for me to understand your enchantment. I thought it amusing as well. Had it worked better, you would have mistrusted your team. I am surprised you know how to trust."

"I know how to do many things," Gavin said. The

strangeness of that whole scenario stuck with him. There had to have been more to it than trying to examine the enchantment and sow discord, though he doubted Cyran would share.

"You could be useful, Gavin."

"What did you want with the Shard?"

Cyran nodded toward the corpse. "Why don't you ask her?"

Gavin smiled. "I'm afraid she won't have much to talk about."

"There are ways to get the dead to speak. I suppose that you never learned those techniques in your training with Tristan." He sneered. "In my case, he made sure my gifts were developed. With my knowledge of medicine and poison and my ability to work through complicated problems, I wanted nothing more than to escape. And escape I did."

Gavin tried to take a step forward, but he was held in place. This sensation felt different than when he'd been frozen by Anna's magic. Instead, the power that wrapped around him now reminded him of what he'd experienced when facing the sorcerer, suggesting that he and Cyran knew one another and practiced the same magic. That couldn't be a coincidence.

"Where did you end up?" Gavin asked.

"I traveled. You know how hard it was to finally escape from Tristan?"

"I know," Gavin said softly.

"After he was gone, everyone scattered. But not you. You stayed."

Gavin stared at him.

Cyran scoffed. "Always the dutiful one."

"I wasn't always dutiful."

"You always did what he wanted. You were always his favorite," Cyran said.

Gavin slammed into some invisible barrier that trapped him in place. "Is that what this is about?"

"If only. Do you think I really care about what happened to me all those years ago? Do you think any of that matters now?"

Gavin could see the lie in his eyes. Cyran might deny it, but it mattered to him. Much like it mattered to Gavin.

*How could it not?*

Everything that he'd encountered over the years since leaving Tristan was tied to what had happened to him all those years ago. He had suffered. The time with Tristan had changed him. It had changed everyone who had trained with Tristan. There was no denying that.

But Gavin had been able to move on. Until coming to Yoran, he hadn't even given much thought to what drove him.

"I think it matters," Gavin said.

Cyran snarled. "You don't understand anything!"

"Help me understand then. Help me know why my friend turned on me."

"Friend? If I were your friend, you would have freed me."

"Did I not?"

"You tried. You failed."

Gavin looked across the clearing. He couldn't move, but as far as he knew, Cyran didn't know that the corpse he had was not who he searched for.

"Who was the one responsible for setting you free?" Gavin asked.

"I was responsible," Cyran said.

"Maybe, but I was the one who took the risk. I was the one who protected you, the others, anyone who needed help. It was because of me that Tristan no longer tormented you or the others."

"The others. Do you even know what happened to them?" Cyran watched him. "In the time he's been gone, have you even cared about what happened to your so-called brothers and sisters?"

Gavin stared at him. "I think about them."

"How often?"

He shook his head. "Probably not often enough."

"Well, I think about them. I think about them every day. I think about how none of them were able to escape. I think about how Tristan tortured them. I think about how he twisted their minds and forced them to serve. I think about the way he turned them into something they were not."

"They lived," Gavin said.

"Did they? What about you? His favorite. Did you live?"

"I've lived."

"Lived by running. Lived by searching for something you never had. I don't see that as living. I'm sure you don't either."

"I've looked for answers. I'm not going to deny that, but he taught me. He helped me to understand."

"He did what he did because he was the one responsible," Cyran said.

Gavin didn't move. Couldn't move. He didn't know if he even should.

There was one more lesson Tristan had taught him, but it was a lesson Gavin was never all that good at taking to heart. He had to act rationally, not let emotion or anger or rage or get in the way. As he watched Cyran, he could feel the emotions rising. For a man who believed in thinking rather than feeling, he was surprised he was letting Cyran get to him.

"Now you're the one who's responsible for using me," Gavin said.

"I must admit I found it a sweet irony that he taught the person I would need."

"For what?"

"For this," Cyran said, gesturing to the body. "You brought me what I wanted. You brought me the Risen Shard."

Gavin shook his head. "I didn't. And that doesn't explain why you needed me for all of those other jobs."

"Part of that was curiosity. I needed to know how skilled you actually were. The rumors of you were quite fantastic. Do you realize that in Berman, they speak about you as a sorcerer?" He smiled, and the bands of power trapping Gavin started to constrict again. "I knew that wasn't true. I knew you would never embrace magic. But I needed to better understand you. You see, when you were younger, there were aspects that always intrigued me. Aspects of your ability, your power, that Tristan never was willing to speak about, but the rest of us did. We understood you were something special. Even as children, we saw it. We might not have known what that meant, but we saw it from you."

Gavin stared at him, his mind racing to understand everything Cyran was saying. "So the other jobs were tests."

"Of a sort. I needed to know if you could be counted on for the most important job. I needed to know if you had the potential to claim the Risen Shard."

Gavin tried to pull on the energy of the El'aras dagger. With its magic, he thought he might be able to use it to get himself free, but he didn't know how to break the magic holding him.

"You see," Cyran continued, "you've also proven to be quite easy to hold with only the faintest magical grip. If you were any more capable, this wouldn't be strong enough." He took a step away from Gavin to stand closer to the corpse. "And now I am going to complete my task."

"What task?"

"The one that must be finished."

"Are you trying to piss me off? I don't really understand. I guess that doesn't matter anyway because you got it wrong. All of it."

"Did I? You brought me everything I needed. First, you brought me the Shard, and I thought that was significant enough. In fact, I was even willing to abandon the other assignment—so much so that I was willing to kill you myself. I admit it was a bit painful. Poisoning you was not something I expected to do, but when you came to my home holding onto the Shard, I knew I had to act. You couldn't have known the significance of what you'd brought and what it meant to me."

Gavin shook his head and looked at the corpse. "You still don't understand."

"And then you completed the task," Cyran continued, ignoring him. "It was on a whim that I went back that evening. I hadn't intended to. I really didn't expect you to show up. I went on the chance that you might have survived." He smiled. "And there you were. I had already known that you and the Risen Shard had spoken, so I knew you were familiar with who she was, even if you didn't know *what* she was. When you completed the job…"

He pulled something from his pocket. It was the glowing crystal—the Shard. He held it closer to the corpse.

"What are you going to do?" Gavin asked.

"The next step in my progression. You see, in order for me to advance my power, I have to steal from another who has it. In this case, I need the Shard. Once she is reanimated, I can take her power. I wasn't going to be able to do it while she was alive, but dead? I doubt she would even have known such a thing was possible."

Gavin had no idea what was taking place, but he knew that if Cyran were to try to use that Shard now, he would realize that he'd been played.

"Are you hearing this?" he whispered into the enchantment.

The voice was soft in his ear. "Yes."

He watched Cyran, waiting for some sort of reaction to indicate that Cyran had heard him talk to Anna, but there was none.

"He never trusted you," Gavin blurted. He needed to distract Cyran from bringing the Shard too close to the body. He had no idea who she was but worried that even a corpse could cause some trouble. He had no idea what would happen if Cyran discovered the truth or how he would react. Worse, he had no idea what Cyran might force him to do.

Cyran turned to him. "What was that?"

Gavin shook his head. "He never trusted you. He didn't trust your desire for knowledge."

"He pushed me into that desire."

"No. He wanted us to understand ourselves. He never forced me to become anything I wasn't anyway. He wanted me to do what I wanted; to understand myself." That wasn't quite the truth, but close enough at this point. All he needed was to delay him a little more.

Gavin held onto the dagger, feeling the strange resistance. He tried twisting his wrist, tried moving it, but he couldn't. Somehow, he was going to have to break out of the magical bands around him. This was the kind of thing he'd trained for. Tristan had taught him to break free from anything holding him, to fight through every bit of resistance. That it was magical didn't matter.

"Understand myself? Are you saying he wanted me to pursue this?" Cyran held his hands out on either side of him. The Shard was in one hand, stretched away from his body.

If Gavin could twist, he might be able to flick the dagger and free himself. Cyran brought his hands back together, and the bands around Gavin constricted again. He couldn't fight that.

Cyran shrugged. "Perhaps that is what he wanted. Perhaps he knew what I was capable of. That might have been why he pushed me the way he did, much like he pushed you the way he did."

"He pushed me to be stronger. Faster. That's all."

"He pushed you to become heartless. To become a killer."

"Only he didn't want me to be completely heartless." Gavin stared at him, shaking his head. "That's something you never really understood. The lessons he taught me and the torment he put me through were to make sure that my heart was solid. That my intentions were pure." He had to stall for time. He wasn't sure whether he could figure out a way to break free of the magic, but maybe there was something in the lessons he'd learned from Tristan that would help.

Even now, when Gavin thought about it, he couldn't help but feel as if the torment he'd endured was more than what he'd deserved. In all that time, he'd never really understood what Tristan had wanted from him. Each time he'd endured a beating, it was as if Tristan was forcing him to turn, to become something else.

Gavin was meant to become a killer. That much was true. But he'd been trained to become the kind of killer who understood the reason behind what they were doing. He couldn't kill indiscriminately. He had to have a purpose for everything he did. It was one lesson he'd failed.

As he looked at Cyran, he realized that Cyran had never learned that lesson.

"You're the reason he died, aren't you?" Gavin whispered.

"Am I? I must admit I wasn't disappointed. There were many who thought you were responsible, especially since you were the one who found him."

"I didn't kill him. You knew that."

"I don't know if I knew that or not. Besides, it doesn't matter. The outcome is the same regardless. He's gone. I am not. And now—"

He brought the Shard toward the corpse.

The body started to shrivel.

Gavin didn't know what was happening at first, but the power was starting to fade. The magic Anna had put around it, the illusion she'd created, disappeared as the Shard approached the body.

Cyran stared for a long moment before turning his attention to Gavin. "You brought me an illusion?"

"You wanted the body."

"The body of the Risen Shard would not disintegrate like this. Where is she?" He looked over at Thomas and carried the Shard toward him.

A dark power began to glow within the Shard. Thomas tried to withdraw, but he was held the same way Gavin was and couldn't get away from what Cyran was doing. Gavin attempted to lunge forward but couldn't.

Cyran placed the dark, glowing crystal against Thomas's neck and pressed it forward. "Where is she?"

"I will not betray the Shard," Thomas said.

"Then you will die."

Cyran pushed the crystal into Thomas's neck. His eyes were frozen in terror, but he said nothing.

Gavin focused on his core reserves. That was what Cyran had tried to suppress. By holding onto that energy, Gavin thought he might be able to find enough power to overwhelm the magic and free himself. That was what Tristan had always taught him. He had to do what he needed to do to find that strength. Tristan had known that power was within him, and he'd trained Gavin to access that energy deep within and fill him.

Gavin sensed the power within him. It was his core. His reserves. His life. All of his training, all of his knowledge, everything came to him. He closed his eyes, letting that energy fill him. And then he pushed outward on the bands holding him. He felt a sense of pressure, and for a moment, he didn't think it was going to work.

Lessons came flooding back to him. Ever since he'd been around Cyran again, those memories were resurfacing more frequently than they had before, and they filled his mind in a way they hadn't in years. By pulling on that power and energy and by focusing on them, he could feel what he needed to do. He hesitated as he let a memory come back to him.

Tristan had bound him with leather straps many times. When Gavin had learned how to overpower the leather straps, he moved on to rope. He broke out of that as well, and then he progressed to chains.

Even they didn't hold him. That's how he earned his nickname when he was young.

It wasn't just that Gavin was strong. Tristan had trained him to be strong and fast— those traits had been part of the lessons that were instilled in him.

*Do not let limitations bind you.*

At the time, Gavin had no idea what Tristan had been trying to teach him, other than that he had to keep moving, that he had to keep fighting. He had to ignore the voices that tried to tell him that he couldn't accomplish something.

He remembered straining against the leather straps, the rope, and then the chains. Each one had been its own challenge. Each one had seemed impossible at the time, but as he'd grown more capable at it, he was able to overpower them.

This was just one more chain. This was just one more barrier that he had to find his way through. He focused on it, and he called upon the core reserves, letting the energy fill him.

The power within him exploded.

The Chain Breaker was free.

## CHAPTER TWENTY-FOUR

Cyran pulled the Shard free from Thomas's neck. Gavin didn't think he was dead—yet. The Shard reflected the light around it, glowing softly with a strange purplish color. He turned to Gavin and held the Shard outward, grinning at him. Everything around Gavin began to blur, as if he was losing focus. Bands of power began to swirl around again. There was energy in the air, but that energy couldn't overwhelm him anymore. This time, he knew he could withstand that pressure.

He glared at Cyran as he held his hands out to either side and pressed outward. He needed to get this over with and make sure that Cyran didn't harm anyone else. The only problem was that Gavin didn't know if he could.

A hint of power flowed from Cyran, and Gavin could feel the bands trying to constrict around him again. The magic was strong, but he was able to resist it now.

"Look at this," Cyran said, taking a step toward him.

The Shard glistened with blood. "What enchantment do you have now?"

Gavin didn't correct him. It might be better for Cyran to think he was using enchantments. As it was, he didn't have any way to explain the power he drew upon. Bands swirled around him again but slipped past him.

He smiled.

*Anna. She had to be the reason that the magic wasn't affecting me.*

"Give me the Shard," Gavin said.

"Or what?" Cyran stared at him. "I'm not afraid of you, Gavin. You might think you're intimidating to everyone else. The Chain Breaker. The assassin. I know you." He turned toward Gavin. The end of the Shard continued to glisten, and Gavin could feel something else too. An energy that came from the Shard seemed to hang in the air. "I know you won't do anything to harm me. You care too much about me."

The way he said it suggested that Cyran viewed caring as a weakness. If it was, then so be it. Gavin didn't mind having that weakness. He'd survived his training to hold onto that, despite what Tristan thought of him.

"You don't want me to be your enemy," Gavin said.

"You didn't even know I was your enemy for all these months. What makes you think I'm concerned about you? You've been working on my behalf, serving as I demanded of you. And in all that time, you had no idea about what you were doing or who you were working for. Do you think I haven't prepared for all of this?"

"Obviously, you haven't. If you'd prepared for all of it, you would've been able to acquire the Risen Shard on your own. You needed me for that, and you needed me to help you remove the El'aras."

"Perhaps I did. It was easier. Sumter failed, so I involved you, my backup, who became my primary plan. This way, I didn't have to risk myself. Why risk myself when I could put you out there? I knew better than to go after that kind of power directly. Then again, that wasn't the way I was taught."

Cyran took another step toward him. The bands of power started to swirl again, and Gavin fought them, trying to pull upon his core energy. The power tightened and constricted around him.

*Would I be able to withstand what Cyran was doing? The previous attack had been deflected because of Anna, but where was she now?*

"Our master taught me to work in the shadows," Cyran said. "He told me that was going to be my strength. I could assist and supplement, but he never expected me to be the one with any real power." He smiled darkly. "Little did he know."

Gavin shook his head. "I can't believe all of this is about revenge."

Cyran laughed. His voice carried into the forest, into the trees, and then faded. "If this was only about revenge, I would have acted long ago. I haven't been afraid of you for a long time, Gavin. In fact, I doubt you could do anything to harm me. No. This has not been about revenge. Not for a long time. This has been about taking my next step."

"You keep saying that, but you don't even know what that means."

"It means I will gain the power to overthrow my mentor."

"Tristan?"

"Tristan is dead," Cyran said. "Thankfully."

"Then which mentor?"

"Who do you think taught me?"

"I don't know. Whomever it was made a mistake," said Gavin.

"A mistake? They pursued me. They recognized my potential. They recognized it in a way Tristan never did. He never appreciated what I did for him, or the power I possessed. He never fully appreciated anything about me."

"You never really understood him then."

"Enough." Cyran held the Shard out and jabbed it toward him. Something surged from the end of it and slammed into Gavin. "You're going to help me use the Shard."

"You've already tried to."

"I tried on an illusion. You're going to help me find the real Risen Shard." He took another step closer with the Shard pointing at him. Gavin tried to stand firm, but the energy that exploded off the end of the Shard slammed into him again, knocking him back.

*Where was Anna?*

He needed her help. He hoped the power she could summon would be able to unravel what Cyran did.

"All of this for power," Gavin said. "You never really understood the nature of what Tristan tried to teach you." And all of this with his master looking for him.

*Did Cyran know the sorcerer had sent Gavin to find him?*

It seemed a stretch, almost too much to believe.

"You think he didn't want us to have power? With everything he taught?"

"He wanted us to have power, but he wanted us to know the proper way to use it. Obviously, that's a lesson you don't understand. Perhaps you weren't smart enough to."

Gavin looked over, and Gaspar and Thomas remained frozen. How much longer would they be able to withstand what Cyran did to them? He had to figure something out—and quickly.

Cyran took another step toward him. Gavin tried to embrace the core energy within and pressed outward. He held onto the same power he used before, focusing on the way he'd been trained and the energy needed to break through the invisible chains that Cyran was holding him in.

Nothing happened. Cyran was using more power, more magic, than what Gavin was able to withstand. It was too much for him.

"Where is she?" Cyran said, looking around. "She's close. I can smell her."

There was a flicker of movement as Anna dropped

down from a tree. She landed in the clearing and turned toward Cyran, unleashing power at him. It washed over him harmlessly.

Gavin could see the look of horror on Thomas's face. Cyran turned toward Anna, a grin splitting his face. With a twist of his wrist, she was thrown back. She gathered herself and stood, and then he knocked her down again.

"I have trained for this day," Cyran said to her. "Obviously, you cannot say the same."

The power he was holding exploded again. It slammed into Anna, a concussive blast that threw her to the ground. She collapsed in the center of the clearing, lying motionless.

Thomas lunged, but Cyran turned to him. He twisted his hand, and Thomas's eyes went wide. Cyran glanced over his shoulder, looking back at Gaspar and Imogen. "I think it's time that your friends were removed from this equation as well."

With another flick of his wrist, each of them stiffened and then went completely still.

Finally, Cyran turned toward Gavin. "I told you I didn't fear you. How could I, when I have far more power than you could even imagine?"

He pressed the Shard against Gavin's neck. The sensation of it was cold, strange, familiar. It reminded Gavin of the sh'rasn Anna had forced him to drink. Energy washed through him now, the same way he'd felt when he drank the elixir. There was a surge of power, almost as if his core strength was restored.

It was a strange feeling, but he was aware of the energy flowing up within him, powering him and restoring his core. There was something more within it too. The magic around him took on a more discrete form, as if coming into contact with the Shard allowed him to feel the bindings that were wrapped around him.

He forced his hands downward. The El'aras blade snapped through the bindings, and Cyran was thrown back.

The others were still motionless. Gavin had to act quickly.

He turned to Cyran and spun. Something started to wrap around him, but he imagined the chains around him and drew upon power, shattering them.

He stabbed with the El'aras dagger. It caught Cyran in the shoulder, and he dropped the Shard. Gavin rolled and picked it up, then held it out toward Cyran.

Cyran clutched his shoulder, glaring at Gavin. "Do you think I need that for power?"

Another band of energy began to constrict around Gavin, but the Shard seemed to protect him. He could feel the power building from Cyran as he started to twist his hands, his lips murmuring wordlessly to form whatever spell he intended to use.

If Gavin waited too long, he ran the risk of Cyran conjuring more power than he'd be able to withstand. He'd gotten lucky so far. His reserves of energy had saved him, allowing him to break the chains of magic.

*Would I be able to disrupt another spell—possibly a more violent and dangerous one?*

He didn't think he would. He needed to act, to disarm Cyran. The problem was that he needed Cyran alive in order to protect the others and finish the job the way he intended.

Cyran began to turn toward Gavin.

Gavin wouldn't wait. He couldn't wait.

He darted forward and stabbed Cyran's other shoulder, rendering his hands useless.

"I think you do fear me," Gavin said as Cyran's eyes widened. He slammed the hilt of the El'aras dagger into Cyran's head.

He crumpled, and Gavin slumped to the ground, exhaustion taking him.

## CHAPTER TWENTY-FIVE

Gavin didn't let himself rest for long. He held onto the Shard, which seemed to give him reserves of energy he didn't have before.

*How much longer would I be able to use that, though?*

Gavin suspected the Shard would eventually be tapped out, and then he'd be drawing upon his own strength. As he'd seen over the last few days, there were limits to how much he could use. He maintained his connection to the Shard and headed toward Anna first.

He touched her shoulder, and she stirred, her eyes snapping open. Something grabbed him around his throat and squeezed, but she relaxed her magic when she saw him. She sat up and took the Shard from him.

Anna got to her feet and hurried over to Thomas. She tapped on his forehead, and when he awoke, he jumped up with his sword out. He made his way over to Cyran and held the tip of his sword to Cyran's neck. Anna then used her magic to revive Gaspar and Imogen. Either that, or she resurrected them. He didn't really know.

"Thank you," she said to Gavin.

"I'm sorry it went that far."

"You don't need to be sorry. You did well. Better than I would've expected without any additional training."

Gavin smirked, not really sure about the nature of the compliment. "I can't let you take him," he said, looking over to where Thomas was wrapping a strange metal band around Cyran's wrists.

"I'm afraid he has to come with us."

Gavin shook his head. "I need to take care of him."

"He attempted to kill me."

"I'm not so sure he wanted you dead, so much as he wanted your power. I don't claim to know what that can do," he said, nodding to the crystal, "but it seems to be considerable power. That was what he wanted. He intended to absorb your power and seemed to think he could use it to strengthen himself."

"It is possible it would've worked," she said.

"It is?"

"The Shard is incredibly powerful."

"Powerful enough he could steal your magic?" Gavin asked.

"There are many aspects of power it can influence."

"Regardless," he said, shaking his head, "I can't let you take him."

"May I ask why not? If this is simply about protecting a friend—"

"Our friendship was destroyed the moment he turned against me." Gavin was going to have to think through everything he'd experienced with Cyran, especially the nature of what he'd gone through. It might be that there was more he'd have to come to terms with. "But I need him because I was hired to collect him."

Gaspar coughed, a look of surprise and confusion on his face.

"The Apostle," Gavin said.

"Are you sure?" Gaspar asked.

"Not entirely, but I think so. I suspect that Cyran is the sorcerer's apprentice. Or had been. He wanted Anna's power and the Shard so he could overthrow his master."

"How do you know he's the Apostle, though?" Gaspar asked. He hobbled into the clearing, his gaze still darting around as it always seemed to do, looking into the shadows as if he could see something hidden there. Imogen leaned on one of the trees, silent as always.

"It was the type of magic he used. The power he used to trap us was the same as the sorcerer's." Gavin turned toward Anna. "I had a job to do. I was hired to find the Apostle."

"After what he did, I'm afraid he has to come with us."

"If he does, then all of my friends will die. I can't withstand the power of another sorcerer."

Anna watched him, frowning. "You might be surprised."

He started for Cyran, and Thomas swept the sword

toward him. Anna caught the blade with her hand. The El'aras sword left no mark.

*Strange.*

Gavin grabbed Cyran and lifted him. "I take it these bands on his wrists, whatever they are, will prevent him from using magic?"

"They are enchantments that will restrict his ability to use his power," Anna said.

"Good. What about you?"

"We have kept the Shard in Yoran for some time now. Unfortunately, it seems as if it has been discovered. The El'aras who attacked you in the tavern proves that. I think it's time for us to move on."

"Move on where?"

She looked over at Thomas before turning her attention back to Gavin. "I don't know, but I don't know that you need to know either."

There was a part of Gavin that felt a hint of regret at that. "I'm sorry for all of this."

"You are not to blame."

"Well, I am a little bit. Had I not broken into your home initially and come after you, you wouldn't have had to move, and the Shard wouldn't have been taken from you. And had I not gone back into your home, I wouldn't have found the Shard, and we wouldn't have had to go through any of this." He flashed a smile and shook his head. "It seems to me that all of this *is* my fault. Maybe I needed to do a better job of picking my jobs. Here I thought you were a slaver."

"When have you ever known the El'aras to be slavers?" There was a real sense of hurt in Anna's question.

"I didn't know you were El'aras at the time. That was one aspect of the job that hadn't been shared with me."

"And if it *had* been shared with you? What would you have done?"

Gavin looked at her, fixing her with a hard stare. The answer was complicated. He didn't know, and he didn't know how to answer her. Perhaps the best response was none at all. At least he wouldn't be lying to her.

"Why have you been hiding in the city?" he asked.

She watched him; her lips pressed into a frown. "I am the Risen Shard."

"I still don't know what that means."

"Perhaps if you begin to understand the El'aras, then you might."

"The El'aras that attacked me in the tavern and harmed my friend weren't with you, but who were they?" She said nothing, and Gavin thought he understood. Cyran had told him about the factions of El'aras. "They were looking for you," he said.

She tipped her head in a slight nod.

Gavin glanced over at Cyran. "Did he send them after you?"

"I suspect they learned of me following your attack. Perhaps it was all part of his plan to draw me out. A complicated one, at that. It means that he is far more attuned to the workings of magic in the world than I would have known."

"I think he's tied to a powerful sorcerer."

"You are probably right, which is even more reason for him to come with us, so we may ensure that he does not do any more damage."

"What sort of damage do you think he might do?"

Her expression darkened. "The El'aras have suffered enough. We do not need to be pitted against each other at a sorcerer's whim."

"Is that what happened?" he asked.

"I don't know," she said. "Regardless, it is time that we move on. We will keep the Shard protected."

"I could help."

She tilted her head to the side and frowned. "Perhaps eventually. For now, Gavin Lorren, you must come to know yourself."

"I'm not sure what you mean by that."

She offered a hint of a smile. "Not yet, but you will. I don't think you have much choice."

He wondered why that would be, though he had a sense from Anna that she wouldn't tell him anything more than she'd already shared. Maybe that was enough.

"Journey well," Gavin said, pressing his fist to his chest and leaning forward. It was a formal departure salute, but in this setting, he thought it fitting.

Anna tapped her ear and then withdrew a small silver circle. She handed it to Gavin. "If you have need of me, use this. Consider it an enchantment."

"About that…"

The forest clearing was bright. Gavin had been unwilling to come at any other time, hesitating to do so unless it was daylight out. He'd continued to knock Cyran unconscious, not wanting him awake when they met in the heart of the forest. He didn't want to talk with him at all. Gavin thought that was the best option when it came to Cyran.

Gaspar was with him, his hand on the hilt of his knives, his gaze darting all around. Imogen moved silently, hidden in the trees. Gavin still hadn't figured out her secret, though he knew she had one.

"Is he there yet?" Wrenlow whispered.

"Would you stop talking?" Gavin and Gaspar said at the same time.

They looked at each other, and Gaspar shook his head. "I'm not sure I care much for this enchantment."

"You'll get used to it," Gavin said.

Gaspar sighed. "I thought *you* were bad."

"I'm not bad," Wrenlow said. "It's just that I get stuck having to stay behind so often, and I like to know what's going on."

"I suppose I could've asked Anna for a different type of enchantment," Gavin said.

Could she have made one where Wrenlow could see what he was seeing? Something like that would've been incredibly valuable. If nothing else, at least it would keep Wrenlow quiet.

He thought that he was pushing by asking her to make

this enchantment, but she had done so willingly. Thomas had been annoyed, but she'd only smiled as she handed one to Gavin and Gaspar, with a third for Wrenlow. They had all been keyed to each individual person so they wouldn't work for anyone else.

"He's not coming," Gavin said.

Cyran let out a moan, and Gavin kicked him, knocking him back again. He flopped over and rolled to the ground. Gavin waited a moment, then kicked again. Cyran didn't get up this time.

"I don't know that he's going to be thrilled that you're bringing him a bruised man." Gaspar looked down, shaking his head.

"I don't care. He told me that we had to remove the Apostle. Maybe it would be better if I just killed him."

"If you'd killed him, then we would've had to drag his corpse."

"I know, and that would've been too much work."

Gaspar looked over at him, studying him.

Gavin suspected that Gaspar knew the real reason Gavin hadn't killed Cyran. He wasn't sure he could. Not in cold blood. Perhaps in the moment he would've been able to, but after Cyran had been defeated, there was really no reason to harm him. The only thing that would've accomplished would've been making Gavin feel a little bit better.

"Are you sure this is where he wanted us to meet?" Gaspar asked.

"You were there. You heard it as well as I did."

"I did. I just... I don't like it."

"Neither do I."

Gavin let out a sigh as he looked all around the clearing. He waited, suspecting that whenever the sorcerer came, he would hold them with his magic and trap them again. He had to be ready for it, prepared for the moment that the sorcerer appeared. He'd been able to escape from the bands of power that Cyran used on him.

*What if I could do the same thing with the sorcerer?*

He had little doubt that the sorcerer would attempt to use the same power against him. When he did, he wanted to be ready.

They didn't have to wait long. Power began to build around him, and soon everyone was frozen. Gavin clutched the El'aras dagger in his left hand, and he felt the power swirling around him. Now that he felt it again from the sorcerer, he was even more certain it was the same type of power Cyran had used.

The sorcerer appeared in a shimmer and strode toward the center of the clearing. He glanced down at the ground, then looked up at Gavin.

"You found him," he said.

"You must have known I knew him. Why not tell me his name?"

"Did you know him?" The sorcerer showed a hint of amusement. Gavin glared at him, but the sorcerer ignored it and chuckled. "Perhaps you did know him, or perhaps you didn't. Had I told you who he was, would you have believed it?"

That was a very different question. Gavin wasn't sure he would've believed it if he'd been told that Cyran was a sorcerer, let alone the Apostle.

"What do you want with him?" Gavin asked.

"I surmise you have already determined what I want with him."

"You were his instructor."

"We call it something else, but yes, I was."

"Are you still?"

The sorcerer glanced down at Cyran, his expression darkening. "He betrayed me. He betrayed his teachings."

"He wanted power."

"All sorcerers want power. It's how he went about gaining it that troubles me."

"You don't care that he came after one of the El'aras?" asked Gavin.

The sorcerer frowned. "Why else do you think I wanted him caught?"

"The El'aras want him as well."

"I imagine they do."

"They're angry with him," said Gavin.

The sorcerer nodded. "I imagine they are."

"Which is why I can't let you take him with you."

Wrenlow groaned from the other end of the enchantment. "What are you doing, Gavin?"

He ignored the question.

"The terms were clear," the sorcerer said.

"They were. I was to remove the Apostle, and I have."

"You have brought him to me, so now that you removed him, I—"

"Now that I've removed the Apostle, I will be the one to decide what happens with him."

Gavin was taking a gamble and knew he had to be careful. He didn't want to risk angering the sorcerer, especially knowing how powerful he must be.

"Why did you bring him to me then?" the sorcerer asked.

"I wanted you to know I fulfilled my end of the bargain."

"What do you intend for him?"

"What would you have intended for him?" asked Gavin.

"With what he did, he must suffer the consequences."

"Is it death?"

The sorcerer watched him, and he said nothing.

"If it isn't that, then I'm not sure he's really suffering."

"You would see him suffer?"

"Considering what he did, he needs to," Gavin said. "Besides, the El'aras want their pound of flesh as well."

"That is what you intend. Interesting."

"You disagree?"

The sorcerer shook his head. "It poses some challenges, but I suppose I will permit it."

"I didn't realize I was giving you a choice."

The sorcerer stared at him and smiled. "Do not mistake my willingness to allow you to do this for weakness, Gavin Lorren."

Once again, he said his name possessively. As before, it left Gavin irritated and angry. During their first encounter, when he'd been trapped by the sorcerer, there hadn't been anything he could do. This time was different.

He focused on his core reserves of energy. Ever since the Shard had been pressed against his neck, the sense of power within him seemed greater than before, as if his reserves were stronger than they'd been. Gavin focused on them, and then he thought about what it would take to break free of the magical bindings that held him.

He took a deep breath and twisted. He used the El'aras dagger to enhance his power and blast free of the bindings. Gavin sprinted forward and brought the dagger up, pressing it against the sorcerer's neck.

"Don't think that just because I don't have magic that I'm not dangerous," he said. With a flourish of the El'aras dagger, he backed away and slipped it back into his belt.

The sorcerer looked at him and smiled. "Yes, you are everything I thought you might be."

"What's that supposed to mean?"

"I will be watching you, Gavin Lorren."

"Watch all you want, but—"

With a burst of power, the sorcerer shimmered, then disappeared altogether.

Gavin took a deep breath. He looked around and turned his attention to Gaspar.

"It's a dangerous game you're playing," Gaspar said.

"It's not really a game."

"I didn't realize you intended to bring him back to the

El'aras."

"I didn't either, but it seems fitting, doesn't it?"

"I suppose it does. What do you think they will do with him?"

Gavin looked down at Cyran, who was still unconscious on the ground. At this point, he wasn't sure it even mattered. "I don't know. We can leave that to Anna."

Gaspar smiled at him. "You do realize that's not her real name."

"I'm sure it's not."

"You also realize she's probably somebody high-ranking within the El'aras."

"Considering the guard she had and the power she possesses, I suspect she is."

"That doesn't trouble you?"

"All of this troubles me," Gavin said. He leaned down, grabbed Cyran, and jerked him to his feet. Cyran started to come around, and he looked up at Gavin groggily.

"You should thank me," Gavin said. "I just saved you from your mentor."

"You don't—"

Gavin slammed his fist into Cyran's temple, knocking him out again. That would work for a while, but eventually he'd need something longer lasting. For now, he took a little pleasure in striking him.

He hoisted Cyran up. "Are you ready?" he asked Gaspar.

"Where now?"

"I intend to signal Anna, and then we can meet her at the Dragon."

"I'm sure Jessica will be thrilled."

"I don't think there will be any fighting this time."

Gaspar looked over at Cyran. "With him, I don't know if you can guarantee that."

Gavin chuckled. He thought he felt something behind him, some sense of energy, but then it faded. If the sorcerer had returned to watch them, he gave no sign of it.

He hesitated as he looked back at the clearing, and he took a deep breath. All this time, he'd tried to avoid magic by coming to Yoran, yet somehow he'd gotten more deeply involved in it.

It probably was a mistake, but at this point, Gavin didn't know if there was anything different that he could —or should—do.

First, he'd find Anna.

Then he would decide what he needed to do next.

---

Cyran leaned back in the chair, his chin resting on his chest. Gavin watched him and clutched the El'aras dagger tightly as he waited. He was using the dagger to detect any magic coming from Cyran, but so far there'd been no signs.

"Maybe she didn't get your message," Gaspar said. He sat at the counter near the kitchen and drank a mug of ale, although Gavin hadn't seen him actually drink from it.

"I'm sure she got his message," Jessica said.

She coughed, and Gavin looked in her direction. She sat at a table near the back of the tavern and didn't get up, but it was enough that she'd come down. After everything she'd been through, it was enough that she'd survived.

"It's not like that," he said. He moved to sit with her.

"No? I hear you've been keeping an eye on her," Jessica said.

"I..."

She chuckled. "You don't have to make any excuses. This is fun. That's all it is though."

"Is that all it is for you?"

She arched a brow at him. "I've been running the Dragon for many years, Gavin. Do you think you're the first rogue I've taken a fancy to?"

Gavin smiled. "That's all I am to you?"

"Perhaps a little bit more than that, but eventually you'll move on. I've known that about you from the beginning. You don't have to make any excuses for it, just like I don't need to make any excuses for my choices."

Gavin reached across the table, taking her hand.

"That doesn't mean that we can't have fun in the meantime," Jessica said.

He laughed.

Cyran started to make noise and stir, and Gavin hurried over to him and struck him once again until he stopped moving. He was going to be bruised. If Cyran ever came around long enough to realize what had happened to him, he was going to be incredibly sore.

Considering what he'd done and what he'd put all of them through, he deserved that kind of pain.

Gavin sat next to Gaspar and leaned back in the chair with the El'aras dagger in hand. He sighed and reached into his pocket, pulling out the small metal circle Anna had given him. This was supposed to be the way to communicate with her, but so far, she hadn't come.

*How long could they keep Cyran?*

Maybe it would've been better to let the sorcerer take him. Gavin didn't have the same knowledge of potions and poisons that Cyran did. It would be easier to give him something that would neutralize his magic rather than to keep knocking him unconscious every time he moved.

"I don't like waiting," Gaspar said.

"I thought that was part of your job," Gavin said without looking over.

"What do you think I do?"

"You're a thief."

"Being a thief doesn't mean sitting around. That might be part of your job, but mine involves action."

They were all restless. Imogen paced, and Gavin kept waiting for her to come over and say something, even though she never talked. Given what they'd gone through, he thought she might, but she'd remained quiet as ever. Even Jessica fidgeted. This was the first time she'd been down in the tavern's main level since her injury.

The dagger started to glow.

Gavin glanced toward the door. "I think we're about to have visitors."

Imogen took a step forward, reaching for the hilt of her slender blade. Gavin had no idea whether she'd be able to do anything against one of the El'aras, but there was part of him that was curious to find out. He'd seen her fight enough to know she had the potential to be dangerous—part of the reason Gaspar trusted her.

The door opened, and Thomas entered first. He left his sword sheathed. Two other El'aras followed. Finally, Anna came in last.

She was dressed in a pale blue cloak, hood pulled over her head. When she pulled it down, her golden hair flowed down her back, giving her a beautiful, almost ethereal quality.

Gavin got to his feet. "It took you long enough."

"It is not an immediate summons. It was never meant that way." She glanced toward Cyran and frowned. "I thought you intended to bring this Apostle to his sorcerer master."

"I did, but then I realized the agreement was simply to eliminate him as a threat. There was another way to remove him that I hadn't considered."

"What way is that?"

"By providing him to you." Gavin glanced over at Cyran. "Seeing as how he was the one who wanted to steal from you and take your power, I figured it would be better for the El'aras to deal with him. I don't know what the sorcerer planned for him anyway."

Anna studied Cyran. The dagger glowed a little brighter.

"What are you going to do with him?" he asked.

"Do you really care?"

"Consider me curious."

"As you should be." She turned her attention to him. "It seems you are not quite as curious as you should be."

"Why is that?" Gavin asked, laughing softly.

"Considering what has occurred, I would expect you to have questions."

"What sort of questions?"

"Such as how you were able to handle the Shard."

"I assume anyone can handle the Shard." She looked at him, and he frowned. "No?"

She shook her head. "Not anyone. It takes a specific person to manage that kind of power. It is why we have kept it in a trunk."

"You can handle it."

"I am trained for it."

Gavin shrugged. "I've trained as well. Not to handle the Shard, but for other things. Pain, primarily."

She started to smile, then shook her head. "That's probably what it is then."

He had a sense that wasn't quite the real reason. "What else should I have been questioning?" he asked.

"Do you not think it odd that you could escape from a fully trained sorcerer's confinement?"

*The Breaker of Chains.*

Cyran had taunted him about that in the past, and Gavin thought it amusing it had been the reason he'd escaped. "I don't know. Am I supposed to find that odd?"

"Perhaps. Or perhaps not. Perhaps that is another part of your training," she said, smiling at him. "Or perhaps you have some magic of your own."

"Why would you suggest that?"

"Seeing as how you're half El'aras, I would not be surprised."

Gavin tensed. "Why would you say that?"

"You are, are you not? You certainly bear the traits of one who is." Anna frowned at him. "Perhaps I have it wrong." She flashed a smile, but it did nothing to take away the chill Gavin felt. "Regardless, it is good you summoned me."

"Do you have something else you want to accuse me of? Perhaps you want to claim I'm a werin. Maybe I'm a sorcerer myself."

She shook her head. "I wouldn't accuse you of sorcery."

"Isn't that what you just did?"

"Perhaps."

She nodded to Thomas, who grabbed Cyran and jerked him to his feet. The two El'aras guards took up position on either side of him and marched him toward the door.

For some reason, Gavin could feel a sense of pressure, which was unusual. It was almost like the resistance he'd felt when he'd been in the manor house and tried to use the El'aras dagger on Anna. It was also similar to the resistance he'd felt when he'd used the dagger to find the Shard, and it was the same sensation he'd felt when he swung the dagger around in the forest.

*What were they doing to Cyran?*

Gavin wasn't even sure it mattered. It was at that moment that Cyran opened his eyes. He jerked and twisted. He swiveled his head, his eyes wide. Cyran turned to Anna, then looked back at Gavin, and something on his face darkened.

"What did you do?" he whispered.

The El'aras guards forced him to stand, and Cyran straightened, somehow making it look as if he wasn't a captive.

"I made a choice," Gavin said.

"You have placed yourself into his service."

Gavin frowned. "I haven't placed myself in anyone's service."

"If I'm here with you, then it's only because he agreed to it. What did you bargain for?"

"I didn't bargain for anything," he said with a smile. "He made the bargain. I was to remove you. Now that you've been removed, or will be, the bargain has been satisfied. That didn't mean I had to leave you with him."

Cyran narrowed his brow. "I'll escape. When I do, I will come for you, Gavin. Don't think I will make the same mistake again."

Gavin walked over to him and shoved the dagger against his neck. "If I see you again, I doubt you'll get the chance."

"You always made Tristan proud," Cyran sneered.

Gavin turned, and it seemed as if bands of power started to wrap around him. He broke free of them, borrowing briefly from the core strength within him. As he did, he looked over at Anna and found her watching him.

*That wasn't magic, was it?*

Tristan had taught him to reach for his core energy, nothing more than that.

*What if it* was *something more than that, though? What would it mean for me?*

Nothing. Gavin had to believe it meant nothing.

The El'aras dragged Cyran out, leaving Gavin alone with Anna.

He took a deep breath, then remembered Anna had been saying something before. "Why was it good I summoned you?"

"Because of something I should've told you before. Perhaps I shouldn't tell you even now, but considering what you offered me, I suppose it is a fair trade."

"What sort of trade?"

"The Apostle for knowledge," she said.

Gavin stared at her, waiting.

"The man you know as Tristan. Your mentor. He lives."

---

Grab book 2 of The Chain Breaker series: The Jade Egg

**A dark sorcerer with a deadly plan attacks his adopted city. The Chain Breaker Series continues.**

After capturing the sorcerer called the Apostle, Gavin decided to remain in the city of Yoran where he's become comfortable. Work that had been plentiful has dried up and comfort becomes complacency.

While new friends help to find jobs, they're not the kind of jobs an assassin trained to be the Chain Breaker should take. He's trained to kill, not track down relics in a city that long ago banished magic.

When pushed to save a young boy, Gavin finds himself dealing with much more than he bargained for. A sorcerer known as the Mistress of Vines has come to Yoran. In order to stop her, he must come to understand a part of himself he was trained to ignore.

It will take an assassin without equal to stop the Mistress of Vines.

Only this time, the Chain Breaker might not be enough.

# SERIES BY D.K. HOLMBERG

***The Dragonwalkers Series***
The Dragonwalker
The Dragon Misfits

***Elemental Warrior Series:***
Elemental Academy
The Elemental Warrior
The Cloud Warrior Saga
The Endless War

***The Dark Ability Series***
The Shadow Accords
The Collector Chronicles
The Dark Ability
The Sighted Assassin
The Elder Stones Saga

***The Lost Prophecy Series***
The Teralin Sword
The Lost Prophecy

***The Volatar Saga Series***

The Volatar Saga

***The Book of Maladies Series***

The Book of Maladies

***The Lost Garden Series***

The Lost Garden

Printed in Great Britain
by Amazon